Cat in the Agrahāram
and Other Stories

Cat in the Agrahāram
and Other Stories

Dilip Kumar

Translated from the Tamil
by Martha Ann Selby

NORTHWESTERN UNIVERSITY PRESS
EVANSTON, ILLINOIS

Northwestern University Press
www.nupress.northwestern.edu

Printed in the United States of America

10 9 8 7 6 5 4 3 2 1

Library of Congress Cataloging-in-Publication Data

Names: Tilīpkumār, author. | Selby, Martha Ann, translator.
Title: Cat in the Agrahāram and other stories / Dilip Kumar ; translated from the Tamil
  by Martha Ann Selby.
Other titles: Kaṭavu. English
Description: Evanston, Illinois : Northwestern University Press, 2020. | "Originally
  published in Tamil as Kaṭavu, copyright © 2000, 2010, Cre-A Publishers"
Identifiers: LCCN 2019038102 | ISBN 9780810141551 (trade paperback) | ISBN
  9780810141568 (ebook)
Subjects: LCSH: Short stories, Tamil—Translations into English. | Tamil (Indic
  people)—Social life and customs—Fiction. | Chennai (India)—Fiction.
Classification: LCC PL4758.9.T42 K3713 2020 | DDC 894.8/11372—dc23
LC record available at https://lccn.loc.gov/2019038102

In memory of John Bernard Bate
1960–2016

CONTENTS

I first met Dilip Kumar in 1986 or 1987, I am not sure exactly when, but I was just following orders: the late A. K. Ramanujan had told me to seek him out, adding, "He's very quiet—he might not say much to you, but he writes very fine stories." I found him in Chennai, behind the till in S. Ramakrishnan's Cre-A showroom, which at that time was located on Royapettah High Road. We shook hands, smiled, and Ramanujan was right: he said very little to me on that first day. I returned to Chennai in late 1988 and began to work in my spare time as a subject expert for the Cre-A Tamil Dictionary Project, and I would see Dilip Kumar from time to time. On a much later trip to Chennai, in the summer of 2000, I stopped by to see Ramakrishnan at Cre-A's new location in Tiruvanmiyur, and that is where I spotted *Kaṭavu*, Dilip Kumar's collected stories, which Cre-A had published in February of that same year. I bought it and brought it back to Texas with me, where it languished on my shelf as a beautiful little object for a while as I worked on other projects, hoping that I would read it "for fun" one day. I went on leave in September 2001, and had it in my head that I would begin each day with a page of Dilip Kumar—and then the World Trade Center came crashing down in a terrorist attack, an event that disrupted us all in strange and unexpected ways. For several years, "a page" was all I had read of *Kaṭavu*, the very first page of "Crossing Over," the title story of the collection. And, for those several years, I was under the impression that Dilip Kumar was a comic writer because of that single, solitary page.

My translation of the Old Tamil anthology of love poetry, *Aiṅkuṟunūṟu*, was almost finished, and before undertaking a translation of a second Old Tamil text, I decided that I needed to step back from classical poetry for a while, in order to come back to it with fresh eyes, and meanwhile to inhabit the world of contemporary Tamil literature a bit more fully. And there sat his book *Kaṭavu*. I wrote to Dilip Kumar in April 2008, and he replied in May, granting me permission to translate his collection. As I quickly found, Dilip Kumar's "comedy" is better labeled "irony," or, perhaps best, one might call him an absurdist, a chronicler of life in Chennai and Coimbatore—a life thick with pleasures and difficulties. In other words, the comic register is only one of many in which Dilip Kumar writes.

The acclaimed author of one novella and numerous short stories, Dilip Kumar is not a Tamil who writes, but a Gujarati who writes in Tamil, the language he has chosen for literary expression. He is also a well-regarded literary critic, the editor of several collections of short stories, and a translator from Gujarati, Hindi, and English into Tamil. Nearly a century ago, the maternal side of his family migrated from Kutch, in the northwestern state of Gujarat, to the southern city of Coimbatore, where Dilip Kumar was born into a prosperous Gujarati business community in 1951. His personal story, which informs and underpins nearly all of his fiction, is one of "from riches to rags." His father died at the hands of a local quack when Dilip Kumar was four: this event appears as a nodal point, with the facts slightly altered, in several of his stories. His mother was subsequently cheated out of their property and business, and they were forced into instant poverty. Dilip Kumar was schooled only through the eighth standard (equivalent to the American eighth grade), and held many itinerant jobs as a "tea boy" and in dry-cleaning shops and tailoring and textile shops until he wound up working for S. Ramakrishnan in the Cre-A showroom. According to many critics, Dilip Kumar is among the best of the living writers of fiction in the Tamil language, crafting his stories in the dialects and idioms of Tamil that are heard in the streets and read in the city's popular dailies.

In his 1985 foreword to Dilip Kumar's first published collection, *Muṅkil Kuruttu*, the late novelist and giant of Tamil letters Ashokamittiran (the pen name of Jagadisa Thyagarajan, 1931–2017), places Dilip Kumar's fiction within the broader sweep of twentieth-century Tamil writing. After describing the rise and fall of Tamil literary magazines and remarking on how Tamil short-story writers had to pin their hopes and reputations on the sometimes precarious nature of Tamil "little magazines," he notes that the release of Dilip Kumar's stories in a published collection was a very special occasion, because it made his stories available to all readers, and not just to those who had access to copies of various little magazines. He remarks on Dilip Kumar's fine eye for description and detail, and his evenhanded and compassionate treatment of even his most difficult and morally flawed characters, noting that this is unique and something that is generally impossible for short-story writers to do.[1]

Ashokamittiran also remarks upon Dilip Kumar's sensitive treatment of poverty among the middle and lower classes, and comments that even though he is not a Tamilian—and most of the characters in his stories are from the North—there is a universality to his portrayals of mothers, sons, coworkers, bosses, relatives, and tenement dwellers. Readers from anywhere can relate to the characters' lives. Even when Dilip Kumar writes about poverty, humor is never very far away, and it is his sense of humor that places him in a class by himself: he can bring out the best of his characters' qualities in the midst of poverty, degradation, anger, hunger, and strife. His stories transcend the "otherness" of cultural difference. For all these reasons, his stories occupy a special place in the world of modern short fiction.[2]

All his stories are structurally complex and elegant in form, and all this for an author whose mother tongue is Gujarati. While the Tamil in which he writes is quite plain, what makes Dilip Kumar unusual is his own identity as an outsider, but one with an insider's perfect fluency in Tamil and an uncanny idiomatic ear. His style is very natural, but he does favor complex verbs and the equally complex temporal distinctions that such verbs in literary Tamil allow. His prose style is tied to what linguists would call his specific "context of situation"[3] or his own distinctive "cognitive orientation"[4] and cannot really be viewed as separate from it, either, especially in regard to issues of register and dialect. In a 2009 conversation, Dilip Kumar informed me that he taught himself Tamil by reading newspapers, referring to his style as "newspaper Tamil." And, indeed, he writes in short, almost telegraphic phrases. There is a great deal of "reportage" in his stories, to be sure, and most of them are pieced together from autobiographical elements, many based on or inspired by actual incidents, with the names swapped around among family members to provide the guilty with the names of the innocent. Many of his pieces employ sequences of conversational vignettes, and his superb control of dialogue and dialect is used to great effect in most of them. A kind of existential rawness emerges in his use of conversation throughout much of his work, and I maintain that it is not just a matter of "content"—of what is said—but of how he positions and embeds direct speech, juxtaposing it with dense and evocative description. Some of Dilip Kumar's stories are experimental, and nearly all of them are emotionally harrowing, but, at the same time, they are leavened with absurdist flourishes and are written in the plainest language possible. He listed his influences for me as Dostoevsky, Raymond Carver, and Erle Stanley Gardner, but Dilip Kumar also owes a sizable debt to the great Tamil writers of an earlier generation, and to Mauni and Pudumaippittan in particular. In other words, to put it in linguistic terms, there is no real linguistic "deviation" in Dilip Kumar's style.[5] Tamil short stories of that generation were not written for the sake of entertainment alone, but depicted "the grotesque truths of life and those matters that are considered unutterable"[6]—in other words, the events that take place in life's darker corners, in urban contexts, in particular. Dilip Kumar's body of work is very much in that same lineage of literary sensibility, as well as being a part of the India-wide turn toward literary realism that had its beginnings in the late nineteenth century.

Publishing and the Emergence of the Tamil Short Story

A. R. Venkatachalapathy has described the emergence of Tamil publishing from systems of patronage and subscription to the establishment of publishing houses and presses, and he tells how the novel became "the bourgeois form par excellence," cementing "the writer's links with the middle class." There ensued a huge "fiction boom between 1911 and 1925," rendering the Tamil book a commodity. The work of author "Kalki" R. Krishnamurthy (1899–1954) and the establishment of the popular magazine *Āṉanta Vikaṭaṉ* rendered fiction respectable, and readership skyrocketed. The reading boom resulted in a widening market and a "proliferation of novels," which also came with great moral reservations, but all of the fears concerning the corruption of the morals of readers were successfully mitigated by Kalki "and his nationalist novels."[7]

Prose literature as we now think of it was late to emerge in almost all of the Indian languages. Even though writing in a fictive vein was nothing new, especially in Tamil and other Dravidian languages, there is a clear generic distinction between the vernacular *katai* or "story literature" in Tamil, and emerging novel and short-story forms that were inspired and influenced by Western styles and genres. Meenakshi Mukherjee describes the emergence of the novel in India in three phases. Prose writing in India began as a didactic enterprise. Mukherjee labels such works "novels of purpose,"[8] exemplified by the first novel to appear in the Tamil language, Samuel Vedanayakam Pillai's 1879 *Piratāpa Mutaliyār Carittiram*, which had clearly didactic intentions. This genre gave way to historical fiction merged with supernatural elements, followed by works that "attempt to render contemporary Indian society realistically in fiction," the latter very much a European move, according to Mukherjee.[9]

In the foreword to his new edited collection, *The Tamil Short Story: Through the Times, through the Tides*, Dilip Kumar himself notes that "the first inheritance from the West was the novel; the short story trotted a little behind." In his three capacities as author, editor, and literary critic, he has a great deal to say about the history of the short story in the Tamil language, as well as the emergence and refinement of its craft. He writes of the pleasing "literary compactness" of the form, and, speaking from his own perspective as an author, he notes that "only the craft of the short story seems to have the benevolence to accommodate the fragmentary realities and truths of our existence." He writes of the "three stalwarts" of the 1910s and the 1920s—Subramania Bharati, Va. Ve. Su. Aiyar, and A. Madhavaiah—who are considered "the chronological pioneers of the Tamil short story."[10]

Casting the Tamil story within the wider context of national literary trends, Dilip Kumar writes that "it is in the short story, undoubtedly the major medium of literary expression in most Indian languages, that the link between modernity and literature best manifests itself."[11] Again, writing from his own perspective as a master of the short-story genre, he discusses the challenges of the form: the writer must strive "to attain the acme of perfection within a very limited space, at once imposing discipline and granting freedom. The essence lies in its precision and unity, revealing in the process the concerns of the writer and his fidelity to the form."[12] Translator Subashree Krishnaswamy also writes of the Tamil short story in terms of "grammar and craft," and definitely as a genre of writing that has to be mastered and practiced. She also remarks on the utter importance and significance of brevity, which proves to be the perfect vehicle to capture "the immediacy of modern life."[13] Dilip Kumar adds, "Contemporary Tamil prose is believed to have evolved from its rich oral tradition of storytelling. But this genre, introduced from the West, was a distinctive, fresh literary form. Unlike the novel, the modern Tamil short story could rely very little on the oral tradition; instead, it had to invent a tenor and a sensibility that was compatible with, conducive to, and reflective of the grammar of the new genre."[14]

The modern Tamil story truly came into its own in the 1930s through the vehicle of *Maṇikkoṭi*, a literary weekly that was published from 1933 through 1939. *Maṇikkoṭi* launched the careers of writers such as Pudumaippittan, Mauni, and Ku. Pa. Rajagopalan. According to Dilip Kumar, it was Pudumaippittan who "honed the idiom of the short story." He and the other authors who collectively came to be known as the *Maṇikkoṭi* group had their fingers "on the pulse of the Tamil experience," but it was Pudumaippittan who set the tone for nearly all that was to follow.[15]

The modern movement in Tamil writing "stemmed from little literary magazines" and served "as a parallel counterpoint"[16] to more popular publications. By the 1940s, reading had become very popular as a pastime. Venkatachalapathy has documented in detail the development of reading practices, such as reading in silence;[17] the rise of reading during hours of leisure, particularly during the monsoon season or to pass the time during train travel; the establishment of lending libraries and reading rooms; and women's reading practices,[18] the last of which we find reflected in Dilip Kumar's stories "Crossing Over" and "The Crowd." By the 1960s, Tamil authors had shifted their focus "from one of the idealism of the *Maṇikkoṭi* writers, and emphasized strong story line, well-defined narratives, and sharp social criticism," which resulted in a "full embrace of literary realism."[19]

The Settings

Many of Dilip Kumar's stories are set in an extensive Gujarati family compound inhabited by orthodox Hindus, adherents of the Puṣṭimārg tradition of Vaiṣṇavism, founded by the philosopher Vallabhācārya (1479–1531).[20] The Puṣṭimārg—the "Path of Grace"—is still a very vibrant and active religious sect whose devotees largely come from the Gujarati mercantile (baniyā) community.[21] Its theological orientation is one of "Pure Non-Dualism."[22] The three-story buildings that house this community are all on Ekambareshvarar Agrahāram Street, located just off Mint Street in the cramped northern neighborhoods of Chennai, and this is no Malgudi, the fictional town in which much of R. K. Narayan's fiction is set: it is not a "fictive" place. The stories connect us not just with literature but with a real place on the map. The agrahāram street wraps around the tank of a 350-year-old Śaiva temple, the Ekāmbareśvara Kōyil. The stories that are set in this very specific locale are, when read together, reminiscent of Georges Perec's 1970 novel *Life: A User's Manual,* which is set in a block of flats in a French city (one would assume Paris), or, to take a more immediate example from an urban Indian setting, of Rohinton Mistry's 1997 cycle of stories *Swimming Lessons and Other Stories from Firozsha Baag.* Dilip Kumar's stories stretch out across buildings, years, different flats, in stairwells and among stories, in lavatories, in kitchens, and across generations, and spill out onto the street. Characters who appear as main protagonists in one story might end up as observers and commentators on the peripheries of others. The contexts of the stories are largely domestic, with all the tensions inherent therein, but Dilip Kumar is also given to political fiction. His stories exhibit a complex "alphabet of themes," as A. K. Ramanujan would call them,[23] including those of abduction and redemption, sexual frustration, humiliation and despair, domestic violence and related issues of identity and wholeness, and those of terror and dread. Dilip Kumar's themes and concerns are simultaneously broadly human—they speak to universal human experience—and deeply private and personal: he writes of the interior worlds of boredom, embarrassment, shame, desire, fear, and affection.

The stories that are set in the agrahāram reflect the values and worldview of an established middle class, and many of them rely on what we can think of as ethnographic detail. In the cycle of stories set in the Ekambareshvarar Agrahāram, he details for us the minutiae of Gujarati family life. The descriptions of the layouts of flats, stairwells, courtyards, and terraces read at times like anthropological field notes, and were sometimes so intricate that I had to ask Dilip Kumar to draw me sketch maps of corridors, showing where doorways were located in relation to wells and staircases, before I could even begin to grasp the movements of his characters through these spaces. His stories document sets of attitudes adopted by a closely knit neighborhood of North Indians, and, in a way, Dilip Kumar uses his stories to explain the intimacies of Gujarati daily life to his South Indian Tamil readers. But this is much more than "tattling": the stories bring us to an understanding of the adaptive powers of a well-off community that has established itself in the midst of working- and middle-class Tamils. We get a sense of where the linguistic borders are, for instance, and of how enclavist upper classes and castes "see"—or "don't see"—the life that swirls around them. His stories are also enhanced with closely drawn descriptions of the inhabitants, often written out in crime-blotter style, as in this description of the pious granny Babli Patti, the antagonist of the 1996 story "Cat in the Agrahāram":

> Babli Patti had a bulky body. A little bun streaked with gray. A big long nose. She wore spectacles with thin steel frames. At her neck, a chain of tulsi beads. She was ruddy-complexioned, like a ripe fruit.

Or here, of Mr. Rao, the violent and overbearing boss of the Coimbatore tailor shop in which the 1980 story "Bamboo Shoots" is set:

> Mr. Krishnaji Rao was a Marathi. Stunted. Fat. He was very foul-mouthed. Though he drank a lot, he was utterly brilliant in his profession . . . Because he'd been out and about in the strong sun, his face had gone as red as an old, bruised apple. With each of his steps, his paunch danced and shook. When compared with all other paunches, Mr. Rao's was one of a kind. It had its mysterious beginnings just beneath his hairless chest: rising up tranquilly, it then formed a lazy half-circle before angling down sharply and disappearing.

Or here, of Dilip Kumar himself, casting himself in the guise of a suicidal poet in the 1992 story "The Scent of a Woman":

> His name is Rahul K. Nayak. He's a Gujarati. Poor. Twenty-four years old. Height 6 feet, 7 inches, emaciated frame. Medium complexion. A long nose, blunted at the tip. There is nothing to differentiate his head from his neck, which stretches upward in a solitary mass. In short, he is about as beautiful as a garden lizard. He is educated only up to the eighth standard. Neither English nor Gujarati comes easily to him. He knows a little Tamil, a very, very, little. You might say that it is only because of this that he dares to write poems in Tamil. And his poems do no harm to the Tamil language, which has been around as long as rock and earth.

In this remark on the resiliency and antiquity of the Tamil language, we get a sense of Dilip Kumar's own admiration for it. It is also worth remarking here upon the author's own knowledge of Tamil convention and literary history. This knowledge emerges most often in moments of humor, as he tips his hat to the *Tolkāppiyam*, the earliest extant text on Tamil grammar, phonetics, and literary usage, in his long story "Kaṭavu," "Crossing Over," published in 2000. He describes a widowed patti, the oldest woman in the agrahāram, who is a survivor of sex trafficking and known for her foul language, which she uses in moments of endearment and expressions of love, in this way:

> Patti didn't have a shred of respect for the agrahāram men. She simply called all of them Da. Behind their backs, without any respect, she would call them sons of whores . . . But Patti really loved Rajni Mama the bier-builder. And so, she would call him a whoreson right to his face. When she pronounced that word with great honey-dripping affection, what occurred was *poruḷ-mayakkam*—a confusion of meaning—a literary device found in the Old Tamil grammar, the *Tolkāppiyam*. Similarly, Patti made beautiful use of vast numbers of Gujarati swearwords, turning them into cubes of jaggery. When she would tell us to shove a fire up our asses, a veritable soothing breeze would caress our hearts.

His knowledge of Hindu philosophy and the differences among the schools of Vaiṣṇava theology also appear in "Crossing Over," but to the most humorous effect in his 1996 "Cat in the Agrahāram." In this story, pious old Babli Patti is terrorized by a cat who has made a habit of stealing the puja milk every morning. Even though the story's overall feel is not funny at all—the starving, thieving cat is a metaphor for Babli Patti's despised, barren daughter-in-law—we learn that cats tend to stay away from the Puṣṭimārg agrahāram because they understand that the atmosphere is not philosophically favorable to them:

> Generally, cats never entered the Ekambareshvarar Agrahāram. In fact, not a single cat had entered the agrahāram in the past fifty or sixty years. All of the agrahāram residents happened to spot cats only in Thangasalai Street, in Govindappa Nayakkar Street, or in Kondittoppu. There had to be reasons other than those of environment for cats not entering the Ekambareshvarar Agrahāram. It appeared that the reasons were ideological, given that most of the agrahāram residents were Puṣṭimārg Vaishnavas. Tenkalai Vaishnavas held cats in high esteem, but there was certainly no compulsion for Puṣṭimārgīs

to do so. Yes, it was true that in the Puṣṭimārg, whose primary deity was the infant Krishna, there were ancillary laws that stated that they must show affection for birds and beasts. However, maximum importance was reserved for the cows, who munched on polythene bags and cinema posters and shat wherever they pleased. Was not the supreme soul Krishna a cowherd himself? It seemed that the cats instinctively understood this higher truth, and followed it with rectitude—until last April, that is.

Dilip Kumar's beautifully sketched, Daumier-like characters move through his thick descriptions of street life, where they engage in transactions of every sort, but if the stories are read in chronological sequence, the reader gains a sense of the layers of community history, especially in the pieces set in the "real streets" of the agrahāram. Other North Indian groups move in, bringing with them their own sets of habits and languages, altering the shapes of buildings and the overall landscape, and force others out: Gujaratis are in, but are overtaken by Marwaris and Rajasthani vessel merchants, and we see all of this happening from the vantage point of an elderly uncle, Mittu Mama, the protagonist of two stories, "The Crowd" and "The Letter." In the 1981 story "The Crowd," we meet Mittu Mama as a fully developed character as he stands on his balcony, surveying the street below him:

> The wind blew in bold gusts. At the temple, the plastic lotuses afloat in the tank had lost their color in the twilight and drifted on the water like black stains. Mittu Mama looked out at the intersection of Thangasalai Street and the agrahāram street. There were rows and rows of people, and rickshaws were trying to cross through them. In the dazzle of the electric light, Thangasalai Street was overflowing with excitement. He could clearly hear the swish of its hustle and bustle . . . all of Mittu Mama's bonds were with what he could see from his balcony: the Ekambareshvarar temple, the temple tower, the end of the street, the street beyond, the temple tank, its algae, its plastic lotuses. Above all of these, the school clock tower loomed.

Compare this passage with the description from the 1993 story "The Letter" as Mittu Mama dictates his complaints to Dilip Kumar, who inserts himself into the story as Mittu's amanuensis. The letter is addressed to Ghanshyam Mama, a well-to-do relative:

> The agrahāram itself has lost its glow. The tank has gone dry. For appearance's sake, they fill it up with a little water, and they float

plastic lotuses on it. They have demolished the saffron-striped wall around the temple tank, constructed a building in place of it, and have rented out rooms to ever-silver vessel merchants. You can no longer see the school clock tower on Ravana Aiyar Street. They've stuck up mikes on the pillars in the temple corridors and play light-music bhajans. In the streets, which used to be frequented by pure Gujaratis, the vessel-shop Marwaris now overrun the place.

There are really no heroes to speak of in Dilip Kumar's stories. Many of his protagonists are either victims of their own circumstances, such as Gangu Patti in "Crossing Over" or Madhuri in "Cat in the Agrahāram," or they are lonely, solitary even in crowded streets or in large, joint-family contexts, victims of their own foibles and self-doubt.

Navigating Fact and Fiction in a Multilingual World

Dilip Kumar's stories also often blur the boundaries between what Mukherjee terms "autobiographical technique" and autobiography itself,[24] and can at times best be thought of as fictionalized personal narratives, but we must at the same time maintain a separation between literary realism and social reality—they are hardly the same thing.[25] Women figure prominently in almost every single story. The younger married women of the agrahāram, whose concerns and struggles as daughters-in-law within the confines of the joint family, coupled with the duties of maintaining orthodox boundaries and religious expression, especially in the performance of vows and the demands of Puṣṭimārg daily worship, are given voice, particularly in the conversational vignettes in part 2 of "Crossing Over." But in these same vignettes, we also hear the voices of unmarried girls as they approach the threshold of womanhood, while they deal with new sets of problems: those of career choice, sexual identity, and the hypocrisies and sexism of religious ideology, with which modernity and their educations have confronted them. These vignettes were particularly challenging to translate because of their intimate nature. The language has a very private feel to it in places, and I found it almost treasonous to bring these conversations into the more public sphere that an English translation provides. Elderly widows rule the roost, and appear either as pious tyrants, as in the case of Babli Patti in "Cat in the Agrahāram," or as frank and loving confidantes, as in the tragic figure of Gangu Patti in "Crossing Over." The agrahāram men, in contrast, are depicted as largely in thrall to their wives and mothers, and as holders of boring salaried jobs. The more classic figure of the "tramp hero"[26] does emerge, however, in Dilip Kumar's more autobiographical stories, as in "The Scent of a Woman" (1992), "A Walk in the Dark" (1980), or in "Bamboo Shoots" (1980). These characters wander through their settings, but they wander with purpose: suicide, hunger, or making a wage. We see the world through their eyes and through their often painful, humiliating interactions with society, or as they quietly observe the daily sorts of humiliations visited upon others.

Dilip Kumar's writing may very well be driven by an autobiographical impulse, but also by an acute documentarian one.[27] He also writes very much within the mode of what Subramanian Shankar terms "vernacular realism." There is a "vernacular specificity"[28] in Dilip Kumar's work that turns not just on issues of the Tamil language, but also on a doubly vernacular specificity—a "cultural duality," in fact.[29] The duality is that of Tamil writing washed through the linguistic intricacies of a Gujarati mother tongue and set within a very specific locale: a small Gujarati neighborhood within the largely Tamil, Telugu, and Urdu linguistic and cultural milieux of north-central Chennai. His stories also exhibit what Shankar calls "vernacular humanism"[30]—the stories mediate among languages, classes, and colors—but even though the stories do display these very particular urban and linguistic specificities, they also transcend the local human condition and speak to more universal concerns, giving voice to a Gujarati subnational identity through the medium of the Tamil language. Most Indians conduct their daily lives through the media of two or more languages, and Dilip Kumar's stories beautifully demonstrate this linguistic complexity and the ultimate "messiness of the world."[31]

I also must admit that during the whole process of translating Dilip Kumar's stories and as I began to write about them, I found very little postcolonial theory to be of much use. Most of the stories are set in Chennai—an urban center with excellent universities where English is very much alive, and where there is a great deal of cultural and political debate. Dilip Kumar's stories are "unfettered by post-colonial angst,"[32] and he is in no way writing back to empire. If he is "writing back" to anything, it is back to his own Gujarati roots, and to his own family. Even though the migration history of his family from Gujarat to South India was very much connected to colonial forces and routes of trade, and although Sowcarpet, the large neighborhood in which the agrahāram stories are set, is rife with architecture and other tangible reminders of empire, there is nothing in the stories themselves that directly confronts its presence. One might assume that he chose to write in Tamil and to live fully in the Tamil world to push back against encroaching North Indian hegemony in the South, but in working with him closely and in coming to understand his own compulsions and literary choices, I found that his move to embrace Tamil so completely was a deeply personal one, and had nothing at all to do with the politics of empire, the condition of the postcolony, or language hegemony. There is, however, one exception in this collection, and that is the case of "Taṭam" ("The Path," 1984), in which Dilip Kumar has certainly "written back" to an oppressive police state during the Tamil insurgency and civil war in Sri Lanka. And very much like Rashmi Sadana in her excellent *English Heart, Hindi Heartland: The Political Life of Literature in India*, I have found reading these stories through an anthropological lens to have been much more fruitful and generative than analyzing them through the lens of literary theory. Being there is critical: we are not just translating words, but ecologies, as Ramanujan once put it.[33]

While Sadana critiques the role of English and Anglophone writing in the world of Hindi writing and publishing, several of Dilip Kumar's stories allow us to see Gujarati migrants—and to a certain extent, the Gujarati language—within a Tamil context. Arjun Appadurai has famously likened the role of fiction to that of myth, thereby linking "fictional content with social mores."[34] Sadana writes that "the world of literary production shows not only how authors, readers, and texts but also how the entire nexus of literary producers and discourse create a social and moral framework that at once reflects and interrogates social norms." Sadana also shows that literature serves as a kind of cultural emblem, writing that through examining "the connections between place, language, and textual production," we can see "what language comes to stand for in people's lives and in society more generally." Her point is not that "authors writing in other Indian languages represent monolingual worlds,"[35] and this is certainly not true in Dilip Kumar's stories: he represents not just a Tamil world, but layerings that include Gujarati, English, Marathi, Christian, and sectarian Hindu worlds; in other words, a very complex and site-specific cosmopolitanism, but one that is "shorn of its elite pretensions."[36]

In many ways, Dilip Kumar is "performing" Gujarati lives for his Tamil readers.[37] His agrahāram stories represent the world of an aspirational Gujarati bourgeoisie, transplanted into a working- and middle-class Tamil urban space. Sadana argues that fiction is "a representation of reality, even when the language of the text matches the language of the street,"[38] and I would say this is especially true in the case of Dilip Kumar's fiction, in which a very specific Gujarati world is expressed in Tamil, the language of that specific world's street. Dilip Kumar's relationship to Tamil is a very subjective one and reflects his own personal linguistic history as well as his family's history of migration from Kutch to Coimbatore to Chennai. In a very real sense, to write in Tamil as a Gujarati is to transform Tamil into a "safe zone"[39] for

Dilip Kumar, since the subjects of his satire do not read Tamil. As a cosmopolitan author and translator, however, he also has a rich relationship not just with the English language, but with contemporary English literature, as well.

Neither does Dilip Kumar's Tamil serve as an example of regional writing. His stories display relationships and histories between languages (Gujarati, Tamil), but they also express the complexities between languages "and their multiple locations"[40] (Kutch, Coimbatore, Chennai). His fiction represents "the dilemma of living in two languages,"[41] but we can even call it three or more, if we add in English, Hindi, Marathi, Malayalam, and Telugu. In the two stories in which Christians are portrayed, "The Miracle That Refused to Happen" (1988) and "The Planet of Old Age" (1997), we see Dilip Kumar's own politics of imagination very much at work, as he deals with the modern problems of divorce, the nuclear family, and caring for the elderly. In a recent conversation, he told me that he found it very difficult to write about these issues—even to fictionalize them—within the Hindu context of the agrahāram, where things such as divorce would be rare, if not unheard of.[42]

In writing about the phenomenon of the autobiography in India, David Arnold and Stuart Blackburn remark upon the compelling truth-telling that we encounter in this literary form. Dilip Kumar's stories are definitely drawn from "life-historical material,"[43] and the agrahāram stories, in particular, function in much the same way as "literary self-narratives." As he mediates between his subjects and his readers, he is in many ways embedding himself in his accounts of lives that are ostensibly about either fictional or real "others," with fiction acting very powerfully as a kind of surrogate voice in which there is a palpable "tension between the desire to tell the truth and an equally intense desire to regulate it."[44] In two stories in particular, "The Scent of a Woman" (1992) and "Five Rupees and the Man in the Dirty Shirt" (1982), we find ourselves reading his own story as an emerging writer of fiction. As Venkatachalapathy notes, the "motif of the ever-poor author" has been a recurring theme in Tamil fiction for quite some time,[45] and in the case of these two stories, Dilip Kumar inhabits and perpetuates that motif very convincingly. His choice of Tamil as his language of literary expression raises questions about concealment, even in the stories in which Dilip Kumar inserts himself as a character ("Crossing Over," "The Letter," "The Solution," and "Bamboo Shoots" are all excellent examples of this), or of the technique of writing oneself into a story by using a deictic, third-person pronoun such as *ivan*—"this man here"—as a stand-in for the first-person "I." Dilip Kumar's choice of Tamil as safe zone—as a "strategy of protection"[46]—serves as a cover for himself, but more so for the family members or for other close acquaintances who populate his stories, of which I include synopses below.

The stories that follow appear in the same order as published in the original Tamil. Even though this takes them out of chronological sequence, with the most recent and longest story appearing first, there are virtues in beginning with "Kaṭavu," "Crossing Over," which introduces readers to the very real place of Ekambareshvarar Agrahāram and many of its inhabitants, upon whom most of Dilip Kumar's characters are based.

The heroine of "Crossing Over," Gangu Patti, is the most senior agrahāram resident. The first section of the story gives the details of her penultimate "death"—we are told that this is, in fact, the twenty-eighth time that Gangu Patti has put her extended family through her final throes, which always turn out to be false alarms. A second plot runs parallel to the main story. Rajnikanth Mama is a childless householder who builds funeral biers to ensure his own passage to heaven upon his death. Whenever Gangu Patti has one of her "crises," Rajnikanth is the first person sent for, and, as it turns out, he is the only man of the extended family of the agrahāram with whom Gangu Patti has a deep and loving bond. The first part of "Crossing Over" is written with light, humorous touches, and readers are left completely unprepared for the tragic details of Gangu Patti's life as they unfold in the second section.

Gangu Patti marries at thirteen, gives birth to six children, none of whom thrive, and she is widowed at the age of twenty-seven. An uncle takes her in, but the family temporarily shifts to a military cantonment for work, where Gangu Patti is abducted by Anglo-Indian soldiers and sold into prostitution in Mumbai (formerly Bombay). She is miraculously rescued and brought back to Chennai to live in the agrahāram, but her mind and spirit have been so damaged by her experiences that it takes her many years to come back to herself fully. As she turns seventy, she befriends many of the younger family women, who then come to her for advice and frank talk, and every afternoon, Gangu Patti holds an "assembly" in one of the agrahāram courtyards, where no topic is off-limits. Advice is given on everything, including sex, religion, pickle-making, and the nature of time and god. In the course of thirteen beautifully realized conversational vignettes, we gain a clear sense of what happened to Gangu Patti, and what her status is in the agrahāram among the older, more pious generation of women. The story ends on a poignant note, when Rajnikanth Mama's own goals suffer a temporary setback.

The second story, "Kāṉal," "Mirage," is a brief sketch of the aftermath of a hasty, ill-fated affair between two anonymous characters. The couple makes use of the privacy afforded them by a friend, and they meet, but things between them go awry, and they leave the flat unsatisfied and humiliated. "Mirage" is very much a mood piece—here, Dilip Kumar's almost cinematic sense of lighting adds to the uncomfortable atmosphere as we join the couple in their stuffy room, the air thick with humidity and frustrated desire.

Mittu Mama, who is mentioned for the first time in "Crossing Over," as a peripheral character, takes center stage in "Katitam," "The Letter." A widower in his seventies, Mittu doesn't get on with his sons and their wives, who confine him to a small room at the front of their flat. But the room has a balcony, and from his vantage point we see the street life surrounding the agrahāram. In "The Letter," Mittu asks Dilip Kumar, who narrates the story in a first-person voice, to take down a letter for him (Mittu's own hands are palsied). Mittu's ultimate goal is to request 100 rupees from his wealthy co-brother, Ghanshyam Mama (the two men are married to a pair of sisters), but as he dictates the letter, he registers complaints about his health and about the members of his own household who have ostracized and insulted him, and in passing, he longs for the past, lamenting the changing times and condemning the encroachments of modernity.

In the experimental piece "Nikala Marutta Arputam," "The Miracle That Refused to Happen," we encounter a most unhappy couple, Mr. and Mrs. James. The story begins as Mrs. James is preparing to leave her abusive husband, her suitcase in hand. She speaks only a few lines, and then goes silent, rooted to the spot, as her husband begs her not to go. Mrs. James is fifteen years younger than her husband, and in what amounts to a lengthy monologue by Mr. James, we are made privy to a history of their entire unhappy marriage—her horrible illness that rendered her bedridden three months into the marriage, his sexual frustration, alcoholism, and sterility, and her kindness and appreciation for the ordinary things in life, serving as counterpoint to his physical and verbal abuse in his drunken rages. The story ends in the midst of his regret at never having fathered a child, with a long meditation on the infirmities and loneliness of growing old. And, as we discover early on in this story, Mr. James is also a poet.

The figure of the poet takes center stage in "The Scent of a Woman." (The Tamil title of this story, "Mannam Enum Tōṇi Parri," is a line from a medieval bhakti poem by a Śaiva saint, and is there to provide atmosphere rather than meaning. Its presence reminds readers of the Tamil lunar month of Mārgaḻi [roughly equivalent to the English months of December and January], during which such poems are sung by the Ōtuvārs, people who have the right to sing Śaiva hymns in the big temple in Mylapore, the center of the city of Chennai, and in many ways its heart.) There is also a reference to Mārgaḻi month and devotional songs in the story's second poem, but the story itself is set in the brutal heat of summer. Dilip Kumar based the poet-protagonist, Rahul K. Nayak, largely on himself, and we find many autobiographical elements in this story—as in many of the others—around which the narrative is built. Here, there are no drunken rages or abusive behavior, but we are confronted with the figure of an overly sensitive, depressed, and now suicidal young man who has gone to the beach to drown himself. Rather than starting off on a maudlin note, however, the story begins with biting self-satire. Rahul K. Nayak's career as a poet appears to be over before it even begins: he enjoys some success, but his empty stomach keeps him trudging around the city looking for work. He finds a job—and a potential lover, Rajakumari—at Prince's Corner, a ready-made shop in Pondy Bazaar. His hopes for himself as a poet clash with the hard realities of his life, and interfere with his abilities to make lasting human bonds. He loses his job, and his state of despair lands him up on the beach, where he then has a surreal encounter with Rajakumari.

In "Agrahārattil Pūṇai," "Cat in the Agrahāram," Babli Patti, a pious old woman, declares war on a stray cat, which has made it a habit to steal inside the flat and lap up all of the milk that Babli Patti has set out in the hall to offer to the infant Krishna, the deity at the center of Puṣṭimārg devotion. Madhuri, Babli Patti's childless daughter-in-law, is a secret champion of the cat, which becomes an apt metaphor for Madhuri's own degraded status in the household. Babli Patti's nephew Suri, the family layabout, hooligan, and dispenser of neighborhood justice, is delegated to get rid of the cat, but by the time the story ends, we see Suri's love for it emerge during the aftermath of an act of terrible cruelty, as well as a fleeting moment of triumph for Madhuri, who stands alone in the middle of the hall, the site of all the feline thievery.

"Mutumai-k Kōḷam," "The Planet of Old Age," repeats a theme that we also see in "The Miracle That Refused to Happen." In the latter, Mr. James describes just such a planet as he rages against his wife, expressing his horror at growing old and likening it to being bundled onto a spaceship and transported to a "separate, desolate planet . . . that planet called Old Age." In the former, we meet Mrs. Florence, a resident of that very planet, as she waits for her son Solomon to come to visit her in a seaside home for the elderly. Mrs. Florence is at the end of her life, her mind wanders, and she suffers from night terrors, which landed her in the home. Her screams at night were terrifying her grandchildren. She consoles herself by looking at the sky, clouds, and stars for hours on end, and much like Mittu Mama, the elderly uncle in "The Letter" and "The Crowd," her bonds are not with people but with things in the world around her within her line of sight, and she develops a peculiar fondness for one solitary star, waiting to see it each night. Solomon arrives, and a difficult conversation ensues, but even though the story ends on a sad, guilt-laden note, it also emphasizes the themes of filial love and maternal forgiveness.

The experimental story "A Walk in the Dark" is another of Dilip Kumar's autobiographical pieces. (The Tamil title, "Nilai," meaning "condition" or "state," is far too ambient a word to move well into English as a title.) The anonymous protagonist meanders over a 2-kilometer path through a marketplace—here, the very specific, very real consumerist space of D. B. Road in north-central Coimbatore—and the reader joins him as he steps out onto the street after completing his first full day at a hard-won new job. The reader is with him inside his head—we see what he sees—and while we quickly realize that he is deranged, the reason is not apparent until we are well into the story. He moves from the glitz and sparkle of the market into a mean little lane, walking through an almost Dickensian scene of a sleeping neighborhood. He then recalls a very disturbing dream filled with sexual imagery, the violent destruction of beauty, and environmental degradation, but as he encounters a threatening stray dog on the street, he snaps to his senses, and it is not until he moves out of the surreal, brightly lit market streets and into its back lanes that we come to a resolution outside of the blinding dazzle and well within the more familiar discomforts of grinding poverty.

"Kaṇṇāṭi," "The Mirror," is an observed story based on a real family of pavement dwellers, whom Dilip Kumar watched through an office window for weeks. Palaniyammal, her husband, Mariyappan, and their daughter Jagadishvari have made a makeshift home for themselves beneath the shade of a City Corporation tree, and a terrible scene over a 25-paisa coin disrupts the mundane pleasures of a sunny morning: Palaniyammal taunts Mariyappan, who cannot speak properly because of his missing teeth, and as her taunts escalate into attacks on his manhood, he pounces on her, thrashing her until he wears himself out. The pair fall asleep in exhaustion, until a Brahmin woman comes by to ask if Palaniyammal can line her brass vessels with lead for her. Hunger is what compels Palaniyammal to rouse and "transact" with the woman, and a walk to the comfortable home—a walk that enunciates caste, the Brahmin woman ahead, Palaniyammal a respectful yard behind—is what makes Palaniyammal's shattering encounter with the mirror possible, an encounter that leads her into contemplating her own fate, and even though she refuses to resign herself to it, the encounter with her own devastating image allows her to feel pity, and even a bit of tenderness, for Mariyappan.

In "Janam," "The Crowd," we return to Ekambareshvarar Agrahāram and to a younger and more fully developed version of Mittu Mama. This is the story in the collection in which we gain the best sense of the ways in which this closely knit neighborhood of North Indians lives within Tamilian spaces. "The Crowd" brings to us an understanding of the adaptive powers—and adaptive failures—of a relatively prosperous community in the midst of working- and middle-class Tamils. The story begins with Oosa, a Tamil man, who has collapsed and lies unconscious on the street. Ranjan Behn, an agrahāram housewife, discovers Oosa lying on the pavement just outside her door, and she doesn't know what to do. She is caught between her urge to help and her fear of being seen in such close proximity to a man who has become a part of the wall; who is darker in complexion and lower in status than she. A crowd begins to gather, and while several young men step forward to help, they are driven by their own selfish motivations, and no one can even bring themselves to touch Oosa to see if he is breathing or has a pulse, save for a character named Avinash, who gingerly grabs Oosa's wrist and hastily pronounces him dead. Mittu Mama, who limps downstairs upon hearing about what has happened from an excited agrahāram child, is the only one who has no compunction about touching Oosa, and, as we learn, Mittu is the only resident in the agrahāram who has bothered to learn Tamil or who has previously conversed in even the most casual way with Oosa at all.

"Mūṅkil Kuruttu," "Bamboo Shoots," is set in Coimbatore in Mr. Krishnaji Rao's tailor shop, and is told in Dilip Kumar's own first-person voice. The story is set in the aftermath of Dilip Kumar's father's death, with the facts changed slightly to accommodate the plot. Right from the beginning, we are plunged into a multilingual context, with mixtures of Gujarati, Marathi, Hindi, and Malayalam within a Tamil setting. Mr. Rao, the foulmouthed and once well-off proprietor, is down on his luck and has fallen deeply into a dissipated state from all of his profligate spending, drinking, and whoring. He is a man with a violent temper, and regularly thrashes his wife, his daughter, and his more vulnerable employees. Dilip Kumar has cast himself in the role of Gujarati accountant. The story begins on an anxious note: Mr. Rao's employees are waiting for their pay, and it is clear to everyone that there has not been enough business in the shop to meet payroll. It is in this context that we learn that Dilip Kumar in his accountant role must bring home enough cash to pay for his father's death-anniversary rites, knowing that failure to do so will bring on the wrath of his widowed mother. He goes home empty-handed, but with the dim hope of collecting lost wages by delivering a stack of blazers to students at one of the local colleges. This story is arguably the most atmospheric in the collection: as the protagonist moves from place to place on his errands, we gain a sense of the brutalities and pleasures of the Coimbatore streets. The tea shops and abattoirs, police brutality, and again, the themes of caste, class, and racial disparities are ever present in the keenly observed depictions of his surroundings, interactions, and daily life.

"Aintu Rūpāyum Aḻukku-c Caṭṭai-k Kārarum," "Five Rupees and the Man in the Dirty Shirt," is an account of an encounter—again, told in the first person by Dilip Kumar as himself—with an author referred to here as "Comrade K.," but who is, in fact, the great Tamil writer G. Nagarajan (1929–81), author of the novel *Tomorrow Is One More Day* and many other brilliant works of fiction. The entire story is set in S. Ramakrishnan's Cre-A bookstore, which in 1982, when this story appeared, was still at its original location on Royapettah High Road in central Chennai. This story will be of particular value to anyone interested in modern Tamil literature, as it provides an extended description of Comrade K.'s state of mind and his horrible dissipation from drink and addiction to hashish in the several months before his death. This story was a challenge to translate: the conversation between the narrator and Comrade K. originally took place in English, but it was written in Tamil for Tamil readers, and translating it back into English proved to be quite difficult, not at all from a lexical point of view, but in attempting to capture the colloquial register in which this historic conversation must have been conducted.

The story opens as the narrator is closing up shop for the night, wondering about a 5-rupee shortfall in that day's accounts. And in comes Comrade K., a shadow of his former self, in a veshti and jibba crusted with dirt, stinking, and disheveled. When Dilip Kumar as narrator realizes who this is, he recalls Comrade K.'s critical accolades and what an important writer he had been to an earlier generation. What follows is a sketch of Comrade K.'s career, his affiliation and subsequent falling out with the Communist Party, a highly intellectual conversation on the uses and pitfalls of doctrinaire Marxism, and the advice of a senior author to one whose career is just getting under way. The conversation quickly becomes personal, and as Dilip Kumar tries to close up shop for the night, we realize the purpose of Comrade K.'s visit: to get money from the till for alcohol. Comrade K. becomes abusive, and after an exchange of words and blows, the two writers—the old and the young—part ways in the street.

We return to the agrahāram streets and apartments in "Tīrvu," "The Solution," and enter into satirical accounts of Gujarati family life. The first-person narrator—Dilip Kumar once more—enters an agrahāram building, only to find its courtyards strangely deserted. He then notices a huge crowd around a well, and discovers quickly that a rat has fallen into it and drowned. An uncle, Babu Bhai, is busily trying to fish the rat out, but to no avail. When the sodden rat is finally extricated, a single problem remains:

is the well water potable? After much deliberation, an elderly, orthodox granny comes up with the answer.

The collection ends on a grim note. "Taṭam," "The Path," was published in 1984, during the "insurgency" period of the civil war between the Sri Lankan government and the LTTE, the Liberation Tigers of Tamil Eelam. The story was inspired by a scream heard emanating from a jail located behind the famous Ice House on Chennai's Marina Beach. Powerfully narrated in the first person, "The Path" is a gruesome story of extrajudicial arrest, interrogation, and torture during a time of heightened emergency and fear, grounded in the suspicion that the LTTE had established training camps and terrorist cells in the forests of the Tamil Nadu mainland. After a particularly brutal beating, the narrator recounts the fate of his Sri Lankan friend and comrade Nayakam, who was one of the leaders of the movement, and fully realizes where he, too, is headed.

A Note on Translation

I can only begin to write about translating these stories in terms of my own initial errors in judgment: I mistakenly thought that I could work on the translations in piecemeal fashion as and when I could, but all I could do was pick at them, and after several years of fumbling, fits and starts, in which I produced what I knew even then were inadequate drafts—translations not fully felt—I decided that a long stretch of time in Chennai was needed in order to "feel" the stories from the ground up and to live and work fully in the Tamil language. The funding for that long stretch came together, and I lived in Chennai for eight months during 2013 and 2014, intensively working on the stories every day, living and breathing them.

The inherent difficulties of translating dialogue were perhaps my greatest challenge. We must translate what is said, but also how it is said. Dialogue is an indicator of all kinds of things, including class, caste, and status. Writing in the voice of a practicing translator rather than her more usual theorist voice, Gayatri Chakravorty Spivak tells us that we must attend to the "'specificity' of language" and any given language's "logical systematicity," but never at the expense of what she terms "rhetorical interference," the ways in which verbal gestures interrupt the logic of grammar.[47] Inflection in voice, register, and tone is crucial, and to this end, I found myself listening with great care to the musicality of any given dialogue during my conversations about the stories with my tutor and reading partner in Chennai, Subasri Raman, and, at the end of the process, during those crucial final adjustments to tone during my sessions with Aniruddhan Vasudevan in Austin. I found myself using the phrase marks of musical notation to make those subtle corrections, and I found this to be the most valuable "method"—if we can call it that—in making adjustments to my final renderings of dialogue.

There is no more intimate act of reading than translation, and in order to make a translated text accessible, "try doing it for the person who wrote it," as Spivak challenges us.[48] And this, indeed, was the final challenge for me, as I sat with Dilip Kumar in his Mylapore office and read out my English versions to him while he sat and followed along with his own Tamil text spread before him on his desk. It was during these initial harrowing sessions that I realized this enterprise was going to be far more difficult than I had ever imagined as I watched him grimace and shake his head, telling me that irony and humor—by far the most difficult aspects of any text to bring across—were just not coming through in my own English. He repeatedly urged me to find my own style. In trying to do so, I discovered that reading the stories aloud—in Tamil and in English, in Chennai and in Austin—and engaging in sustained conversations about them with the author and with other readers were essential and crucial components of my work.

Translators must be writers and rewriters, and it is not just words that we are translating, but their "emotional impact, the social aura that surrounds them, the setting and the mood that informs them, the atmosphere they create":[49] their context, in other words; Ramanujan's "ecology." Edith Grossman tells us that translation is an "interpretive performance," and that the goal is "to speak the piece in a second language."[50] A good translator is, in practice as well as in effect, the "second writer."[51]

I very strongly agree with Subramanian Shankar's contention that "translation practice" must become "a rich and pluralizing critical provocation," and that one must view translation as "opportunity rather than problem." But I am not so sure that I can agree with him on the whole issue of translatability. Shankar writes that "modernity lends itself to easy translation; tradition resists it in a variety of ways,"[52] but due to my own training in the classical languages of India, and with the objectification of texts that unfortunately arises from vast temporal gulfs—sometimes as wide as two millennia or more—I have personally found it much easier to translate "tradition" and "convention" than to translate modernity. I have found it far more difficult to read—let alone translate—modern Tamil fiction at a remove than the texts I have translated that are composed in classical languages, along with the certain amount of license that the ambiguity of poetry offers the translator. It is far easier to wallow in what Aamir Mufti has termed "the philological sublime," which, in effect, renders philology a "homeless practice."[53] With fiction, you are either right or you are wrong, and the only way to make a viable translation of any modern story is to live within the specificity of its writing; to live in its language and the milieu of its progeny. As Shankar remarks, "translation is often theorized as if the social dimension were of no consequence," but he and I would both maintain that the social dimension of translation is of every consequence when it comes to modern fiction.[54] As translators, we must solidify what Mufti describes as the "ghostly" presence of the vernaculars, and not leave it to Anglophone authors such as Salman Rushdie or Arundhati Roy to perform the vernaculars for us as they bend their English toward other languages.[55] If there is any "bending" at all in Dilip Kumar's fiction, it is the bending of Gujarati toward Tamil. But simultaneously, we must never forget the imbalance of power that is fostered by translating vernaculars. It is one thing for Dilip Kumar to "translate" Gujarati experience into Tamil, but it is another thing again for me to translate that duality into English: we must fully acknowledge the "directionality in which creativity flows,"[56] as well as the flows of our own scholarly and creative investments as translators. And finally, speaking from the other end of the process, a translation must stand on "independent, English-speaking legs,"[57] and it is my hope that the stories that follow stand tall and straight.

Notes

Transliteration of Tamil words adheres to the scheme as set out by the editors of the *Tamil Lexicon* (Madras: University of Madras, 1982).

1. Ashokamittiran (Jagadisa Thyagarajan), "Muṉṉurai," in Dilip Kumar, *Mūṅkil Kuruttu* (Chennai: Cre-A, 1985), iv–viii.

2. Ashokamittiran, "Muṉṉurai."

3. Donald C. Freeman, "Linguistic Approaches to Literature," in *Linguistics and Literary Style,* edited by Donald C. Freeman (New York: Holt, Rinehart & Winston, 1970), 9.

4. Richard Ohmann, "Generative Grammars and the Concept of Literary Style," *Word* 20, no. 3 (1964); quoted in Freeman, "Linguistic Approaches to Literature," 14.

5. Freeman, "Linguistic Approaches to Literature," 5.

6. A. R. Venkatachalapathy, *In Those Days There Was No Coffee: Writings in Cultural History* (New Delhi: Yoda Press, 2006), 79.

7. A. R. Venkatachalapathy, *The Province of the Book: Scholars, Scribes, and Scribblers in Colonial Tamilnadu* (Ranikhet: Permanent Black, 2012), 75–98.

8. Meenakshi Mukherjee, *Realism and Reality: The Novel and Society in India* (Delhi: Oxford University Press, 1985), 16.

9. Mukherjee, *Realism and Reality,* 16.

10. Dilip Kumar, *The Tamil Story: Through the Times, through the Tides* (Chennai: Tranquebar Press, 2016), quotations on xv, xv, and xvii.

11. Dilip Kumar, *The Tamil Story*, xvii.

12. Dilip Kumar, *The Tamil Story*, xvii.

13. Subashree Krishnaswamy, "A Note on Translation," in Dilip Kumar, *The Tamil Story*, xxv.

14. Dilip Kumar, *The Tamil Story*, xvii.

15. Dilip Kumar, *The Tamil Story*, quotations on xviii, xviii.

16. Dilip Kumar, *The Tamil Story*, xvii–xix.

17. Venkatachalapathy, *The Province of the Book*, 98.

18. Venkatachalapathy, *The Province of the Book*, 230–41.

19. Dilip Kumar, *The Tamil Story*, xx.

20. Shandip Saha, "A Community of Grace: The Social and Theological World of the *Puṣṭi Mārga Vārtā* Literature," *Bulletin of the School of Oriental and African Studies* 69, no. 2 (2006): 225.

21. Shandip Saha, "The Movement of *Bhakti* along a North-West Axis: Tracing the History of the Puṣṭimārg between the Sixteenth and Nineteenth Centuries," *International Journal of Hindu Studies* 11, no. 3 (2007): 299–318.

22. Saha, "The Movement of *Bhakti* along a North-West Axis," 303.

23. A. K. Ramanujan, "On Translating a Tamil Poem," in *The Collected Essays of A. K. Ramanujan*, edited by Vinay Dharwadker (Delhi: Oxford University Press, 1999), 230.

24. Mukherjee, *Realism and Reality*, 86.

25. James Wood, quoted in Sadana, *English Heart, Hindi Heartland*, 150.

26. Mukherjee, *Realism and Reality*, 113.

27. Rashmi Sadana, *English Heart, Hindi Heartland: The Political Life of Literature in India* (Berkeley: University of California Press, 2012), 69.

28. Subramanian Shankar, *Flesh and Fish Blood: Postcolonialism, Translation, and the Vernacular* (Berkeley: University of California Press, 2012), 12–16.

29. Sadana, *English Heart, Hindi Heartland*, 160.

30. Shankar, *Flesh and Fish Blood*, 99–100.

31. Shankar, *Flesh and Fish Blood*, 136.

32. Sadana, *English Heart, Hindi Heartland*, 67.

33. A. K. Ramanujan, "Form in Classical Tamil Poetry," 218.

34. Arjun Appadurai, *Modernity at Large*, quoted in Sadana, *English Heart, Hindi Heartland*, 7.

35. Sadana, *English Heart, Hindi Heartland*, 7–9.

36. Sadana, *English Heart, Hindi Heartland*, 93.

37. David Arnold and Stuart Blackburn, "Introduction: Life Histories in India," in *Telling Lives in India: Biography, Autobiography, and Life History,*

edited by David Arnold and Stuart Blackburn (Bloomington: Indiana University Press, 2004), 13.

38. Sadana, *English Heart, Hindi Heartland*, 9.

39. Sadana, *English Heart, Hindi Heartland*, 26–30.

40. Sadana, *English Heart, Hindi Heartland*, 105.

41. Sadana, *English Heart, Hindi Heartland*, 134.

42. Dilip Kumar, personal communication to the translator, Chennai, July 2014.

43. Arnold and Blackburn, "Introduction: Life Histories in India," quotations on 1, 3.

44. Sadana, *English Heart, Hindi Heartland*, 17.

45. Venkatachalapathy, *The Province of the Book*, 109.

46. Arnold and Blackburn, "Introduction: Life Histories in India," 17.

47. Gayatri Chakravorty Spivak, "The Politics of Translation," in *Destabilizing Theory: Contemporary Feminist Debates*, edited by Michèle Barrett and Anne Phillips (Palo Alto, Calif.: Stanford University Press, 1992), 178.

48. Spivak, "The Politics of Translation," 189.

49. Edith Grossman, *Why Translation Matters* (New Haven, Conn.: Yale University Press, 2010), 7.

50. Grossman, *Why Translation Matters*, 12.

51. Grossman, *Why Translation Matters*, 49.

52. Shankar, *Flesh and Fish Blood*, 107–10.

53. Aamir Mufti, *Forget English! Orientalisms and World Literatures* (Cambridge, Mass.: Harvard University Press, 2016), 200.

54. Shankar, *Flesh and Fish Blood*, 112.

55. Mufti, *Forget English!*, 160–63.

56. Sadana, *English Heart, Hindi Heartland*, 168.

57. Grossman, *Why Translation Matters*, 99–100.

Cat in the Agrahāram
and Other Stories

Crossing Over

1

This time, it seemed that Gangu Patti was not going to let anyone down, that she was definitely going to die, but no one could say for sure. As on all the other days, at a few hours past midnight, Gangu Patti's breathing grew labored. As was her custom, Patti extended her legs, pressed the back of her head up close against the wall, and with her gaze fixed on the crossbeam, she opened her mouth and noisily sighed with a great show of effort.

Sharada Behn and Pushpa Behn from the neighboring flat were seated right across from Patti. To ensure a smooth passage straight to heaven for Patti at the moment of her last breath, Natti Behn had spread open Dongre Maharaj's *Bhāgavatam* on a wooden reading stand, and began to recite from it in the corner. Patti's nephew's wife, Surekha, began to give Patti's back a gentle massage.

I was out in the courtyard, lingering near the door with Patti's nephew Gopal Bhai. Trambak Bhai, Babu Bhai, and Pran Jivanlal from the adjacent flats were conversing with a couple of teenagers in low voices. A 25-watt bulb yellowed with grime cast a gloom, hanging there shrouded in cobwebs.

As usual, Trambak Bhai looked at me and said, "*Dey,* her condition isn't good. You'd better go get Rajni from number 31." I hesitated, and moved slowly toward the stairs that led to the ground floor.

In the Ekambareshvarar Agrahāram, this very scene had been staged many times in the front room and courtyard of flat number 22, on the second floor of Building number 25. There is no rule stating that those who have lain down to die are actually obliged to do so. Nevertheless, Gangu Patti had violated deathbed decorum far too many times. She had done this not once, not twice, but she had wakened and panicked every single one of the twenty-four Gujarati households in that building twenty-seven times, and she wouldn't even die at the end of it all. Show up at the agrahāram, and just try saying to anyone: "Gangu Patti is 'serious.'" They'd slap you on the cheek, albeit gently.

In the few moments before she would start to struggle for breath, every time Patti would open her eyes wide and stare out into the void of the front room. Then she would movingly proclaim, "My boy Gopal, today my spirit is in peril! The time has come for me to go to Goloka, Da! Bring some Ganges water, fast!"

As soon as the eighty-year-old Kannadiga Ramchandra Sharma, the chief Ayurvedic doctor at the Marwari Hospital in Kontittoppu, was plunked on a scooter and brought to the house, he would check Patti's pulse. "It's true that Ma-ji's heart is weak, but there's nothing to worry about. She's probably had some deep-fried snack or other in the evening," he would nonchalantly say. (Patti must have polished off some bondas from Natti Behn's house, or some samosas from Madhuri's flat downstairs.) Removing his cap and rubbing his bald pate, he would think for a moment. Then, he would stick his hand inside his coat pocket and take out little packets of powder in bunches. Selecting one among them, he would tear it open and pour the contents into Patti's open mouth. He would give a few more packets to Surekha and say, "Thrice a day, for three days. She shouldn't take food. Only barley water and rice kanji, no salt." Then, collecting his 15-rupee fee and saying his namastes, he would leave. Before the *Bhāgavatam* recitation could even get to the point where Parikshit Maharaj was subjected to the curse of the serpent's bite, Patti would let loose tremendous belches with noisy *aaaa*s and *uuuu*s, and *trrr* and *brrr* with innumerable farts. All this would take only four or five minutes. Afterward, all would be well. Drinking down a mouthful of water, Patti would then drop off to sleep like a baby. Cursing the old crone left and right, the building would once again fall into restless hen-sleep.

As I stepped down into the street, the agrahāram looked desolate in the moonlight. A small electric light glittered at the top of the Ekambareshvarar temple's gopuram. A cool breeze spread out over everything like a secret. As I drew closer and closer to Building 31, Rajnikanth Mama's face appeared in my mind.

An absolute master in the building of traditional Gujarati funeral biers, Rajnikanth Mama worked as a sales representative in a wholesale bicycle shop on Broadway. On most days, he would head out at the crack of dawn for the towns that surrounded Chennai to take orders for spare bicycle parts, tires, and tubes. It was just him and his wife. They didn't have children. He was very affectionate with a touch of the rowdy in him.

Someone told Rajnikanth Mama that after death, those who have no heirs to perform funeral rites and offer rice balls to them will wander about as ghosts. They had also added that, in order to counteract that misfortune, if he were to build 108 funeral biers, all would turn out well. From that moment on, Rajnikanth Mama threw himself into the building of biers. He studied it as a true art form and became a master. People would say that even the giant Ghatotkaca could be laid out and borne along on a bier that he had built. Whenever a Gujarati died anywhere in the Sowcarpet neighborhood, the first call went straight to Rajnikanth Mama. Up till now, in his forty-fifth year, he had built 102 biers. As far as he was concerned, one bier was just one step closer to heaven.

Rajni Mama lived in the back portion of Building number 31, and in order to rouse him, I had to grab the iron knocker of the ancient door, like that of a temple. When I knocked, calling out to him at the top of my voice, in addition to the three dogs and the two bandicoots I annoyed at the side of the street, I managed to rouse Mittu Mama, Lakku Mama, and Suri Chittappa, along with everyone else in the family. Even though Rajni Mama was half-asleep, when I relayed the matter to him, he spoke like a man a bit possessed: "*Adey*, are you nuts? So that old lady-shmady is going to die-fie?! Even if the whole town dies of plague and is heaped up on biers, she won't die; you can count on it . . . okay, okay, who sent you here? Was it that fool Trambak? That rascal will have me to deal with if that old lady doesn't die today."

When I returned to number 25 with Rajni Mama in tow, the courtyard was empty. No one was there except Gopal Mama. The doctor had come and gone. Having passed gas, Patti was peacefully sleeping away. "Didn't I tell you? That old thing has made a face at the God of Death yet again," Rajni Mama said with a soft laugh.

2

Now, it had occurred to no one that Gangu Patti had once been an innocent toddler, a young girl, an adolescent, a young woman, a married woman, or even an older woman before she became an old lady, a patti. Most of Patti's contemporaries had died. Now, even the old women and men who still had life running in their veins were eight to ten years her junior. Gangu Patti had been married off at thirteen. She reached puberty at fifteen, gave birth to six children before she turned twenty-two, was robbed of all six of those children one by one, and was widowed at the age of twenty-seven. Gangu Patti was the daughter of Gopal Mama's aunt once removed. Her parents and her siblings had all died right before her eyes, without a single person remaining. After she was widowed, only Gopal Mama's father would take her in to live with his family. But Gangu Patti's sorrow didn't end with that. It so happened that in the following year, Gopal Mama's father had to shift to Renigunta for several months for work. At that time, there was a military barracks across from the place where they had come to live. In addition to the locals, there were Anglo-Indian soldiers coming and going in lorries and trucks. One evening, Gangu Patti suddenly went missing. People said that only those soldiers could have abducted her. After that, Gangu Patti was lost for four or five years. What happened to her is still a mystery even today: we didn't know where or how she was. When Gangu Patti was found again, she was in Bombay, along the side of a street in Bhuleshvar, where she was roaming, pregnant, her left knee twisted, her mind muddied. Someone from the agrahāram who had gone to Bombay spotted her, and sent word. Gopal Mama's father went there and rescued her. Right there in Bombay, she had an abortion and was given a bit of treatment for her leg. She was then brought back. During those days, as if she was suspended in a state of shock, Gangu Patti would lie staring vacantly at the ceiling, or she would weep into her hands, choking with sobs. Her mind cleared a little after eleven years of treatment at the Marwari Ayurvedic Hospital. Yet they said that she was not the old Gangu Behn anymore. But those who spoke this way knew absolutely nothing about the old Gangu Behn.

In her youth, Gangu Behn was so beautiful to behold. Except for her nose, she looked exactly like the Hindi film actress Nargis. A fair complexion, full breasts, gorgeous eyes, slightly plump lips, blouses with puffed sleeves, a bag worked with imitation pearls slung from her shoulder—if you looked at the color photograph of her from that time, your heart would skip a beat. Her youth sparkled; her proud bearing mocked the whole world! It made you want to spit right in the face of the man who said that the body is an illusion, but also embrace him in the same breath.

After her treatment, even though she was found to be a bit more cheerful, the despair and the cruelty in her wilted heart were always lightly at play on her face. She wouldn't talk much to those near her in age. She would only say things to little kids and youngsters. In the evenings, she would do little tasks around the house. She taught music to the neighborhood kids. If Suraiya's songs were playing on the radio, she would listen and sing along with them (the two Suraiya songs she loved best were "Sōchā thā kyā, kyā hō gayā" and "Ō Dūr Jānēvālē . . .").

Unlike the other widows of the agrahāram, she wouldn't knead dough for chappatis, or dice vegetables, scour pots, or go to the haveli to string flowers. At one time, like a woman possessed, Patti immersed herself in reading books. At a young age, she had studied through five levels of Gujarati and two levels of English. Asking Gopal Bhai to borrow books for her from the Gujarati Mandal Library, she began to read. She read a huge number of books: collections of folk songs, essays, novels, religious texts, short stories, books on the culinary arts. Finishing her chores, she would read right through from noon on into the night. For a whole year, she read heavy,

heavy tomes without stopping. Then one day, all of a sudden, she gave up on all of that. From then on, she sat, eyes closed, resting her head against a wall along the side of the front room. What was Patti thinking about in those days? What was she contemplating? Even though the years had ground to a halt for Patti, Gopal Mama finished college, went to work, got married, and fathered a child. Both of Gopal Mama's parents had gone to Goloka. After she turned seventy, Patti's mind suddenly returned to her one day. Patti went uninvited to everyone in the building and began to chatter affably. One fine morning, she finished her bath, tied on a dazzling white sari, planted her cane firmly with every step, and went to every single flat in the building, inquiring after everyone's health and wealth. She fondly stroked the heads of unwashed children, still dull with sleep. She even kissed some of those kids. Patti stood in the courtyard and delivered a moving preamble to all of the family matriarchs who had gathered in their doorways, addressing everyone generally, but also singling out individuals:

"Dear daughters! Though I have been here for a long time, I have not spoken to any of you. Such has been my state of mind. True, I am older than any of you. But it's not like the elderly can never make mistakes. Am I right? It's for you to say. Don't be small-minded. Good or bad, whatever occasion it may be, don't forget this old wretch. Know that your aunt and I played together as children. If you need any help at all, just ask; don't be shy. I will help in whatever way I can. Whatever is on your mind, don't hold back! In the end, tell me, what do human beings need, other than love? In the world, true love alone is greater than anything else. What's left for me in life now, tell me. I am a woman who needs to be gone. And all of you must stay behind. Be happy. You are well aware of the suffering I've endured. This is a body that has been ripped to shreds by hundreds and hundreds of male dogs. But it has still not occurred to that blind god to fell this wreck of a body. Remember that as long as there is life in me, I am sitting here, a woman alone, and older than any of you. All of you are my children, children who were lucky enough not to have been born from my ruined womb. Be well. Okay, tidy up your kitchens and come on upstairs after lunch. We can chat."

Patti finished up her goodwill tour in four laps and came back. Hearing Patti's address, the members of all twenty-four households of Building 25 stood wonderstruck. Though there were many who could see the real truth in Patti's speech, there were others who did feel that Patti clearly had a screw loose.

It has to be said that the women in the building gradually responded to Patti's appeal. After lunch, the women started to gather in the courtyard of Gopal Mama's house by the staircase. These were mostly unmarried girls, young women, and middle-aged women (all except for Madhuri, Tram-bak Bhai's daughter, who was younger than everyone else. She would only come on Saturdays. She was thirteen, and on the chubby side.). None of the elderly women came. Gangu Patti leaned against the wall, her spectacles sliding down her long nose, and held court. For many years, Patti had never spoken, but now she spoke nonstop. She told stories from the books she had read. She sang songs, she posed riddles. She hennaed their hands. She plaited their hair. She put their hair up in various types of buns. She taught them all sorts of things: how to embroider, knit sweaters, draw kolams, draw pictures of peacocks on glass, make pickles, bake biscuits and cakes. Everyone thought that there was not one thing Patti didn't know. And within a week, Patti took all of the agrahāram women under her wing with the enthusiasm of a new bride. Patti considered herself to be well read and spoke about nearly anything and everything because of it. She spoke with-out any guile or hesitation about topics that were delicate to speak of for orthodox Gujarati women, especially widows. She even spoke cheekily—without any shyness—about everything having to do with sexual organs, instincts, and intercourse. At first, the women of the building were shocked to see this side of Patti. But gradually, they came to understand Patti's child-like heart and keen sense of humor, and they ceased to care about it. Even though her audience would squirm with shyness, they relished her words deep down inside and felt a private thrill. What is more, the fact that Patti would say what they were unable to say made them happy, too.

Patti didn't have a shred of respect for the agrahāram men. She sim-ply called all of them Da. Behind their backs, without any respect, she would call them sons of whores. The Gujarati word *rāṇṭnā* can be trans-lated into Tamil as approximately "son of a whore" or "son of a slut." But Patti really loved Rajni Mama the bier-builder. And so, she would call him a whoreson right to his face. When she pronounced that word with great honey-dripping affection, what occurred was *poruḷ-mayakkam*—a con-fusion of meaning—a literary device found in the Old Tamil grammar the *Tolkāppiyam*. Similarly, Patti made beautiful use of vast numbers of Gujarati swearwords, turning them into cubes of jaggery. When she would tell us to shove a fire up our asses, a veritable soothing breeze would caress our hearts.

Patti conferred a nickname upon every woman who came to her assem-bly. The names for each were as follows: Little Bum, Big Bum, White Pig, Fat Rani, Cobweb Broom, Frog, Yardley, Double Roti, Style Mami, Lalitha-ji, and Chandrababu. Patti also gave herself a name: Bad Omen. In addition to this, names were given even to the sex organs. She dubbed the penis Vastu, the vulva Kapila-vastu, and the rump Deksa. At first, even those who felt shy took into account the subtle benefits of these code words and in time got on board with them. Every day, she would always begin with "What did you cook in your house today?" Then, the conversation would range over all topics: ration cards, milk cards, Panjabi wheat, puja, mothers-in-law, sisters-in-law, the severe heat, the naked torso of Salman Khan, the water problem, clothing. But no matter what, Patti would provoke someone to talk about Vastus and Kapila-vastus every single day. At first, even though those who were thus cornered by Patti felt embarrassed, they later went to her of their own accord and began to talk about sex. Their shame subsided, and the young women in particular joined right in with gusto. And since Patti enjoyed this image of herself as a well-read intellectual, she felt free to say shocking things that unsettled everyone. (The minutes of Patti's assemblies are provided below, in brief.) The sharp and witty things that Patti said were beautiful to hear and to behold. The agrahāram women were moved by Patti's genuine love and titillated by her coarse talk.

And there had not been a change in Patti's program until recently. For the past several months, the state of Patti's health had become a cause for some concern.

* * *

"Lalitha-ji, it's been six months since your marriage, yet you're just as you were—why no baby bump, Di? Isn't the vastu paying visits to the kapila-vastu? Or is it you who have closed the kapila-vastu gates?"

"I just hate it, Patti—when I see the vastu, it scares me."

"It's been six months. And you're still afraid, Di? Be brave. But if you need to, go see a doctor. Don't keep on saying that you're afraid—you'll mess things up. There are just two things that are important to our Gujarati men. One is chappatis; the other one, kapila-vastus. Keep this in mind and be smart."

* * *

"Patti, have you read all of the books on vows?"

"Oh, I've read them all right, Chandrababu. Tell me what you need."

"Teach me a helpful vow."

"Why?"

"There's always a problem in the house."

"What, can't the vastu stand up straight?"

"*Chi*, the things you say!"

"No, Di, there are vows for all of that, too—didn't you know?"

In the midst of this, White Pig interrupted: "Is that true, Patti? Tell me, tell me!"

Patti smacked her on the back and said, "*Chi*, bitch! You're not even married yet, and until then, what's all of that to you?" Frog stretched out an ear and said, "Tell *me*, Patti—I'm married." Patti whispered something in Frog's ear. At once, Frog shrieked, "*Aiyye, chi*, how can you call this a vow?" Patti said, "Why not?" Turning to Chandrababu, she asked, "What's going on in your house?"

"No matter how much money comes in, there's never enough. There is never a surplus in the house."

"*Adiye*, there is no vow for any of this. But even if there were such a vow, it should be Chidambaram observing it. (Pa. Chidambaram was the finance minister of India many times.) The entire country has your problem."

Chandrababu said nothing further. But when the assembly began to adjourn, Patti told Chandrababu about two or three vows. But at the same time, she also said this: "Look here, only women have to suffer with vows. Only women have to undertake all of the vows in this world. There isn't a single vow for men. Those dogs just eat and gad about—that's all they're good for. So think before you act."

*   *   *

"My mother-in-law heaps abuse on you nonstop. What's going on between you and her, Patti?"

"What did she say?"

"She calls you an unlucky, foul-mouthed, shaven-headed widow, and that your body and mind are filthy."

"If she says that, it must be true. My body *is* covered with filth. Every single species of dog in India has utterly ruined me. Why, even a white man lay down on top of me. That's what she means. What she wants to talk about is my body, but what could she know about my mind? For days on end, they kept me naked and would go on shoving their dicks alternately up my vagina and in my ass, they crammed rum and biryani into the wailing mouth of this shaven Vaishnava widow, observant and ritually pure . . . all of these troubles . . . tell me: could she ever understand them, this mother-in-law of yours who is all wrapped up in a sari and safe inside the agrahāram, only unwrapping herself a little for her husband? Don't mind her, let her be."

"Don't cry, Patti."

"How can I cry? Where's the time for all that there is to cry about? I finished with my crying long ago."

*   *   *

"Patti, they say that the soul never dies. So what is this thing called 'soul'?"

"Who told Fat Rani about all of this?"

"A big man who was discoursing on the *Bhāgavatam* said this yesterday."

"What did he say?"

"He said that even though the body dies, the soul never dies."

"He said that, did he? Did he say it directly to you?"

"No, he said it to everyone in general."

"Oh, you've misunderstood. Women don't have souls, didn't you know that?"

"Why are you talking like this, Patti? Don't I have a soul?"

"Don't feel bad about it. I don't have one, either. No one who is here with us has a soul. Women don't have souls."

"But then why did he say that our bodies will perish, only our souls will never die?"

"He must have said this only for the men. Not for us. Only those who have souls need to be concerned whether it dies or doesn't die. We don't have to worry about it. No souls for us!"

"But if that's the case, then how can those of us without souls take on our next births?"

"Who said this?"

"The same guy."

"Do you want to be reborn?"

"Yes . . . but you just told me that I don't have a soul."

"That's a good thing, in a way. Even if you do have a soul, and if you could take another birth, let me tell you from my experience: you would only be reborn as a milk cow in Haryana. For you, this birth itself is plenty. Just look at how beautiful you are—so fine! Don't worry about all of this soul-schmoul stuff. One good body is all you need to live. Okay, leave it be. In this life, what do you want to become?"

"I want to be a doctor, but I don't have a head for science."

"All of it will come; study carefully. If you put your mind to it, you can accomplish anything."

"If I put my mind to it, can I get a soul?"

"Girl, have you gone mad? If you put your mind to it, you can even *die* if you want to. But a soul is the only thing you can never have. Long ago, god decreed that women have no need for a soul. If you don't have a soul, there's no harm in it. Be happy."

Half believing what Patti said, Fat Rani left, a bit disappointed. Double Roti then said to Patti, "Why did you deal such a fatal blow to the poor thing?" Patti said, "What, then? All of these good-for-nothing swamis—they keep denigrating the body by saying over and over again that the body will perish. If you trust what they say, will it ever occur to anyone that they need to take care of their bodies in order to be healthy? If the body is happy, only then, Di, will the mind be happy, and self-confidence will come. If the body is degraded, then there won't be any progress—neither in your material life, nor in your spiritual one. We will only be left with a bunch of fat lazybones. She's a thirteen-year-old kid, and she prattles on about her body dying, she wants a soul, she wants another birth. What rotten times we live in!"

* * *

"Patti, how many green chilis should I put in dried mango pickle?"

"That all depends on how much fire your ass can handle."

(Even though she spoke like this, Patti would properly indicate the correct proportion of green chili at the end of the assembly.)

* * *

"There is neither pleasure nor satisfaction in my kapila-vastu. So what's the use of even having one?"

Patti would begin haughtily, speaking like someone being interviewed on TV: "This is a very good question. Cobweb Broom, the main reason for lack of happiness in the kapila-vastu is due only to the ignorance of the vastu wielders. Without knowing the kapila-vastu's subtleties, what's the use if you just rush in and out like an impatient idiot? According to the opinion of gynecological specialists the world over, generally, problems with the kapila-vastu are very rare. Maybe somewhere, in one or two cases in 100,000, there might be natural dryness. But there is treatment for that. Otherwise, general lack of comfort and smoothness in the kapila-vastu is caused by the haste of the vastu-wielders. You yourself should teach your husband the proper ways for entry into the inner chambers of the kapila-vastu."

"Oh my god, how can I talk about any of this?"

"There is no other way. You have to talk. In these times, things are so much better, Di. In my time, we wouldn't even look at a vastu, but we just kept on having kids."

* * *

"My mother-in-law is being such a pest, Patti."

"She's a real wretch, that one—what did she do?"

"She's always irritable and scolds me constantly. She makes me slog all day. Yesterday, she handed me 12 kilos of wheat and told me to have it all cleaned by evening. She's breaking my back."

"I've known her since the time she was married, Di. No one has ever seen her smile. Even if she ever did smile, it was like the grin of a Sivakaci calendar cat."

"Can a cat smile, Patti?"

"Don't be silly. Does a cat ever smile? They just draw it that way. Okay, so what does your husband say to this? He's such a simpleton!"

"He doesn't know a thing about all this. Because of her, there is trouble between us. He says that he wants it every day. But I can't cope, Patti."

"Oh, you poor things. You're just kids. If you can't be happy now, then when?"

"She told me that my boobs bounce too much, like a prostitute's, so I shouldn't wear a maxi."

"There's nothing wrong with them, Di. Your breasts are just the right size—like fine copper pots. Don't cry. Your mother-in-law is jealous, that's all. She's never had such breasts. She has always been as flat as a chappati pan. Listen to me. For three days, mix a laxative in her tea and give it to her. Only after she runs to the toilet forty or fifty times and curls up in a heap will she come to her senses."

"But isn't that a sin?"

"If you see everything as sin and merit, will you ever get what you want? If you ask me, you could even poison your mother-in-law. Don't cry. Go. What did that shaven widow ever do to deserve a smart daughter-in-law like you?"

*　*　*

"Come, Di, how was your college tour and everything?"

"First-class, Patti. The whole week was terrific."

"Did you go around Ooty and see all the sights?"

"Who cares about Ooty—I've seen a whole new world, Patti."

"What, Di? Tell me."

"She has proved to me that from now on, women don't need vastus."

"Who is this 'she'?"

"Akhilanteshvari. She's my classmate."

"What did you two do, Di?"

"*Everything* . . . I can't put any of it into words. You just experience it."

"*Adiye*, Di, keep it clean, you two."

"I'm not afraid of anything. From now on, I'm at no one's mercy. Akhila is the only one for me."

"And that mother of yours: will she simply let it be? Won't she find a plowman suitable for the field?"

"None of that is going to work with me. You will see. Anyway, Patti, what do you think about this?"

"Di, get lost, you wretched creature. Here I am: I can't even bend my hand to scratch an urgent itch on my own ass, and you talk to me about this? What does it matter what I think? Would they make it into law . . . you Saturn!"

"And Akhila wants to meet you, Patti."

"Are you making fun of me? *Adiye*! I'll give you one swift kick in the ass, and that'll teach you."

* * *

"Gangu Patti, do you believe in god?"

"Sometimes I believe; sometimes I don't."

"So you are not certain."

"Nothing at all is certain in this world, Di. When I am afraid, or when I can no longer stand myself, I believe in god. But otherwise, I don't."

"Why is it that way?"

"That's just the way it is. Tell me more."

"What do you think about our Puṣṭimārg?"

"The Puṣṭimārg belongs to the past."

"What are you saying? Just yesterday, that swami said that the Puṣṭimārg is spreading throughout the world."

"Oh, my dear daughter! These swamis who have paunches and bellies like the head cooks at Udupi restaurants—they don't know a damned thing. They're driven around in the cars of the richest man in each town, and they're floating in money. What would they know? Only you and I know that there is no Puṣṭimārg beyond this agrahāram, all there is is Central Station."

"How can you talk such sacrilege at your age?"

"There isn't any sacrilege, Di; I'm just telling the truth. From the very moment that Vallabhācārya reached liberation, there have been innumerable complaints about Puṣṭimārg."

"In that case, what is the path for Vaishnavas like us? Which other path can we follow?"

"There are two important streams in the Hindu religion. One says that you yourself are god, the other one says that god is one thing and that you are another. There are several sects in the second one—that you go in search of god, or that god will come looking for you, or you go halfway, and you stop and ask, and god will come the remaining half of the way and will redeem you. Don't get caught up in all of this bother. In order for you to be a good woman, there is no need for any of this. We can be good people even without god, or we can be bad people."

"In those 'sometimes' when you do believe, which god gets your prayers?"

"Me? I just think upon the infant Krishna. But only through force of habit, Di, let's not make an issue out of it. Mostly there are lots of advantages in not believing in god."

"How can you talk this way? You're not making sense. You've read so many books."

"Who told you that people who have read a lot of books have any sense?"

"Don't make fun of me, Gangu Patti. My intentions are pure. Not just from time to time: I want to believe in god all the time."

"You wouldn't be wrong even if you asked me with impure intentions. Now, what's the issue . . . do you want a god to worship, or do you want a path to follow?"

"I want both."

"For that, you need to go join some mutt or other. I'm telling you the truth, my dear, the time of mārgs is over and done with. All you can do now is join a crowd and chant 'Govinda, Govinda.' You're a young woman. Why are you fussing over mārg-schmārg? You can worship all the gods you want, or you can pick one among them and worship that one. And just for people who are like you, they've arranged the Hindu religion just like a supermarket. You can just pick what you like."

"Aren't you afraid to say all these things, Patti?"

"Why should I be afraid to say what's on my mind?"

* * *

"Patti, he wants to put his vastu in my Deksa."

"Who, that husband of yours? I'm not surprised! He is capable of anything. But then, why don't you just try it once?"

"Patti, what, you're just totally rotten!"

"*Adiye*, don't get so upset, girl. Nothing is sacred in this world. Your deksa is certainly not sacred. What does the Hindu religion say? That the body is impure, and that it also perishes. If a kind of joy can be had in this way from a perishing body, so be it."

"You are truly perverted. I don't know why I came to you!"

"Perversion that is bottled up inside is far more dangerous than perversion that is let out. Besides, tell me where there is no perversion. In fact, there is perversion in everything. Listen to me. If you definitely don't want it, then refuse it decisively! But if there is any hesitation and you are of two minds, then give it a go. And who knows? There might be a few benefits for you in that."

"Old lady, you're headed for hell."

* * *

"I'm going to go kill myself."

"Why are you so sad, Big Bum?"

"Nothing is right. I've given up on this life. I don't like anyone. It's as if I want to punch and beat everybody."

"How old are you, Di?"

"Forty-seven."

"That's how it is at this age. You're going through 'the change.'"

"What change? Go on, Patti, I just want to die."

"Don't talk like that, Di. That isn't easy. You need a lot of cowardice to commit suicide. You're a brave one. You won't die anytime soon. Only after you've had lots of grandchildren will Yama come for you—he'll ceremoniously entice you with a plate of betel leaves and nuts, then drag you off. Besides, if you really want to kill yourself, you have to do it before you turn thirty. After that, there is no use. It will only make a mess."

*   *   *

"Patti, the vastu can't enter the kapila-vastu like before."

"Why? What's happened?"

"It slips out within a minute."

"Oh, no, poor thing, he's become an old stodge . . . he's not even forty-five yet . . . he's so tall and handsome, like a basketball player. And it's like this for *him*? Okay, okay, don't you go and find yourself another vastu. Your husband is innocent."

"Yes, but Patti, I hear that in Burma Bazaar you can get a machine that's just like a vastu!"

"You can even get a *real* vastu in Burma Bazaar. Listen to me. These machine-kichines don't work. And they're expensive, too. If your mother-in-law finds out, she'll tear you a new one. Here's what you should do: Let the vastu come inside the kapila-vastu once a month. At other times, try something with your hand."

"Patti, you have a superb brain."

"Why are you suddenly praising my brain, Di?"

"You said exactly what I thought you'd say."

"Is that so! Well, aren't you clever, Di! *Chi*, bitch! Shove a fire up your ass . . . I said what she thought, it seems!"

*   *   *

"Patti, do you remember your childhood?"

"What about that *now*?"

"Is it true that you were very beautiful when you were young?"

"Is that so! Who said that, Di? Even a camel is beautiful when it's young."

"Right now, if you could all of a sudden change yourself into a young girl, what would that be like?"

"If I wanted to change into a young girl, you would have to crawl back into your mother's womb, and your mother into your grandmother's womb. Don't blabber like a lunatic."

"But don't you ever think about your past?"

"What's passed is past. If you or I think about that, what will come of it?"

"But don't you cherish the time of your youth? Aren't you sad or happy or whatever about anything?"

"There is no time that people should cherish. As a matter of fact, don't you know that there is nothing called 'time'? Like 'god,' time, too, is nothing but a figment of the human imagination."

"If time is imaginary, then yesterday, today, tomorrow—all of these—are they nothing?"

"All these time measurements are only like a cave hollowed out in a vacuum. If you want to, you can see that cave. You can even see that cave's roof. But if you aren't keen to, then it's all nothing."

3

The next morning, Rajni Mama came back to look in on Patti. Patti was sitting in the front room, slurping her tea from a saucer. As Rajni Mama was taking off his chappals, he said, "Patti-ma, did you cancel your ticket again yesterday? It looks like I'll be buying my ticket before you buy yours."

He came in, and Patti raised her head to look at Rajni. "*Adey*, you son of a whore, what inauspicious things you say first thing in the morning! When an old hag like me is still around, how can you talk of dying, you senseless dog?"

As he came close to Patti, Rajni Mama bowed his head, folded his hands, and sat down next to her. "Patti-ma, keep this in mind. Don't forget: your bier will be built only by my own hands."

"Happily, my boy. I will only climb onto a bier that you have built, and only then will this old crone's heart be soothed."

In a voice that was suddenly filled with concern, Rajni Mama said, "What happened, Patti-ma? You gave us all such a scare yesterday." As he said this, he gently caressed Patti's head.

"Nothing was wrong with me, Da, just gas trouble. Yesterday, Mandakini from the downstairs flat said, 'Patti, I've made black-gram vadais, and they are just like the ones from Ratna Café. Here, take two.' And this shaven old widow greedily gobbled them down."

"What! Two . . . *two* vadais? Have you gone mad? Are your guts made of iron? Not even a horse could digest two of those deep-fried, black-gram vadais. You should be controlling your palate in the first place. It will be good for you, and good for all of us, too."

"I'll do it, I'll do it. Leave it be. What is your little donkey doing at home?"

"What does she do, other than cook?"

"What's it to you, Pa? There are only the two of you, a master and his mistress. You can cook and cook all of the tasty stuff you want. Always . . . a jolly good time for the both of you."

"Wha-a-a-at, jolly?" As Rajni Mama began to speak, Gopal Mama came in with newspaper in hand. When he saw Rajni, he said, "What, Da, when did you come?"

"Just now. Patti seems better. I am going to Andhra on business. I'll be back in ten days."

Gopal Mama sat down in a chair and shouted, "Surekha, did you give Rajni any tea?"

"What, Da, I hear that your boss is going to feed the poor to the tune of one lakh rupees on Gandhi's birthday."

"What else could he do with that black money he's been hoarding? He can't eat it, he can't shit it. He has to spend it, and this is the only way," said Rajni Mama.

He finished up his tea, took Patti's hand with affectionate concern, talked for a bit, and said, "Patti, I'll be back. Take care of your health." He then bowed his head again, and folded his hands to Patti. Patti blessed him, saying, "Live long, my boy."

Patti then took the powders that the Ayurvedic doctor had given her, and slept until the afternoon without taking any food. The assembly didn't meet that afternoon, just as it hadn't when Patti had been "serious" the previous twenty-seven times. She took rest the next day. Madhuri (aka Fat Rani) came home from school at four o'clock and woke Patti up. Patti sat up and embraced her.

"Patti, I heard that you were very 'serious' yesterday."

"It was nothing, Di. Look at me: I'm just fine."

"They said that you wouldn't make it this time."

"They said that. But if I had died, it would have been just fine."

"Are you telling the truth, Patti? Aren't you afraid of dying?"

"What's there for me to be afraid of, Di? I myself have witnessed so many deaths. You're just a little girl. You won't understand."

"If you say that you're not afraid, then it must mean that your mind isn't willing to die."

"But even if your mind *is* willing to die, is that enough? Death has to make its way to you, too."

"But you yourself once said that if we put our minds to it, we could even die if we wanted to."

"Really? Did I? . . . I said that? When did I say such a thing?"

"No, you said it. It just seems to me that perhaps you are afraid."

"No, Di, no, darling girl. I'm not afraid at all. Dying is not in our hands."

"Can't you die if you put your mind to it? It looks like you want to hang around for a little longer."

Patti suddenly grew quiet. After a couple of moments, she answered.

"Tell me what I get by staying alive if I do stay. My soul is endlessly yearning for death to come."

"Do you have a soul? You said yourself that women don't have them."

"When did I say that?"

"You said it."

"I really said that?"

"Yes, you did."

Once again, Patti fell silent for a short time. Then she spoke once more.

"Will you be sad if I die?"

"Won't I be sad if anyone dies?"

"How will you cry if I die?"

"Die first."

"After I die, how can I see you crying?"

Now it was Madhuri's turn to fall silent. After a short time, it was Patti who spoke again.

"If I die, you have to wail out loud. No sniveling, no soft little sobs."

"Why like that?"

"It has to be that way. Children should not cry softly. You really need to wail."

"Patti, don't mistake me. You shouldn't die. Patti, please be with us for a little while longer."

"*Chi*, what kind of talk is this, Di? Why would I mistake you at all? You always say such smart things. Okay, okay, go, change your clothes, drink your tea, and study! Come back tomorrow," said Patti.

That night, Patti couldn't sleep. She tossed and turned all night. She woke up very early. When it turned five, she got up as usual, rolled up her mat and put it away, had her bath, sat down along the side of the wall, and facing north, she leaned back. She closed her eyes, and she lay there for a little while, just like that. Suddenly, a noise much like a hiccup erupted from her, and with that, Patti's life left her.

Hearing the news that Gangu Patti had died, the entire agrahāram gathered together. No commotion, no ruckus. Everyone was wonderstruck: that old woman just lay down and died so suddenly, as if she had climbed into a rickshaw and gone off to the beach. Because Rajni Mama was not in town, someone else had to build Patti's bier. When Patti's body was removed from Building number 25, the women stood sobbing, their voices subdued. In a mix of peace and bustle, Patti's funeral procession began.

Rajni Mama returned from Andhra and made straight for Gopal Mama's flat. He saw Patti's photo in the front room and began to weep. "In the end, you've tricked me, old lady. From now on, whom can I scold as I wish? From now on, there is no one like you who will call me a son of a whore with such love and affection," he lamented. Gopal Mama's wife, Surekha, sat shuddering in a corner, her face covered with the end of her sari. Was she laughing? Was she crying? No one could really tell.

Mirage

Very slowly, they became aware of the stuffiness of that room, and the silence that had suddenly settled around them. They lay there, congealed like black shadows in the faded light of the small blue lamp, burning in a corner of the room. Their naked, fair bodies also looked like corpses, in a way.

They lay there with their hearts wilted from dissatisfaction. The stench of sweat dripping from their bodies and the slight dampness that had gathered on the bed were unbearable. Even so, they yearned to stay there, without disturbing the prevailing silence. It was as if they were trying hard to dissolve the feeling of extreme emptiness that had arisen from the turmoil of disappointment in the darkness and the silence of that room.

She lay stretched straight out with one leg over the other, staring vacantly at the ceiling. Save for the slow and even movement of her breasts as she exhaled, she lay there motionless. Reclining on his side, he had nestled his face in her shoulder. From that angle, he was watching her. The way she was lying there, and her nakedness coupled with her dissatisfaction, troubled his heart. He could sense that her eyes were moist.

Only on that afternoon had it been confirmed that there would be some privacy for them at this place. When he had informed her of that, she consented, without any hesitation at all. There was never any great attraction between them, but enough temptation not to let go of an opportunity if it ever came their way. They could read each other's minds, somehow.

After a little while, as if she had slowly made up her mind about something, she moved away from him a bit. He, too, shifted silently. It occurred to him that they could talk about something or other, but he didn't speak. He was unable to decide what would be appropriate for the moment: to speak or to keep quiet. He was trying to figure out what she might be thinking. It was confusing.

She had arrived at this place before he did. When he knocked at the door, she appeared before him in a light blue sari, her hair done up loosely, smelling of talcum. Letting him inside, she bolted the door from within. Looking meaningfully into his eyes, she smiled merrily, her face aglow.

Her body appeared as if there was a strange eagerness emanating from the whole of it. It seemed as if a lovesick light with the sheen of the moon was spreading in the pupils of her eyes. Without saying a thing, they tightly embraced. He planted kisses on her forehead while gently stroking her head. She was like a gorgeous animal, and becoming hot with desire, she melted into his hands. Like little children, they tore off their clothes impatiently and reached the bedroom.

She lay there like a dried-up log of wood.

She was the first to speak.

"Let's get up. I think it's getting late." She then asked, "Should I switch on the light?"

"No," he answered.

After that, they both got up slowly. He looked at her. Her beautiful body looked like a marvelous sculpture. With a sudden desire to embrace her, he touched her shoulders longingly. Pushing his hands away sharply, she said, "Enough," in a voice full of frustration. He withdrew from her, and walking past her without saying a word, he went to the front room.

He put on his clothes and waited for her. A photograph was hanging in the front room, of the friend who had given him the use of the house, along with his wife. Both of them were smiling beautifully. He stared raptly at his friend's wife's face. It was as if that woman's face were jeering at him, looking out at him from behind her simple smile.

Confused, he tightly shut his eyes. Yet again, inside his closed eyes, a vision appeared from just a little before, that of a youthful body sliding down on him. He had thought that nothing would go wrong on that day's union. When he had begun to kiss her beautiful little breasts, she embraced him tightly. As the intoxication and frenzy of heavy breathing feverishly spread out everywhere, they dissolved and became extinct. Very slowly, when those gentle leaps toward fulfillment started, the world itself spun. At that very moment when the final throes were reaching their highest point—Now! Now!—it all suddenly changed; the flow ebbed. The waves receded, and he collapsed. Her face and her body were shaking violently in protest, wanting to keep going. She had not expected this in the least, and refused to take this disappointment. With a mixture of guilt and affection, he held her fast. Like a fish suddenly yanked out of water, she stopped moving after a few thrashes.

Letting her go, he quietly moved away. It had all happened within seconds, and it was all over. She suddenly started to cry with soft sobs.

He lay there silently.

As she came to the front room, he was preparing to leave. Her face was unclouded. The depth of the dissatisfaction in her eyes had lessened. Looking at him, she smiled slightly.

Locking the house, they both came out to the street. The street wore a desolate look. The moon was afloat in the sky. They walked toward the bus stop slowly. When the wind blew, rustling the leaves of the trees that lined the road, a certain feeling of freedom arose in him. The tension in his mind lessened.

Please forgive me.

SHE: For what?

. . . no . . . it's never happened like this. I know how you must be feeling.

SHE: Never mind, I have no regrets.

I don't need to prove anything to you, but let me tell you that this is the first time it's gone like this.

SHE: Never mind.

Maybe today I was just overwhelmed by the suddenness of this opportunity.

SHE: Okay, never mind, let it be.

I am feeling sad that your courage was all for nothing.

SHE: Enough, stop talking.

You really hate me, don't you?

SHE: No.

You must be having doubts about my prowess, too.

SHE: No.

You're lying.

SHE: Enough, stop.

Please don't try to compare me to anyone else. Especially to your husband.

SHE: . . .

Next time . . .

SHE: Enough of your nonsense.

They walked along silently. They had to walk a few minutes further to get to the main road where the bus stop was. He walked gazing at the sky. She walked observing her own long shadow that fell on the street. Suddenly, he started to talk again.

We really shouldn't have met today.

SHE: We never should have met at all.

The bus stop was deserted. They just stood there in silence.

The Letter

"Come at 3 P.M. sharp," Mittu Mama had said just yesterday. As usual, he needed to write a heart-rending letter to ask Ghanshyam Mama for some money. Mittu Mama was my grandmother's brother. He was very poor. Ghanshyam Mama was Mittu Mama's co-brother, and a very wealthy man.

For the most part, the letters that Mittu Mama dictated to me were not all that interesting. But, because of the visible palsy in Mittu Mama's aging fingers, I had agreed to write out one or two letters a month for him. Besides, since these documents were of a very personal nature, I alone was appointed to handle them. As a consequence, an affectionate mutual bond was established between us—like that between a gentleman and his mistress, full of tiny little secrets.

When I arrived, Mittu Mama was lying down with his head on a big bolster. His legs had been wrapped in polythene bags, and were propped up on a small pillow like two clumsy bundles. When he saw me, he affectionately greeted me: "Come here, Champ!" Mittu Mama was in his seventies. Big eyes, sunken cheeks, thick eyebrows, a long nose, a skinny body, handspun dhoti, handspun vest, and a fraying sacred thread. Mittu Mama's wife, Jamuna Mami, had died many years ago. His sons lived in the back part of the building along with their wives, and they didn't get on with him. They had confined him to this front room, which looked out onto the street.

With his usual pomp, Mama began: "Take this down!"

He also warned, "Don't even try to interrupt me!"

Respected Ghanshyam-ji,

Please accept the greetings of your co-brother Mittu, resident of Sowcarpet, Chennai. Here, we are all joyful and happy. I would like to receive the news that you and all of your family members are likewise joyful and happy.

Why I am writing just now is that, for some days now, my mind has been very uneasy. To be precise, for the past one week. Everyone here wants me to die. And I, too, want to die. But to live or to die, is it in our hands? I could even commit suicide. But for me to commit suicide, there are one or two obstacles. First of all, my age. If a man at seventy-three commits suicide, no one will bother. They will just feel that the Saturn is gone at last. Second, my legs. You know that there are cracks in my feet and eczema on my knees. And with legs such as mine, how and where can I go to commit suicide? Besides, should I die with such stinking legs that leak pus and fluid, would *that* be nice? You know this, too. But anyway, I want to die just as my relatives wish.

Thanks to the money that you so kindly sent last month, until the day before yesterday, I had been going to the Gujarati Charitable Hospital in Ravana Aiyar Street for my medicines and bandages. But this month, instead of Dr. Tamaraikannan, the dermatologist who comes on the third day of each month, a new doctor has come. His name is Sanatkumar Jain. A Marwari. His father, Sukanmal Jain, has a whole-sale ever-silver vessel business on Thangasalai Street. His shop is right next to the New Ananda Bhavan Café at the corner of NSC Bose Road. If you see the man, you will recognize him. There is no way you wouldn't know him. Dr. Sanatkumar is a young man, but he is other-wise capable. He received training for several years under the famous dermatologist Dr. Thambaiya. He examined my legs and changed the medicine. He gave me some topical ointment and several tablets to take. As for the bandages, he said that it is enough to change them every other day. He said that the itching and leaking of fluid would cer-tainly clear up six months from now. As you know, while the treatment is free, I can only take a rickshaw to the hospital. Kattavarayan the rickshaw man is the only one who will steady me with his hands and take me. We had agreed to 2 rupees to go and come. But he is taking me on credit because the money ran out last week. I owe him 6 rupees now. The word came just this morning that Kattavarayan's mother had fallen ill, so he has left for Chengelput. There is no saying when he'll be back. I can certainly make an alternative arrangement. But could I find anyone like Kattavarayan? Besides, where's the money to give to a new rickshaw man?

That is why I am saying that I'm completely frustrated. Only my death would be good for everyone. As for you, you'd be relieved of the burden of sending me money month after month.

As you know, none of my sons are any good. The oldest one plays the bulbultara all the time, and just trails behind his wife.

His wife—you know how she is—that squat little queen? She looks like a harmless cat, but what trouble she makes! One day last week, I said that there wasn't enough salt in the gravy—in the plain dal that she gave me along with my chappatis. I asked her to bring some. Is this a crime? She dismissively turned her face away in the style of Lalitha Pawar and left. And that useless dog—my eldest son—comes in support of her, saying, "So what, if you have less salt at your age?" And you surely know my youngest son's story. He has a bank job, true, but what's the point? He doesn't have an ounce of gratitude or loyalty. Who does he think he is? He finished up his B.Com. only because of your good graces. Now he has become a big devotee. Every Saturday night, he arranges for bhajan gatherings, and is tearing the house apart. With that tabla and those wooden clappers, the havoc his friends wreak is not little. So when they finish their bhajans, all of these dogs set out after midnight to have puris, lassis, and paan at Maheshvari Bhavan. How many puris I must have eaten at Maheshvari Bhavan! How many of those paans I must have had! He knows all too well that I crave Maheshvari Bhavan puris. But this rascal hasn't brought me any even once. He thinks he's a big governor. When I say "governor," I am reminded of our governor, Prabhudas Patvari, who came to the temple of our Shrinath-ji. Modesty, what modesty! He bowed his head before our Natti Behn, took her blessings, and left. He said, "We don't have a grudge against Indira Gandhi." That woman is always full of false pride.

Only my number two son, Rajni, is any good, that poor fellow . . .

At this point, I interrupted and asked, "Mama, do I have to write 'number two'? Ghanshyam Mama surely understands!"
"Just shut up and write what I say!

He can't make enough to meet the needs of his wife and children, and cannot rest. Something happened the day before yesterday. As I dictate this, my eyes are brimming with tears.

I looked at Mittu Mama's eyes.
"What are you looking at, Da? Write!"

There was no coconut oil in the house. He's just using water to comb his hair. Although the oldest and the youngest blow all of their money on cigarettes and paan, they won't buy any oil. Now, everyone in the house is getting by, taking a daily head bath and putting off oiling their hair until evening. Without oil, my bald pate has dried out, and it's like my head is on fire. Whatever is left of my hair is sticking out like coconut fiber. I am afraid to even look at my face in the mirror . . .

I had a look at Mama's head, and confirmed that this was true.

Before I die, there are a few things that I want to put in order. As you know, I have no property at all. I am a veritable pauper. When your sister died—that is to say, my wife—I bore the responsibility of continuing to worship her deities. You would know that. Before I pass away, I want to give these deities to you. They have been passed down in our family from generation to generation. My mother (and my grandmother before her) would rise before dawn, bathe, and after bathing, she would do the puja for these deities on an empty stomach. And only then would she drink water. After her, your sister, too, did it in the very same way. After your sister died, I now do as much as I can on my own. But you know that I am unable to bathe every day. I can only bathe on the days on which my leg dressings are changed. So I do puja only every other day. My real sorrow is that even on auspicious days, I can't make proper offerings to these deities. I can only offer the food that comes to me daily at eleven o'clock: three chappatis and a little rice, and in the evening, just the two idlis and the one vadai that come from Ambi's Café. I believe that God will accept this, too. What really counts is that it's done with true devotion.

You can't trust my daughters-in-law. They don't know the value of these. They'll just chuck them out. Or they'll give them to the children to play with. There is one among these deities that is particularly important. And that would be the 5-inch-tall image of Balakrishna, crawling with his flute. It is a beautiful thing to see. If you dress him up in his silk clothing and his cap with the golden thread and put some kumkum on him, it's Krishna himself, right before your eyes, as if he has come crawling right into our courtyard. Before I die, I want to entrust these Thakur-jis to your care. Please tell my sister, that is to say, your wife, that this is my last wish. After our time is over, you can't say that the children will do anything properly. Let my sister perform the worship of the Thakur-jis, to the extent that she is able. After that, you can consign them to the well or to the river. Apart from this, I have a few holy books and some Ganges water in a little pot. I want to give all of these things, too, only to you. Among the books, you should certainly keep the *Hanuman Chālisā* and the *Bhāgavatam*, which was blessed by Dongre Maharaj. With the *Hanuman Chālisā*, your house will be free of ghosts and demons, and the *Bhāgavatam* will ensure prosperity.

By now you will have understood that I'm ready to die. But I cannot see how death will come, or from where. You know that even if we go willingly, death will not concede to us until our lives are finished on this earth. Last week, Jivanlal's eight-year-old son was flying a kite, and he lost his balance and fell from the second story. But, his good luck, he fell right on top of the big bundle of dirty clothes saddled on the donkey belonging to the Ekambareshvarar pinman. Not a scratch, not one mark on him. But too bad for the donkey, which stumbled when the boy fell—its hind leg was fractured. And you know what a big cheapskate Jivanlal is. He said that he would not give so much as 1 paisa for the donkey's treatment. Getting 3 rupees from him to take the donkey in a rickshaw to the veterinary hospital was such a terrible task. Before he left, with one choice obscene phrase, the dhobi cursed our entire Gujarati lineage.

What do you say to this?

But still I think that I just really need to die and be done with it. When I think that with so many reasons for me to die—and here I am, not dying—it just makes me want to laugh and cry at the same time. Ranjit Broker, who studied with me, went and died ten days ago—in just one breath—without any trouble at all. Like this, I have heard that three elderly people have died, right here in this street, within the space of a single month.

Diabetes and heart attack joined hands as a couple, and like a husband and wife, they came for a visit, and dragged each one of them away. Even my daughter-in-law Subhadra has these two diseases. But for me, except for my petty maladies—eczema, cracked feet—there is not one thing wrong. Just like my eldest daughter-in-law said last week, I am nothing but a limping dog, and I feel just like one.

Now, there is no one left in the Ekambareshvarar Agrahāram who would mourn my absence. The agrahāram itself has lost its glow. The tank has gone dry. For appearance's sake, they fill it up with a little water, and they float plastic lotuses on it. They have demolished the saffron-striped wall around the temple tank, constructed a building in place of it, and have rented out rooms to ever-silver vessel merchants. You can no longer see the school clock tower on Ravana Aiyar Street. They've stuck up mikes on the pillars in the temple corridors and play light-music bhajans. In the streets, which used to be frequented by pure Gujaratis, the vessel-shop Marwaris now overrun the place. The temple peepul tree is the only reminder of the old layout of the agrahāram. It still gives shade. But the people who would appreciate that shade have all vanished. The peace that this peepul tree used to give is now gone. They have sold off the building on the eastern end, where my sister Natti Behn lives, for 60 lakhs. Because of this, thirty families will be out on the street. Like birds whose nests have been torn apart, they are just waiting to be scattered. The mood here is about to change. The whole meaning of life is in the atmosphere of a place, and if it goes, life goes.

I pray daily, but rather than to god, to the god of death: Drag off this wretched old man—it won't wreck your noose. When I have died, please arrange to have the *Bhāgavatam* recited for the liberation of my soul, in my house or even in your house, it doesn't matter.

Apart from the above, there is otherwise nothing more to tell.

I await the news about your joy and happiness.

As ever,

Manmohan Das Dwarka Das
(Mittu)

P.S.: If it is convenient for you, please send me 100 rupees via money order.—Mittu.

I put the pages in order, and then folded the long letter. And as usual, Mittu Mama took the tiny key that hung on his sacred thread, opened his tin treasury, and gave me a large envelope and postage stamps. I wrote out the address, and, as I was taking it away, he said, "Don't be lazy—don't put that letter in any random mailbox you see on the street, but go straight to the Park Town Post Office. After you've sent it, come back and tell me." As he gave me a 50-paisa coin, he said, "You keep this for yourself." I set out.

Three or four days passed, and one night at eight o'clock the news came via telegram. I rushed to Mittu Mama to tell him the news.

Mittu Mama was sound asleep. I shook his shoulder and woke him up.

"What's the matter, Da?"

"We've been ruined, Mama."

"What's happened?"

"A telegram came from Udamalaipet. Ghanshyam Mama has died."

Panicking, Mittu Mama got up: "What are you saying?"

"Yes, Mama, it's a fact. He came home from the office today at noon. He chatted with everyone as he ate, and had a good laugh. And he read your letter two or three times. He went to have a short nap and never got up. He passed away in his sleep. Heart attack."

Mittu Mama stared blankly at his legs, and after a long silence, he philosophically said, "Those who are fortunate enough to die, die. But there is no other option for those of us who stay behind. We just have to keep on living."

All of our relatives who had gone to take part in Ghanshyam Mama's funeral rites had also read Mittu Mama's letter. They openly expressed the opinion that Mittu Mama should have died in Ghanshyam Mama's place. Mittu Mama's sons and their wives were extremely humiliated. In particular, Mittu Mama's eldest daughter-in-law was bursting with rage. She wished that the old man's tongue be drawn out and cut off, and, for having been in cahoots with him and for writing that letter, both my hands should be sliced off. But luckily, no such disaster happened. However, I've had to stop writing letters for Mittu Mama.

The Miracle That Refused to Happen

Mrs. James was setting out, her little suitcase in hand.

"I'm leaving," she said.

Regarding her for a short time, James then asked, "What, is that all? Really? Don't you have anything else to say to me before you go?"

"I can't think of anything at all."

"Where will you go?"

"Somewhere. Far away. To a solitary place with no people. At least when I die, I want to do so in solitude, with a heart that is free of anguish."

"Don't blabber on like a lunatic. We all have to die in that very way. One by one. Alone, and in total isolation. Even if the whole world gathers around you, death herds you off into solitude and deals with you."

She said nothing.

"I didn't at all expect that you would want to do such a foolish thing in your forty-second year. Listen to me! Just stay."

"No, I have to go."

"Even if that's the way you feel, tell me how there is any lack of solitude here. You and I have lived for so many years in this same house, but we have come to live separately, like two ancient animals. If you wish, we can sleep in separate rooms from now on."

"No, I have made up my mind. I'm going; I must go."

For the past two months, the idea had been growing secretly within Mrs. James. Slowly, slowly, it took on blood and flesh, and, like a strange goblin, it latched onto her. The night before, as she sat in the courtyard staring vacantly at the sky, Mrs. James had decided that she would leave the next day. It seemed as if someone were calling out to her again and again from beyond the cloudless sky.

Stroking his gray hair with both hands, Mr. James contemplated the floor. Mrs. James just stood there without speaking. After a few moments, she began to move slowly toward the door.

A bit overcome by his emotions, Mr. James lunged at her, as a child would.

"Wait a little. Our life together, which has lasted for twenty-five years, and our bonds—don't make them meaningless."

Mrs. James said nothing. There was nothing for her *to* say. Further, as a matter of fact, from now on there was not a single thing for her—not only to say, but to share, to think, to contemplate, to laugh about, to grieve over—there was nothing at all. She had dried up completely.

"Think it over. We've shared everything for twenty-five years. From that first night filled with desires and urges, up until this evening filled with grief, which has hardened and dried out our veins. You can leave me, you can disappear, but what will you do with your burden of memories?"

Mrs. James said nothing.

"Today I still remember your face from those days. I will never forget your splendor as you stood before me, like a miraculous flame, with your cheeks awash with fairness and sheen. Do you know how much I loved you at that time?"

Mrs. James said nothing.

"I have forgotten nothing—the unique intoxication of your hot sighs that spread all over my body, and how you coiled around me like a plump red serpent."

Mrs. James said nothing.

"But look, time changes everything. Nothing leaves its mark in the flood of emotions."

Mrs. James said nothing.

"Do you remember . . . within three months of our marriage, you were bedridden. That horrifying lump was growing in your stomach. Pus and blood had formed a mass, like a huge, disgusting rotten egg."

Mrs. James said nothing.

"During those nights, do you know how anxious I was, up until the doctors told us that the mass in your stomach was not malignant?"

Mrs. James said nothing.

"I wonder if you even knew how many sleepless nights I spent before your surgery. At that time, you would sleep on peacefully without a care, like a child next to me."

Mrs. James said nothing.

"I sat gazing at you as I listened to the sound of your regular breathing. Then, all of a sudden, I would be seized by passion and love, and I would plant kisses on your cheeks and forehead. I would grasp your palm and press it to my chest. You would sleep peacefully on, your slumber not disturbed in the least."

Mrs. James said nothing.

"Do you remember? We couldn't have intercourse for the three years after your surgery."

Mrs. James said nothing.

"How many nights, cruel nights, nights that mercilessly destroyed the passions and desires of my youth!"

Mrs. James said nothing.

"At that time, you lay there sleeping like a wilting, trampled creeper. And right next to you, I lay there like a block of steel forged in passion and dissatisfaction."

Mrs. James said nothing.

"Before your health improved, I was completely diminished. What is more, as a matter of fact, there was never a full chance for us to enjoy ourselves sexually. Experiencing the powers of my youth, immersing myself in it, joyful entrancement that would leave you wilted—all of it was just a mirage. Before reaching the peak of sexual union, it just slipped from my hands every single time. Even now, I remember every inch of your body that glittered with youth. Do you realize how much I loved your breasts that looked like marble—they kindled such longing—and your robust thighs that nourished my mad passion?"

Mrs. James said nothing.

"Back then, I, too, was handsome. I was so proud, looking at and admiring my arms and the thick black hair on my chest."

Mrs. James said nothing.

"I know what you're thinking. But what's the use? You think that we've just lived as mere bodies. And that's true enough. We *have* just lived as mere bodies. Two mere grown-up bodies. And only after seven years was it known that I was sterile. And only then did I understand why your womb had remained silent for so long, like a bottomless well, despite taking in my lifeless sperm time and again."

Mrs. James said nothing.

"It's the truth. I'm just a sterile man. I'm just a drunk. Do you know that there are fewer sterile men than there are barren women in the world? And how can it be that I am one among those few men?"

Mrs. James said nothing.

"Sterile men can either commit suicide, or they can make themselves useful to society. I don't have the guts to commit suicide. So I started to drink. And since you can't occupy yourself in service to society while you're drinking, I wrote poems. Worthless poems steeped in self-pity. I'm still writing them now. I wrote one just yesterday."

Mrs. James said nothing.

> All of life's seasons are finished
> and gone.
> The pollen has dried up in the flowers.

Lush green leaves have wilted and died.
The fluttering of wings has ceased.
Look, dusk, too, has fallen.
As veins wither
nerves fray, and the body grows cold.
As night and death cover everything
it will all go cold.
Certainly,
like a mist, blankness will spread out,
and will obliterate everything.

Mrs. James said nothing.

"It's true. I really drank a lot. Without regard for night and day; without regard for whether I was home or outside."

Mrs. James said nothing.

"I left my job, too. Urchins on the street mocked me. I was abused and beaten up by one and all—from rickshaw men to arrack-shop bouncers. Yes, it was true. I had become an irredeemable drunkard."

Mrs. James said nothing.

"And on top of it all, I hated you. Whom did I *have* to hate, other than you? Who else would have taken my hatred seriously?"

Mrs. James said nothing.

"Your empty womb mocked my impotence. I hated you so much. I even wanted to tear apart your intoxicating body. I wanted to kick your taut belly. Sometimes I even did."

Mrs. James said nothing.

"I know what a good woman you are."

Mrs. James said nothing.

"It was you who went out to get our rations every month, you who went out to buy our vegetables."

Mrs. James said nothing.

"It was you who went to the Marwari shop to pawn our goods, only you. It was you who went. You did everything alone. You were always there—to wash, to cook, to get beaten up, and even to starve."

Mrs. James said nothing.

"Even after all of this, it didn't seem to me that I was such a bad man."

Mrs. James said nothing.

"I know very well the joys and travails of women."

Mrs. James said nothing.

"But tell me why you put up with the injustices I meted out to you?"

Mrs. James said nothing.

"In truth, I know that you're such a tender woman."

Mrs. James said nothing.

"It thrilled you to see the blossoms from the red tiger-claw tree of our house, scattered like a beautiful kolam."

Mrs. James said nothing.

"On rainy days, the drenched crow on the terrace of the opposite house—its fluttering was a great miracle to you as it ruffled up its damp wings, beating them with a fluttering sound, and craning its little neck this way and that."

Mrs. James said nothing.

"I could see how much you savored the sight of that mouse that would fearlessly hang about in the kitchen, cramming grains of cooked rice into its mouth and darting its beady-eyed glances here and there."

Mrs. James said nothing.

"You even loved that ash-colored lizard, heavy with eggs, which would lie motionless on top of the partition wall in the bathroom."

Mrs. James said nothing.

"The coconut tree right next to our compound wall that stood there season after season, having been robbed of its nuts in the dark of night—you made me understand the beautiful sparkle that the stupid tree acquired on rainy days."

Mrs. James said nothing.

"I have learned so much from you."

Mrs. James said nothing.

"Even though I cannot deny the joys that you have shown me, your world is uncomplicated. It's filled with blooming flowers, and with damp crows, and with mice, and with mother lizards, and with stupid coconut trees."

Mrs. James said nothing.

"But my world isn't like that. It is far beyond mice and mother lizards. It's replete with pain, unsteadiness, and disappointment."

Mrs. James said nothing.

"When the mountain breeze blows, you feel its coolness. But I feel only sorrow. Time lies hidden within the wind, and within time, nothing but emptiness."

Mrs. James said nothing.

"I know what you're thinking. That I am a drunk, that I am a poet, and therefore I'm spouting nonsense, that my feet never touch the ground, that I just float!"

Mrs. James said nothing.

"It's true. Suppose that I do blather away in euphoria. But only while floating can you see the meanness of life tethered to the ground."

Mrs. James said nothing.

"But I don't say all this because you are about to leave me and go your own way."

Mrs. James said nothing.

"It's only fair that you would want to leave me. Perhaps if I were you and you were I, I would definitely have left you and gone my own way long ago."

Mrs. James said nothing.

"On most occasions in life, we could only think about the right things, but we couldn't act upon them. You don't know how cruel life is."

Mrs. James said nothing.

"But no matter what, there is no atonement for the cruelties that I inflicted. I'm impotent, but what could you do about that? I take responsibility for my failings. But what's to be gained by just owning up to my faults?"

Mrs. James said nothing.

"Perhaps . . . perhaps if I had had a child, if I had fathered just one child, you might think that I might have lived an entirely different life."

Mrs. James said nothing.

"I've tried to think along those lines. But it is not possible to say if I would have been any different. Compared with my life up to now, I might have lived as a slightly more decent man. Even so, then, just as today, I would still have been a suffering soul. Then, just as now, I might have noticed the emptiness that lies behind the veil of time."

Mrs. James said nothing.

"Do you know? It isn't possible to set things right by filling up life's void with experiences. It seems that we can't even fill it up with love."

Mrs. James said nothing.

"In old age, there are no opportunities left for experiences or love. Old age dries up all of it."

Mrs. James said nothing.

"When your calf muscles shrivel, your legs stop running. Then, that whore called time will come and stand nude in front of you and pick you clean."

Mrs. James said nothing.

"Do you know how merciless old age is? It will take you a little longer to realize that. You are fifteen years my junior. There is still strength in your legs to walk, to move past things. So you don't get it."

Mrs. James said nothing.

"Does it seem to you that I am being overly dramatic? Life is always like that. But we pretend that it isn't so, and we try to put up a good front."

Mrs. James said nothing.

"Do you know how old age happens? Like the first beam of light in the tender predawn darkness, it suddenly pierces deeply into you, secretly, and without a noise. And it dries up your veins. It will make your beautiful black hair fall out. It will frost your temples with gray. It will snatch out your teeth and cast them away."

Mrs. James said nothing.

"Suddenly, very suddenly, it's as if someone bundles you into a spaceship and transports you to a far-off place, off-loading you onto a separate, desolate planet. You're all by yourself on that planet called Old Age, and that's where you will end up."

Mrs. James said nothing.

"Even though the world, filled with youth and speed, continues to function and writhes on right before your eyes, you can't go near it. Between you and it, a giant glass scrim will descend."

Mrs. James said nothing.

"Even if you leave me, you will still definitely come to experience what I'm telling you."

Mrs. James said nothing.

"Listen to me! Even though, in a way, it would only be fair for you to leave me, please don't. Don't embrace the vacuum and the loneliness of old age. It's really terrifying, and rather than go through it, you can kill yourself; I would be very happy for you."

Mrs. James said nothing.

"The effects that the loneliness of old age have on a human being are very strange. When the sun sets in the evening and darkness begins to cast its shroud, everything changes. The allure of the solitude that you are now imagining will suddenly vanish. Clouds will gather, and as yellow and red hues spread out in them, a profound sense of bitterness will grow in that small span of time. Then, your heart will stand impatiently, clamoring for human company."

Mrs. James said nothing.

"Look here: Nature is not as pleasant as you think! Outside, the cold season has finished; spring has begun to arrive. The green spreads everywhere and laughs at us. But what? What will it do to you? It won't do a thing. Spring won't do a damned thing for old people. In the face of life's void, nature has no role to play."

Mrs. James said nothing.

"Why, even Christ has no role to play in that void. Other than handing it to you, perhaps."

Mrs. James said nothing.

"I am a man who is terrified of life; a man who always stands wringing his hands before the void. Do you remember? The lines of those psalms you used to sing each and every Sunday! I recite those often, even now."

> Out of the depths have I cried unto thee, O Lord.
> Lord, hear my voice: Let thine ears be attentive to the voice of my supplications.
>
> Lord, my heart is not haughty . . . neither do I exercise myself in great matters, or in things too high for me.
>
> Surely I have behaved and quieted myself, as a child that is weaned of his mother: My soul is even as a weaned child.
>
> Keep not thou silence, O God: Hold not thy peace, and be not still, O God.

"In a way, the void of life is like the vague and unsure grief of a child weaned of its mother, feeling it over and over again."

Mrs. James said nothing.

"Listen to what I say. Just stay. Our separation will only give both of us more sorrow. In your forty-second year, don't just walk off like a young girl."

Mrs. James said nothing.

"Either time will heal everything, or it will cause us to forget."

Mrs. James said nothing.

"Look: the chilly mountain breeze has begun to blow sharply. Outside, the night's become completely cold, and has spread out. Like a limitless secret, the moonless, starless, misty night has enveloped us. There is not a thing there, save for darkness; only silence and emptiness have gathered everywhere."

Mrs. James said nothing.

"The silence of this ancient house will terrorize and kill me. Please don't leave me, just look at my sagging face. Look at my shriveled, trembling hands."

Mrs. James said nothing.

"It isn't possible to share old age and the void with anyone. Even so, the consolation known as 'mutual companionship' is certainly there for us. Like two drunkards, we can come together and drink down our very own poisons from two separate cups, at least until my poison kills me or your poison kills you."

Mrs. James said nothing.

Suddenly, Mr. James began to cry, weeping softly as he hid his face in his hands.

For a long time, Mrs. James looked at her husband intently. She then put down her suitcase, moved slowly to his side, and supportively gripped his shoulders. When he felt his wife's hands on him, Mr. James cried even more loudly and held her tightly.

And Mrs. James said not a word.

The Scent of a Woman

He is sitting on the beach. Today is the last day of his life. Today he is going to commit suicide. And yes, your guess is correct: he is a poet. And this you will know for sure: great poets never die of illness. They only commit suicide. Even if someone is not a great poet to begin with, he might become great just by killing himself. But it appears that our friend has all the characteristics of a great poet: face brimming over with grief, eyes clouded with dismay and fear, and he gives you a philosophical smile without showing his teeth. What is more, no one understands his poems: they are only published in magazines with print runs of 300 copies. Were he to live, it would just be for his 300 readers. In fact, if he were to die, those 300 people might well be responsible for his death in some way—that is, besides Rajakumari.

Who is this Rajakumari, you might ask. Rajakumari is a simple girl of modest looks. But she has no taste for poetry. The fact that Rajakumari has no interest in poetry does not bother him at all. After all, there is no rule that states that girls of average beauty have to like poetry. However, it was Rajakumari who said that she was in love with him. He didn't say that he loved her in return. This doesn't mean that he didn't like Rajakumari; neither could it be said that he liked her. It was just that his poetic mind was not accustomed to making decisions. He regarded the beauty of life as residing in its impermanence. Who has said that a man's mind is a decision-making machine?

But in the end, he, too, was forced to make a decision, unfortunately. He rejected Rajakumari's love (and in a voice that had an almost final ring to it). Why did he do it? He didn't understand. Basically, there's not a big difference between decisions based on clarity and those based on compulsion. You can always prove that any decision could be wrong at one time, and right at another, including his decision to kill himself today.

Even before this, he had come to this same beach many times—to this very same spot!—to commit suicide, and he returned alive every time. In order to commit suicide, you need utmost courage, and if not that, utmost cowardice, but it seemed that he had neither. But today, it wouldn't go like that. He would definitely commit suicide today.

He stands up and walks toward the sea. Reaching the edge of the shore, with the waves dashing against his shins and receding, he sits down at the very edge of the water and stretches out his legs. After gazing out at the sea for a while, he would definitely commit suicide.

The sea! The sea is such a wonder. The sea stretches on as far as the eye can see, and even beyond that. Gigantic waves furiously pounce on the shore. He loves the noise that the small waves make as they come rubbing against the big ones as they crash on the shore and scatter. The flutter that stirs within his heart from the big, muffled boom is so fascinating. In that half second of calm that exists just as the waves recede, he imagines the turbulent silence that comes after death. In the end, the sea always reminds him of death itself. Nature's grandeur is always an unnecessary annoyance to man. In a single moment of confrontation, it will start ridiculing man's helplessness.

As if to signal its setting, the sun spreads out a light red-gold color in the sky. Off in the distance somewhere, two boats can be seen. On the shore, a few fishermen have spread out their dry nets, and are mending them. Reeking of beedi smoke and sweat, they wander here and there around the spot where he is sitting. One among them, an aging man with a graying moustache and gleaming eyes, sees him and gives him a smile. While returning the smile, he considers the smell of sweat that is emanating from the fisherman's body.

The smell of sweat is the reason for the friction that had arisen between him and Rajakumari. He remembers that the time he had first encountered her happy face at Prince's Corner, there was also a sweaty smell emanating from her. The poor thing! An innocent girl. What on earth did she see in him? Thinking about his mean little life, it makes him want to laugh out loud dramatically. Opening his mouth and gazing at the sea, he lets out a loud laugh.

In truth, his life is really quite trivial.

His name is Rahul K. Nayak. He's a Gujarati. Poor. Twenty-four years old. Height 6 feet, 7 inches, emaciated frame. Medium complexion. A long nose, blunted at the tip. There is nothing to differentiate his head from his neck, which stretches upward in a solitary mass. In short, he is about as beautiful as a garden lizard. He is educated only up to the eighth standard. Neither English nor Gujarati comes easily to him. He knows a little Tamil, a very, very little. You might say that it is only because of this that he dares to write poems in Tamil. And his poems do no harm to the Tamil language, which has been around as long as rock and earth.

Six months before, he arrived in Chennai with the hope that by writing poetry, he might become a big man. But right when he got down at Central

Station, he knew that his dream would not come true. So far, none of his dreams have come true. A widowed mother back home, an older sister who had run off with a tailor, very young brothers—with such a background, dreams could only be just dreams.

A comradeship with poverty is certainly not new to him. From his thirteenth year, he had been experiencing the intense provocation of hunger, commencing like mice running rampant in his empty stomach. He had worn nothing other than torn shirts and tattered chappals, but he took on these degradations quite naturally. He knew that Indian poverty was just as boundless as all of those Indian theories on spiritual awakening.

Staying at a relative's house, he trudged around daily, looking for work in many places. In between, he wrote a lot of poems. Wandering from shop to shop, at last he found a job in that ready-made shop called Prince's Corner in Pondy Bazaar. 250 rupees per month. Ten hours of work per day. And it was here that he met Rajakumari.

In addition to Rajakumari, Jeyakkumar, Kaja, Rattinasingam, and Venkatesan worked along with him. Except for Rajakumari, all of the others thought that they were working at Prince's Corner because their circumstances were not good. Rattinasingam had come from Sri Lanka to write dialogues for Tamil movies. Jeyakkumar couldn't get a job in the fire brigade. Kaja just missed out on getting a job as a Class Four employee for the City Corporation. Venkatesan thought that he deserved to make a thousand rupees a month at Ashok Leyland. But he was paid to slog away at Prince's Corner for a mere 300 rupees.

Only Rajakumari seemed to have undiminishing gusto, as if she had taken on this incarnation only to work as a salesgirl in a ready-made shop. Rajakumari was a tad on the short side. She was a little over 4 feet, 7 inches. Curly, thick hair. But she had a fair complexion. A beautiful face. If only she were a little taller, she would have been a great beauty.

Within just a few days after he had joined, his co-workers easily accepted him. But he was beneath Rattinasingam's contempt. Rattinasingam just took him for a fool. Rattinasingam believed that only intelligent men could write screenplays for Tamil movies. Yet, you could say that those days passed pleasantly enough. On Sundays he sat in Natesan Park and wrote poems. He ate three square meals a day. And he roamed, walking alone past midnight in Pondy Bazaar, where the branches of the trees met to form a canopy over the street. He saw European films at the foreign consulates. He went to all of the literary meetings. He made friends. And his poems began to be published, and one poem in particular that he had written about trees caught everyone's attention:

At night
Trees reveal a rare beauty
(like wives)
The banyan looks down
But the palmyra looks up
As the coconut tree bends its fronds
It sieves the moonlight
Eyes haggle with sleep
But the trees
Refusing to dissolve into darkness
Flaunt their beauty
In dense green
Always
Trees reveal a rare beauty
Like wives at night . . .

But at Prince's Corner, no one liked this poem, including Rajakumari, and curling up her lip, she laughed: "Is this what you call a *poem*?"

Then one day, just like that, Rajakumari fell in love with him. That day at noon, she took him to Jiva Park (he usually ate in a restaurant). She gave him tamarind rice and curd rice that she had brought from home, and also declared her love for him. He was astonished that there was a girl who would have the heart to love him. But he hid his happiness at once. A strange pride abruptly possessed him. In a voice dripping with bitterness and vanity, he said, "Look here, Rajakumari! We are from different worlds. You are an ordinary girl. But I am a poet. I don't have much of an inclination for love. I am somehow here because of fate's sway. In regard to life, rather than wrecking myself like this in a clothing shop, I have very lofty goals. As I bound toward those summits, love would only be a burden to me. Please forgive me."

Rajakumari, who didn't at all believe what he said, opened her mouth and grimaced sarcastically.

He continued, "That aside, there is another hurdle that will make it hard for me to love you. You sweat horribly. The sweat that oozes from your body reeks of garlic. Before you can love anyone, you need to take some kind of medicine to remove the stench of your sweat."

When he said this, Rajakumari's face fell.

From the next day onward, Saturn caught hold of him! The creaky old proprietor of Prince's Corner suddenly began to get after him. If he came five minutes late, a scolding. If customers left without buying anything, a scolding. If he took a little rest after lunch, a scolding. If he stood up, a scolding. If he sat down, a scolding. His co-workers said that all of this was Rajakumari's handiwork. (Rajakumari was in the good graces of the proprietor.) The day before yesterday, he had agreed to give a 5-rupee discount to a customer who had bought 305 rupees' worth of clothing, and that was an enormous blunder. A heated row ensued between him and the decrepit old owner, and in the end, he was suddenly thrown out of his job. In the space of five minutes, it was over and done with.

Being stripped of his job was surely a huge blow to him, but what seemed so absurd to him was the manner in which he lost it. But even then, he imagined to himself that the boundless love that Rajakumari had for him had manifested itself in boundless malice. Until last week, he didn't think that life could be so cruel to him. Today, absolutely everything seemed to have gone beyond the limit. It was as if everything had dried up for him.

On the seashore, people thronged to enjoy the breeze. The boats were brought back to shore. The fishermen left. Young lovers were hunkering down in the dark. The stars bloomed in the sky.

He is sitting there, staring blankly at the sea. As he teeters at the brink of death, the awareness that there was nothing at all to think about in that final moment offers him some relief. From that morning on, he had put himself in the right frame of mind to commit suicide. Today, he spoke to no one, so that the tension in his heart would not go slack. He hasn't smiled at anyone. He wouldn't even look at his own face in the mirror. But now, though his face wasn't particularly interesting, he wonders just how it would look in a mirror. The human face does not reflect everything. It can paint in bold strokes, as with makeup, such blunt feelings as desire, love, affection, and sorrow, but could hardly touch the grief and the perversity entombed deep down inside that heart. Just as a flower's pollen waits to be randomly disturbed by a bee, one has to wait for the hands of death to rap on the doors of one's innermost heart. The naïveté of a man's life is beyond the realm of the emotions.

Facial expression is not crucial for a person who is about to die. Only the state of one's mind is important. And in any case, death is a good thing. There is no great difference between death without a reason and death with a reason. Why? There is no big difference between life and death itself. It is death that is vindicated in life.

Sliding backward and lying flat, he looks at the sky. His thoughts surge up randomly: the moon, the stars, his childhood, his mother, his poems. Finally—again—he thinks only about Rajakumari: "Come to think of it, Rajakumari really is a good girl, perhaps. I should have just accepted her love. She definitely has the allure befitting a lover. And more than that, I have seen an innocent passion sparkling in her eyes, the passion of a heart under the sway of love. What a fool: I did not understand that universal love and romantic love spring from the same source. And what right did I have to make fun of her body odor? It is through the body that the beauty of youth finds its sparkle, and a young heart's dignity, too. In truth, Rajakumari is a marvelous girl." As the sea waves lap gently at his feet, he shuts his eyes tightly, then opens them. The sight of the glittering sky, brimming with stars, creates a great ecstasy within him. It is as if he wants to wail out loud. He closes his eyes once more.

A little later, it seems as if someone is walking toward him. He senses a sound very close to his ears, the muffled sound of footsteps in the wet sand. It appears as though someone is standing very close to him. He slowly opens his eyes and looks. It is as if Rajakumari is standing there. With astonishment, he opens his eyes wide and looks again. Without a doubt, it is Rajakumari herself. He rises abruptly and sits upright. Rajakumari looks so beautiful in the moonlight. Looking at him, she smiles. He moves a bit, and gestures to her to sit down close to him. She sits down.

HE: Why are you here?

RAJAKUMARI: It is sultry. So I came.

HE: Same here.

RAJAKUMARI: It's summer.

HE: Yes.

RAJAKUMARI: Are you sweating, too?

HE: Understood. Please forgive me. I really should not have spoken to you like that.

RAJAKUMARI: It's all right. Anyway, you were only telling the truth.

HE: I regret it very much.

RAJAKUMARI: That's the way it is.

HE: I'm not as bad a man as you think.

RAJAKUMARI: I know.

HE: You won't believe this. I came here today to commit suicide.

RAJAKUMARI: Oh, is that so?

HE: Don't mock me. I've already lost all hope.

RAJAKUMARI: You are a fool.

HE: That's the truth.

RAJAKUMARI: You're a coward, a complete fraud.

HE: That, too, is the truth.

They both fall silent.

RAJAKUMARI: Have you ever loved anyone in your lifetime?

HE: No.

RAJAKUMARI: Is falling in love a crime?

HE: No.

RAJAKUMARI: Is it a crime if your lover sweats?

HE: No, definitely not.

RAJAKUMARI: Speak, and be honest: Don't you love me?

HE: Yes. I admit it. I love you.

RAJAKUMARI: Then why are you putting on this act?

HE: I don't understand it, either.

RAJAKUMARI: What don't you understand?

HE: Maybe I just don't like the fact that I love you.

RAJAKUMARI: Why do you talk such nonsense?

HE: It's not like that. You're an innocent girl. You don't know anything about life. "Love" is a feeling dependent on circumstances.

RAJAKUMARI: So?

HE: The circumstances are not right for love now. At least as far as I'm concerned, they aren't. I only want to die. And I have written my final poem, too.

RAJAKUMARI: Don't blabber.

HE: Listen to this poem. I'm not blabbering, and you might just understand it.

He recites the poem.

On a Mārgaḻi dawn
A devotional song is faintly heard from somewhere.
The world goes on without changing.
Like the semblance of a familiar face,
Life dissolves inside me and torments me.
Like fragments of form that flutter in a painter's imagination,
Faces, voices, emotions
Are fanned out everywhere on my table.
Whose face should I see,
Whose voice should I hear?
Where do I begin?
But you never succeed
If you try to weave a magical nest like a sparrow
By gathering up the dried, fallen leaves of the imagination.
The heart—that gland of sorrow—that is about to run dry
Releases its final drops with deep bitterness.

In the stifling afternoon
Life seems ancient, knitting together its immovable aerial roots.
I know the wings of desire,
And also the pathway of love.
In a world encased with shadows
There is a small corner that glows with light.
It fills me up
Like the first smile of an infant.
No,
It mocks me.
The world goes on without changing.

He looks at her and gives her a hopeless smile.

RAJAKUMARI: I'll say it again: You're babbling. But there's a clarity to your babbling. There is no salvation at all for people who perceive an infant's first smile as mockery.

HE: Pardon me. I really don't understand, and for me to love you, there are so many inconveniences.

RAJAKUMARI: What inconvenience?

HE: You don't know about my mother. At your age, she had given birth to five children, and had already become a widow. She is a very angry woman. The poor thing, she had such hopes for me. I was everything to her. I saw her bare forehead for years, and I lost faith in all of it: love, affection, attachment. Listen to me without cringing. Poverty is capable of drying up everything. Humans are all about needs. Their inner lives are made of nothing but needs: you will learn this when you get to know them intimately. Men are mere bundles of needs . . . but still, you're a marvelous girl. You have no big complaints about life or men. You have immense love to give to people, and so much to share with them. But I have nothing. My world is loveless. There's so much bitterness and restlessness. I have no interest in knowing what is real and what is fake. I have stopped paying attention to that. I don't even know whether my sorrow is genuine or false. If you choose to be with me, your very life will be wasted. The best thing for you is selling "gowns" at Prince's Corner.

RAJAKUMARI: You're blabbering too much.

HE: I agree, but I am unable to bear the fact that I love you.

RAJAKUMARI: You really are crazy.

HE: We all are.

RAJAKUMARI: I really hate you.

HE: And that is what I beg of you: that you hate me.

RAJAKUMARI: What will happen if you die?

HE: Nothing will happen.

RAJAKUMARI: Then what are you waiting for? Die and be done with it. Look, the sea is waiting for you.

They both fall silent again.

HE: It's become very dark.

RAJAKUMARI: Yes.

HE: The stars are glittering so beautifully.

RAJAKUMARI: Yes.

HE: The full moon is shining so wondrously.

RAJAKUMARI: Yes.

HE: The sea waves have become huge and are roaring.

RAJAKUMARI: Yes.

HE: The cool breeze offers happiness.

RAJAKUMARI: Yes.

HE: In the moonlight, your face looks beautiful.

RAJAKUMARI: . . .

HE: Your curly hair is waving in the breeze, and you're such a beautiful sight when it tumbles into your face.

RAJAKUMARI: . . .

HE: I can see the ocean in your eyes.

RAJAKUMARI: . . .

HE: I really like your long fingers.

RAJAKUMARI: . . .

HE: Your fingers are so soft.

RAJAKUMARI: . . .

HE: This is the first time for me. Your touch is so warm.

RAJAKUMARI: . . .

HE: Can I pinch your palms?

RAJAKUMARI: . . .

HE: I want to take you onto my lap and tenderly stroke your head.

RAJAKUMARI: . . .

HE: If you permit me, I would like to plant a kiss on your little lips.

RAJAKUMARI: . . .

They tightly embrace. And time comes to a complete halt. After a while, they speak in soft voices.

RAJAKUMARI: Can I ask you a question?

HE: Mmm.

RAJAKUMARI: Do you like me?

HE: Mmm.

RAJAKUMARI: Do you like me a lot?

HE: Mmm. Mmm. Mmm.

RAJAKUMARI: The smell of my sweat . . . ? Is it okay with you?

HE: Mmm.

RAJAKUMARI: Am I beautiful?

HE: Mmm.

RAJAKUMARI: Do you love me?

HE: Mmm . . .

RAJAKUMARI: Are you sure that you love me?

HE: Mmm . . .

RAJAKUMARI: No confusion?

HE: Mmmhmmm.

RAJAKUMARI: Promise?

HE: Promise.

RAJAKUMARI: See? I knew my love was true.

HE: You're a crafty one.

RAJAKUMARI: Enough, don't hold me so tightly. How many more times are you going to kiss me?

HE: This one is the last one.

RAJAKUMARI: *Chi*! You're a beast. With all this lust, after so much drama?!

They both laugh.

RAJAKUMARI: Okay. Shall we leave? It's become late.

HE: Mmm.

RAJAKUMARI: Okay. Take your hands off me.

They stand up and walk toward the street.

HE: When will you come again?

RAJAKUMARI: I don't know.

HE: Tomorrow?

RAJAKUMARI: No.

HE: Next Sunday?

RAJAKUMARI: Mmm.

The street is deserted. At the bus stop, one or two people can be seen waiting for the last bus. The two of them cross the street, and just as they reach the stop, the bus comes.

In the empty bus, they confine themselves to a corner. As the conductor comes close to them, Rahul holds up his index and middle fingers and says, "Two for Pondy Bazaar." The conductor looks at him oddly, tears off only one ticket, and gives it to him. He turns to Rajakumari to say something. Rajakumari, who had been sitting by a window to the side, has suddenly disappeared.

The bus races along quickly, bumps into a pothole, and shudders.

Then, it begins to run smoothly again.

Cat in the Agrahāram

"Death refuses to come for this old hag. This makes the seventh time!" Smarting, Babli Patti muttered words of scorn.

Madhuri understood the situation as soon as she stepped out of the kitchen. "Did it drink it all up again?"

Babli Patti cursed, "The damned thing, in this house, it is impossible to move from one side to another for a single minute . . ." Then, abruptly and cleverly, she changed tack, looked at her daughter-in-law, and jeered at her in chaste, grammatically correct Gujarati: "Well, Maharani, what have you been doing that the cat could slink inside an open house like this without your knowing it?"

Madhuri knew that she didn't have to provide the old lady with an answer to this. It was Babli Patti who had said a while ago: "Roast the besan flour and finish making the drumstick curry before I complete my puja." Surely the old thing could smell the tantalizing fragrance of roasting besan flour. Madhuri pinched her veil with two fingers without letting it slip, and stood calmly right next to the kitchen door in her usual posture.

"Okay, okay, what are you looking at? Go, get another cup of milk and bring it here! . . . Today, when Nattu comes, we'll need to figure out a way to deal with this Saturn of a cat somehow," said Babli Patti.

Gopal Bhai was rinsing out his underpants, and Sharada Behn was scrubbing her pots. They heard Babli Patti's outburst in the house from the first-floor courtyard and came to see what was going on. Cupping her chin in her hand, Sharada Behn politely lamented, "That's one smart cat! I see it here and there, and in the next moment, it just vanishes mysteriously." Without answering, Babli Patti turned toward the puja cupboard.

The Ekambareshvarar Agrahāram was behind the Ekambareshvarar temple in Thangasalai Street, surrounding the temple tank on three sides in the shape of the Tamil letter *pa*. Generally, cats never entered the Ekambareshvarar Agrahāram. In fact, not a single cat had entered the agrahāram in the past fifty or sixty years. All of the agrahāram residents happened to spot cats only in Thangasalai Street, in Govindappa Nayakkar Street, or in Kondittoppu. There had to be reasons other than those of environment for cats not entering the Ekambareshvarar Agrahāram. It appeared that the reasons were ideological, given that most of the agrahāram residents were Puṣṭimārg Vaishnavas. Tenkalai Vaishnavas held cats in high esteem, but there was certainly no compulsion for Puṣṭimārgīs to do so. Yes, it was true that in the Puṣṭimārg, whose primary deity was the infant Krishna, there were ancillary laws that stated that they must show affection for birds and beasts. However, maximum importance was reserved for the cows, who munched on polythene bags and cinema posters and shat wherever they pleased. Was not the supreme soul Krishna a cowherd himself? It seemed that the cats instinctively understood this higher truth, and followed it with rectitude—until last April, that is.

In May, the aforementioned old female cat accidentally entered the agrahāram, and, just as accidentally, no one took notice of it. In Building number 25, where twenty-four middle-class Gujarati families lived, on the first floor, in flat number 9, Babli Patti had taken some milk to the front room and had kept it there for puja, and in the one or two minutes it took for her to go back inside the house to rinse off a betel leaf to make a paan for the baby Krishna, the cat appeared, coming inside without hesitation and lapping up an entire cup of milk completely. It was when it turned to go out, acting as if nothing had happened, that the cat was spotted for the first time.

At first, at the moment she saw the cat, Babli Patti was beside herself. She mostly blabbered in Gujarati, "Are . . . are . . . Madhu, cat . . . Madhu, cat." Hearing the racket, the cat turned around and looked, and unfazed, it stopped in the middle of the hall for one or two seconds and looked Patti right in the eye. It then strolled off indifferently. From right next to the door, Patti quickly grabbed her small bamboo stick with which she kept impurity at bay and randomly hurled it at the cat. The cat tactfully stepped aside and vanished.

At first, Madhuri, who had come running from the water tap with wet hands, was only tempted to laugh, but when she saw the upset face of her mother-in-law, she suppressed it. Babli Patti was standing there in desperation, her lips pursed. Madhuri said, "Let it go, Ba. Leave the poor thing be. It's a creature without a voice." Patti shouted at her with malice: "*Chi*, shut your mouth, you barren donkey!" Madhuri just stood there, feeling small.

Babli Patti had a bulky body. A little bun streaked with gray. A big long nose. She wore spectacles with thin steel frames. At her neck, a chain of tulsi beads. She was ruddy-complexioned, like a ripe fruit.

She got up early in the morning at four o'clock, bathed, tied on a white sari, and with her bare forehead, she went to the temple five houses down from her building, and would return only at the stroke of ten. Then, she would begin to perform an elaborate puja for her family deities. She would sit before a teak cupboard set in a mirrored frame adjacent to the kitchen door. If you were to open the cupboard door, miniature deities would be sitting there atop their tiny cushions, all decked out in their clothing shot through with gold thread. Patti would take all of them out, one at a time. Removing their shimmering garments, she would bathe these deities. Wiping them down with a velvet cloth, she would take out fresh clothing from a large biscuit tin and carefully dress them. For the main deity, the infant Krishna, there was even a thumb-sized golden cap. After fixing dots of kumkum on them, she would seat them once more on their little cushions. Then, she would arrange in a circular fashion, in small cups, the types of food prescribed for the day on a big salver, placed on a plank in front of the cupboard. In one cup, there would even be tiny rolls of paan. After a while, she would wave lighted lamps, ring a bell, sing a bhajan to the tune of "Jaya Jagadishvara Hare," and would then close the cupboard. Only after that would she even take a sip of plain water.

Thanks to Babli Patti, a superb reputation had been established for the Ekambareshvarar Agrahāram. In all matters spiritual, she made a name for herself as the ultimate authority. But more particularly, there was no disputing her word in regard to Puṣṭimārg daily observances. She was the supreme authority on all of the prescribed ceremonial rules and on the remedial subsidiary rules, as well: she knew what fast was to be observed for what trouble, and what good fortune followed which puja; and she knew thoroughly the rules and rituals for death anniversaries, for weddings, for bangle ceremonies, for Navaratri, and for the well-being of potential brides and grooms. She could repeat from memory the *Bhāgavata-purāṇa* backward and forward. In addition, she could argue right down to the bottom line in philosophical debates. (A few weeks before, a student who was conducting doctoral research concerning the Puṣṭimārg faith had come down all the way from Baroda, and had had her doubts cleared up.) If she were present at a ceremony, even the Brahmin priests who chanted mantras were cautious. Even though Babli Patti had so many things to her credit, her daughter-in-law Madhuri obstinately refused to recognize her greatness. Madhuri's opinion was that the old crone was not all that innocent.

But even so, she felt sorry for her in terms of the cause of the frequent obstacles to her mother-in-law's puja. It had happened in just this way the last six times. It was as if it were planned: within the one or two minutes in which Babli Patti had gone inside, as she was preparing the lamp wick, or mixing the dal and rice together, or cutting the fruit, or picking up the matchbox, that trickster cat would come, and in the blink of an eye, it had finished its work and gone.

That evening, Babli Patti's son Nattu (whose full name was Natvarlal) finished up at the office, and when he returned home, Patti complained to him about the cat.

"Nattu, I don't know what you will do, or how you will do it, but that damned old thing must somehow be eradicated for good."

Though Nattu was tall and well built, like a policeman, he was actually a simpleton. He was even afraid of speaking out loud. He maintained a number two account for a Marwari merchant in Sembudass Street. From the number one account, Nattu received a salary of 1,000 rupees, and another 1,000 rupees from the number two account. He didn't indulge in idle gossip, he didn't smoke beedi-cigarette, he didn't go to cinema-drama: Nattu had none of these vices. He kept to himself and just did his job. Once he came back from work, he would change his clothes, finish drinking his tea, and go off to the temple. He would return in the evening only after eight o'clock. Only on Saturday night would he go for bhajans at ten. On Gujarati New Year's Day, he would take Madhuri to the movies or to the beach.

Nattu trembled and said, "What are you saying, Ma? Isn't it a sin to kill a cat?"

"Eh, you useless fellow, did I tell you to kill the cat? I say to just chase that donkey away somewhere and come back. Do I not know that killing a cat is a sin? The nonsense you spout."

"Where do I go to chase it off, Ma? First of all, I have to see the thing in order to chase it. All of this is due to your own negligence. Why do you need to set the cup of milk out first before you start the puja, and put it in the center of the hall? After that, all you do is yell 'Hoy, hoy!'"

"Enough is enough. Don't be such a smart aleck. It's as if I now need to learn how to do puja only from you."

"Okay, okay, leave it. I'll talk to Suri. He's the one who is fit for this sort of work."

"You must be crazy! Is that wicked fellow the only person you can think of for the job? That sinner might really even kill the cat. Be careful."

"Don't worry about it. I will look after everything," Nattu said decisively.

Suri was Babli Patti's nephew Surendran, the eldest son of her younger brother Ranjit Singh. He didn't have a job. He wore neat clothes, and, accompanied by his friends, he unceasingly stuffed his face with Calcutta paan and loitered about eagerly. He could swear in Gujarati and Tamil with amazing facility, and without a care. He didn't like god and rich men, but he was bound by love. He was a one-man kangaroo court for all of the wrongdoing in the agrahāram. On the basis of "Justice before Caste," a few days before, in punishment for harassing a girl who had come to sell flowers in the agrahāram, he had lifted up and flung a bicycle that belonged to a middle-aged Gujarati man into the muddy temple tank, which was covered with slime.

In the kitchen, Madhuri was kneading chappati dough, and she overheard the conversation between mother and son. She was thinking about that white cat. The old cat's face was sunken, its skin withered, its fur falling out, and it looked as if it was in distress, in a posture of waiting for its own death. When its eyes keenly met her own, it seemed to her that it was suddenly about to say something. On the many occasions when Babli Patti was not at home, it came near the front door, where it cracked open its mouth and uttered a "meow" in a weary voice. And without fail, Madhuri gave it some milk, each and every time. She felt that there was not much difference between herself and the cat. And just like that cat, she, too, had to live in the shadows. Did the cat have kittens? Surely it must have given birth to at least one or two kittens during its prime. Or perhaps it, too, was barren, just like her. Madhuri thought that the little acts of stealth that made up its own unprotected, short life were quite like the ones in her own. A cup of milk for the cat was equal to a sari for her, or an evening at the beach, or a Hindi film. And just like that cat, it seemed that one day she, too, would get old and fall to ruin. Just like that cat, one day she, too, would be tormented by loneliness. In old age, there is certainly no chance for love. Was someone storing up love, waiting to shower it on her? Where is it, in Babli Patti's heart? In her husband Nattu's heart? Where, where is the absurdity called love hiding? In the pale eyes of that old cat?

Madhuri rolled out the kneaded chappati dough and loudly smacked it onto a plate.

For Nattu, the cat issue was no big deal. He immediately forgot about it. But he remembered it as soon as he saw Suri on his way back from the temple.

"Just leave it to me, Nattu Bhai! Consider the job done," Suri cheerfully said. "Why just send that cat away from the agrahāram? If you give the word, I can even pack it off to America." Nattu said with trepidation, "No, no, don't do all that. Just send it away from the vicinity of Building number 25. That will be enough."

"Done, Nattu Bhai, done," assured Suri in English.

The next morning, Patti's son-in-law Hansraj arrived from Cochin on work. It was always like this with him. He would just show up without any notice.

Babli Patti held her son-in-law in very high esteem. As far as she was concerned, the only disagreeable thing about him was his snuff habit. Hansraj was only thirty-eight years old. With his moustache, the thick beard that concealed his face, and his long hair cut in a Bhagavatar crop, he looked like a swami in pants. Everybody said that he became this way only after his marriage.

Nimmu—Babli Patti's daughter—was quite all right before her marriage, but after the wedding, her body suddenly began to swell. At first, they all thought that perhaps she was growing fat due to sheer wedded bliss. Then, little by little, when she had become horrendously fat, it was discovered that she had some sort of disease. In addition to the money that Hansraj had inherited, he also earned an enormous salary. He spent money like water on his wife, but it was of no use. By the age of thirty, Nimmu had become unimaginably fat. It took 2¼ meters of cloth just to stitch a blouse for her. She had to sit by herself in an auto-rickshaw. She gasped for breath after walking ten steps. What is more, in the house, she could only go about her tasks while either sitting or crawling. The peaceable Hansraj modified the kitchen in a suitable arrangement for the convenience of her body.

Nimmu was not overly worried about her weight. She lavished affection on everyone with her constant laugh. Even those who had made her acquaintance for only ten minutes would be so moved by her love that they would long to see her again right after they left. When guests came, she would crawl around like a little child inside the kitchen, seeing to her tasks and attending to their every need. The doctors had said that she would only live for another ten years maximum. "If I die, you will need sixteen men to lift me," Nimmu laughed with a cackle. For Hansraj, his whole life was Nimmu.

For the entire week during Hansraj's stay, the cat did not come near Babli Patti's house. She was so busy showing hospitality to her son-in-law that Patti had completely forgotten about it, too.

When Hansraj was leaving for home, she put some favorite treats for Nimmu into a big tin and gave it to him.

She said, "At least for this Deepavali, see if you can bring Nimmu here."

"You know very well what her condition is. If she were to come, I would have to load her into a van to bring her. Why don't you just come to Cochin instead and stay for a week? It would be a change for you, too."

"What change? Will it happen just because you say so? If I were to leave, who would look after the house? Madhuri is incompetent. Governor Patvari might manage to find some spare time, but where is it for me?" complained Patti.

When she saw Nattu at the door, she said, "Okay, then . . . Nattu has come back with a rickshaw." Coming as far as the door to see him off, Patti thought of her daughter and fought back her welling tears. Hansraj looked at Madhuri, said, "Okay, see you, Sister," and left.

Ten days passed. Suddenly, one Sunday morning, Suri came to Building number 25 along with that old cat. By the time Suri reached Babli Patti's house, children and grown-ups had crowded around him. Under Suri's folded left arm was the cat, which was leaning its head on his chest, resting there just like a baby.

Babli Patti wondered, "What kind of magic is this? That thieving Saturn has gone limp on you like this!"

"That's Suri for you! Within these ten days, this cat has wolfed down 5 liters of milk and eight double omelettes. Is it so easy to cast a spell on a cat? I've come to show it to you before I leave it somewhere. Tell me, Auntie, where should I take it? Should I leave it in Tiruvorriyur, or in Tirunvanmiyur?" While Suri kept on stroking its back with his right hand, the cat shyly snuggled up against him, looking like a new bride.

Keenly looking at the cat, Babli Patti suddenly decided on something, and said, "*Dey*, Suri, don't leave. I'll be right back," and went inside. She was looking for the snuffbox, which her son-in-law had forgotten and left behind.

Returning quickly, she came back to the door. Conspiratorially waving her hand, she told Suri to come close to her. Then, in a low voice, she told him to bring the cat up close. Suri was holding the cat by its stomach, and he held it out before Patti. Patti had kept her fist closed at her waist, and all of a sudden, she brought it next to the cat's face, and in that second, she opened her palm, put every bit of snuff on the cat's nose, and rubbed it in.

In the next moment, as if it had received a jolt of current, the cat leaped from Suri's arms, fell down, and lay on its back. It appeared to be dazed. The cat tried to stand up, but it convulsed again and fell down in a heap. It then dashed itself into the foot of the hand pump, then the gutter, then the toilet door, one after the other, and it fell down again. Its voice was terrible, rising strangely. Each and every time it recovered, it would get up, and when it tried to walk, its legs weakened and crumpled. Turning its little head this way and that, it sneezed and sneezed pitifully, and then fell down.

Babli Patti dusted off her hands. Aside from the cat, the remaining snuff was sent up into a cloud in the breeze, and all of the many people who had gathered there began to sneeze, Suri included. A few of the grown-ups and children who were standing a little way off looked at the sneezing, staggering cat, and shook with laughter. The cat clambered onto the one-brick-wide wall at the edge of the first floor, sneezed again, and fell with a splat to the lower floor. It then got up slowly and ran off, leaving the building.

Looking at those laughing people, Suri showered them with filthy abuse, and then ran down after the cat.

A sudden stillness spread there. One by one, everyone began to disperse. When Patti turned to go back inside the house, Madhuri was standing in the middle of the hall. Suddenly unable to face her, Patti lowered her head and slowly passed in front of her.

That evening, someone came to see Babli Patti, and she began in her usual way, "What the Puṣṭimārg tradition says . . ."

The Planet of Old Age

At that seaside home for the elderly on the day before her death, Mrs. Florence finished her lunch and was settled into a reclining chair on the tinnai. The other old people who stayed in the home had gone on a picnic today with the manager. They would not come back until nightfall. Only the watchman was there, sleeping in the shade of a tree right next to the outer gate.

Mrs. Florence was waiting for her son Solomon. Today was Sunday, the day on which he was supposed to come. He would certainly come. It had happened that Solomon had missed a few Sundays in the past, but as of today, her medications would run out, and this Solomon knew. If not for any other reason, he would at least come to bring her medications. He would definitely come.

The street was drying up peacefully. The sky was glittering like a vast, blue sheet of thin steel. In one of its far corners, a big, white cloud was gleaming, having become even whiter in the heat, and looked as though it were oozing something from its vast middle. The sea breeze had not yet begun to blow.

For several months, in order to cope with her feelings of loneliness, Mrs. Florence had developed a unique craze for looking intently at the sky. During the day, except for the time of her afternoon nap, she would gaze at the sky. She would keep on watching for hours without tiring. It was sheer happiness for her to look at the many little white clouds. She did not much care for the dark, gray clouds. Florence's vision and mind were always wandering somewhere in the sky, following the clouds as they took on form and then disintegrated. The shapes, the angles of the clouds: she would concentrate with care on these things. She imagined that in accord with the sights in the changing sky, her mind, too, experienced drastic shifts and emotions. On the few, rare occasions where she happened to be staring blankly at a cloudless sky, she became quite withdrawn. The vacuum reflected by the sky affected her very badly.

On summer nights, she would ardently look at the sky. First, she would take it all in, in a single glance, that surface of the sky aglitter with the moon and with thousands of stars, and she would experience rapture. Then, she would look keenly at each individual star. She would look with deep interest at a few stars that, having appeared in the netting of the black clouds that had gathered them up, were twinkling from within them. She thought that it was impossible to describe her state of mind while looking at the stars in this way, individually. When her eyes grew tired of all of that fervent looking, she would again look at the sky in its totality. Then, any previous joy would vanish, and sorrow and helplessness would suddenly overpower her. She would laugh, thinking bitterly that she was just a speck in the cosmos.

Two months before, Florence had been captivated by a single, tiny star in the sky one night. Far away from the rest of the stars in the west, it shone beautifully. Either by chance or because it was her wish, on that night, that star fell into her vision and she looked at it many times. At first, Florence was not interested, but suddenly, she began to be engrossed in it without a reason. She was surprised at how it constantly attracted her. That night, before Florence went to sleep, she inscribed that star in her memory. The next night, she saw it again. Then, she remembered to look for it every night. In a few days, a passion for seeing that tiny, solitary star engulfed and possessed Florence. Every evening, as the stars began to bloom, Florence would impatiently wait to see that solitary star that so attracted her mind. In the daylight hours, from time to time, her infatuation with that little star seemed ridiculous to her. But at night, she fervently hoped that the star held some secret—or even a miracle—for her.

With fatigue, Florence blinked once. She rose, and, going out, she opened the gate and glanced searchingly up the street for a little while. Then she returned and sat down.

From a coconut tree in the yard of the opposite house, a crow, gliding very low and without moving so much as a feather, perched gracefully atop the compound wall. It looked Florence right in the eye. She, too, looked at it in return. With its little legs, the crow took one or two steps and moved slowly along the wall sideways. It then gently bobbed its head two or three times and turned. Then, straightening up, it opened its beak and cawed. A gray color spread lightly over the back of its little neck and shone beautifully in the sunlight. Florence was looking at it fondly. After a moment or two, the crow spread its wings fully and flew away. As it flew upward, its legs brushed against a rose bush that was growing inside the wall, and the bush shook. One yellow rose was blooming on the bush. It, too, shone beautifully in the sunlight. Feeling satisfied, Florence reclined.

One night, three years ago, Mrs. Florence had been suddenly struck by an illness. Late in the night, she began to speak softly in her sleep. Like a snippet of a conversation that was about to end in a scuffle, her voice began as a murmur before words started spilling out loudly. Finally, a terrifying scream! Solomon and his wife and children woke up in fear. The children began to cry. After that scream, Mrs. Florence somehow went back to sleep again with a groan.

The next morning, when Solomon told his mother about the scream in her sleep during the night, she refused to believe him. "Did I? I screamed?" she mocked. But the following night, in the same way and at the very same time, Mrs. Florence let out a horrible scream. At first, Solomon thought that perhaps it was a hallucination, that everything would just take care of itself. But, as bad luck would have it, the next night, and the night after, and on every subsequent night, Mrs. Florence kept on screaming. Solomon tried everything: prayer, medicine, pills. But nothing worked at all. Finally, on the advice of his wife, Solomon brought Mrs. Florence to this home for the elderly and admitted her.

Near the tinnai, a big, black bee flew in circles, buzzing loudly. Mrs. Florence kept on sleeping, disregarding the slight wakefulness that was stirring in her consciousness, and she made a great effort to drown herself even further in her sleep. But that torturing buzz had already begun to ring in her ears, and now it sounded loudly. Her sleep was disrupted. The many black and gray shapes that floated inside her eyes disturbed her a lot. But when she opened her eyes and squinted, there really was a bee making circles above her head.

For a moment or two, Mrs. Florence stared keenly at the bee. Then suddenly, she raised herself up straight and sat down again. At once, the bee flew upward a little and hovered. Flying even higher, it hit the roof, knocked against the eaves, and, darting out, it vanished.

Because she happened to wake up so suddenly from her sleep, Mrs. Florence's head began to ache. She got up, washed her face, and came back. The heat had quickly dissipated, and the sun was setting behind the tall buildings. Mrs. Florence was staring off blankly somewhere in the western sky, and she didn't notice that Solomon had opened the gate and come inside. Even when Solomon came up very close to her, put his hands on her shoulders, and called out, "Mother?" she stood there motionless. Then, as tears suddenly welled up in her eyes, Mrs. Florence began to cry.

Perplexed, Solomon looked at his mother, embarrassed for her. After a few moments, Mrs. Florence dabbed at her eyes and struggled to regain her composure.

"What is this, Mother? Like a little child . . ."

"I thought of something, and the tears just came. Okay, leave it, how are you?"

"How am I? I am quite fine. How are you? Tell me that first. Are you sleeping well? Are you taking all of your pills?"

"Didn't you bring the children along? What is David doing?"

"Glory has a music class. The little one has a slight fever. Don't worry about a thing. Everything will be okay."

"It's been two months since I've seen the children. Every single week, you evade me by coming up with some excuse or other. Why doesn't your wife want to send the children?"

"It's not like that at all. I'll definitely bring them with me next week."

Solomon looked at his mother's faded face. Her face had lost its color and had become wrinkled. Her lips had gone slack and were drooping. Over three-quarters of her hair had gone gray. She looked pitiful.

After a short period of silence, Mrs. Florence suddenly spoke.

"I cannot stay here. Take me back home."

"Be a little patient, Mother. As soon as we know that your body is sound, I'll definitely take you home. It will just be another two or three months. That's what the doctor is saying. By this Christmas, everything will be okay. Be patient."

"There's nothing wrong with me. I am just fine. That doctor doesn't know anything. I can't take the pills he gives me. They make me really dizzy. And my chest hurts."

"Don't worry about it. It will all be okay. Just manage somehow. Just another two months."

"I am not as mad as you think. No one here says that I scream in fear at night or that I make trouble for others. If you wish, just ask and see, you can ask anyone. You're the only one who is saying that I'm mad."

"Who is saying that you're mad? Stop imagining such things. All you have is a very common mental illness. The treatment for it is quite simple. Be a little patient."

"If it's a common disease, then why can't I take my medicine at home? Why have you confined me in this hell for two years like this? I know everything. It's clear that you're not going to take me home. I'll die right here."

"You don't understand. Solitude is necessary for you, only then will your health improve."

"What's so great about solitude? I don't need any solitude. I will be all right as soon as I come home and see the children's faces."

Mrs. Florence bent her head low. She sighed heavily and grew pale; her face sagged. She was about to cry again.

Solomon held his mother's shoulders. He said, "Don't cry, Mother, everything will be okay. It will be all right. I am praying to Jesus for you every single week," speaking as if he were consoling a little child. "Look here, I've brought you some raisins; you love those."

Mrs. Florence said nothing. Then, gently supporting his mother, Solomon took her back to her room.

As Mrs. Florence lay in her bed, Solomon sat in a chair at her side. Mother and son didn't say anything for a long time. Mrs. Florence looked keenly at her son's face. Solomon's nose was broadening, and his chin had begun to sag. His temples had started to go gray. Helplessness and emptiness were etched on his face. "Solomon is growing old himself," thought Mrs. Florence. "Poor thing, what can he do? Does time spare anyone? It spares no one at all. How can I ask him to show love toward me? Love is a matter of chance. And it appears now that there is no occasion for love."

Mrs. Florence suddenly laughed. Solomon was startled, and understood nothing. But he, too, joined her in that laugh. It appeared as if the tension that had spread between them had suddenly vanished.

Afterward, Solomon and Mrs. Florence talked casually for a long time. Solomon promised that he would come with the children the following week, and took his leave.

Mrs. Florence came as far as the outer door to see him off, and she stood there for a little while, watching him go. Then, she raised her head and looked at the sky. The western sky had grown dark, and had obscured her favorite, solitary star.

Solomon learned the news the next day, and by the time he came, they had washed Mrs. Florence's dead body, had changed her clothes, and had neatly put things in order. Irutayaraj, who was staying in the room next to Mrs. Florence's, mentioned: "Last night, the light kept on burning in her room for a long time. After midnight, I heard the sound of her crying—she wept and wept. I knocked lightly on the door to her room. She refused to open it. And she immediately put out the light. After that, I went back to bed, thinking that she would be fine after a night's sleep. I came to know about her death only this morning."

Solomon looked upon his mother's face, her eyes closed. He remembered how she had seen him off: she had smiled at him, like an ancient child with tear-filled eyes, on just the day before.

A Walk in the Dark

He began to walk slowly. All of the shops in the right-hand corner of that broad market street had been shuttered. And just a moment before, they had closed the shop where he worked. He could see from here that the many fabric shops, fireworks shops, and sweet shops were still open at the other end of the street. It was after 2:30 A.M. As the streetlamps burned, spreading out their light at regular intervals, the street itself was immersed in gentle darkness and gave off a peaceful sight. Along both sides of the street were huge trees, which were spreading out lots of shadow. In the middle of the street as well as along the side, some donkeys were sleeping, sitting close together at various angles, grouped in twos and threes. A donkey foal was grazing nearby.

He found that, walking past those tall, lush trees, their protective covering was of great consolation to him. The trees danced and swayed. The leaves frequently murmured in the quick gusts of cool breeze. Lowering his head, he walked on, listening to their murmur with careful attention. For some reason, while that sound spread through his mind soothingly at first, it then started to torment him deeply. He thought instinctively that within the sound and the faint vibration of those little leaves was the life of the sea waves themselves, as they rose up and engulfed you. Following this, he perceived that his consciousness was expanding. As the dense agitation of the leaves rang in his ears, he raised his head and looked at the street.

With its pitiful, sleepy face, the street wore a desolate look. The closed shops looked like prostitutes who had done their work in haste, and were now worn out and drowning in sleep. The hustle and bustle of the street's daytime hours cast a shadow in his mind. Drawing clear pictures of the forenoon's frenzy and the calm which had spread now, he fixed them in his thoughts. Then, he began to compare them carefully. He became quite engrossed in this. With swelling excitement, he suddenly changed the tempo of his mind, and alternated these two scenes back and forth in rapid succession. Then, in a single moment, he finished his mental picture with night's tranquil scene, and became one with it. The street became even more peaceful than before.

Slowly raising his head, he looked above the trees and on to the expanse of the sky. The moon was hiding somewhere behind a dense cloud. But the stars were shining everywhere, scattered like nature's riddles. He stared at them blankly for a little while. But the sky stretched on beyond his limited gaze. Suddenly, before nature's guileless greatness, he began to shrink to the size of a mean little dot. A thirst spread from somewhere in his mind and rattled him. He went dry. In the next moment, unable to bear the sight of that long, endless sky that reflected every little bit of emptiness inside him, he shook with fear, lowered his head, and began to walk quickly.

This consciousness which had dawned well within him now engulfed him completely. His brain felt a leaping urge to constantly chew on one thing or another, like a cow chewing her cud. But within him, all of his collected thoughts and baseless memories flew off and scattered, like snapped threads, vanishing quickly. He then fully realized the agony of his condition. His brain sent constant shivers of fear. He softened into a thin, liquid state, overflowed, and dissolved. Then, somewhere in the distance, the sound of fireworks exploding suddenly disturbed him. It stopped even before he could curse about it. He attempted for a moment to figure out from which direction and street the sounds of the crackers had come, and then he gave it all up. He took another look around the street. Then, he turned his head and walked on, staring with disinterested focus at his own shadow, which at first grew quickly, and then slowly shrank. Behind him, a donkey began to bray.

At the left end of the street, there was lively movement. Laughter and smiles pervaded the faces of men and women who roamed here and there, their eyes sparkling, their arms filled with bags and children. There were huge crowds in the doorways of the shops. A few shops were closed, and in those doorways, idle darkness was pitifully scattered in the light. Embossed letters on the nameboard of a large shop were blinking on and off in a beautiful red color, indicating that the shop was open. Tiny electric lights that adorned the name-boards of nearly every shop flashed on and off. Paying attention to the way that light and darkness were alternately heaped up together in the street, he walked on.

His feet shuffled along slowly, and stopped naturally in front of the corner petty shop. He bought a cigarette, lit it, and drew on it with an extraordinary yearning. The smoke completely filled his chest and soothed him. He turned and began to look at the bazaar. It was sparkling beautifully, with the gaiety it had assumed to greet tomorrow's festival. Even though people were exhausted by their running about here and there, the thought of the approaching festival was gladdening their minds. From this angle, he really savored the beauty and the commotion of the street. For a short while, he stood there looking, lost in it. Then, right next to him, a long string of fire-crackers began to explode. His mind absorbed that sound and was engulfed in happiness.

It seemed to take a long time for that string of crackers to finish. Within seconds, as it began to explode, his expanding self-awareness began to toss him about in its waves. The moment the crackers stopped exploding, the beauty of the illuminated street suddenly became cloying to him. The speed of his mind, which had galloped and plunged like evening waves, now slowed down. His enthusiasm dissipated, and he was stripped bare of it. His mind, estranging itself, went away from him and was lost somewhere in the joyful sight of the night. Little flames, which had failed to swallow the darkness completely, veiled the night around themselves and winked their eyes at him, tormenting him. He dejectedly watched the people who were roaming about, having hastily thronged in the street.

There were crowds at the entrance to the fireworks shop. People were mashed together there, in that radiant, bright light, and to him, they were mere forms. While taking another deep drag on his cigarette, he indiffer-ently merged with those bodies. Slowly drawing faces for them in his mind, he began to match the faces to those bodies, according to their shapes and heights. Then, for those faces, he created minds and emotions that would resound in them. Then, as if he were counting stars, he imagined their little desires and fears that were flourishing there, running in their minds. Then, he plotted out their brains to boss around those little minds, and having determined their countless turnings, unreal journeys, and rhythms, he then felt a rush of pity for them.

Once more, a cracker exploded somewhere very close to him. As the faces that had appeared before his eyes scattered, he again became con-scious of the bazaar and looked at it. The bazaar briskly functioned on, without being aware of him. He crossed the street and slipped inside a little lane. In a corner of that lane was his house.

As he entered the lane, he slowed down his gait, and decided to have a fresh look at everything. The lane was not yet awake. There were trees lin-ing both of its sides. A donkey was standing motionless in the middle of the lane. When he walked past it, it tilted its left ear slightly.

He began to look at the houses carefully; all of those tiny houses were inhabited by middle-class people. He began to think about those people who were slumbering away inside those houses. He tried to imagine their faces and the various postures in which they were sleeping: some sleep-ing straight on an incline, some with their heads bowed, others sleeping on their sides with pillows stuffed between their legs; some had their heads slightly turned, and leaking drool from their mouths and drenching their pillows; girls aged ten to twelve had gone off to sleep, giving off the lovely smell of wilted flowers; children smiled, sucking their thumbs. He, too, smiled fondly.

From the tinnai of one house, he heard the coughing sound of an old man who was sleeping there. The man began to cough repeatedly. Thinking that the man could have tuberculosis, he felt pity for him. After the sound of coughing subsided, he had barely walked on when he heard another voice. When he looked in that direction, he saw a young man muttering away as he slept on a tinnai. Stepping softly, he approached the outer wall of that house. Suddenly, that young man blabbered out loud. "So she went to the temple, it seems . . . to the temple . . . what, woman, such a big deal, the temple! . . . we don't know where our next meal is coming from, and yet, she goes to the temple. Who needs the temple? The temple . . . you Saturn, what, woman, why do you scream *Aiyo, Aiyo*, I'll break out all of your teeth . . . rascal . . . so she went to the temple . . . donkey." The young man slowly went quiet. When he thought for a moment about that young guy's babbling, it made him laugh. Just like this young man, many among those who were sleeping on that street must be dreaming one thing or another. He recalled one of his own recent dreams.

It was a vast, dense forest. In the center of the forest were seven or eight trees that had grown here and there, and very close to them some bushes, together with a small rock, and a pasture that surrounded it in a half circle. The time could either be daybreak or nightfall. In the pasture, two elephants were copulating. The enormous bodies of the elephants were in a very easy harmony. One or two moments later, the speed of the elephants began to increase. Then, a wild buffalo which had come from somewhere, stood watching the elephants with wonder. The buffalo was standing right behind the male elephant. Then, suddenly, it sank its teeth into the tail of the male elephant and bit down. The male elephant increased its speed and moved away a little. The buffalo bit down again. This time, it bit the elephant on its broad rump. The wild buffalo was repeatedly biting all over the elephant's rump. And the elephants just went on copulating at a tremendous speed. Then suddenly, both elephants vanished, and only the wild buffalo stood there, gazing blankly at something. A black hare was sitting by itself atop the little rock in the direction in which the buffalo was staring. The hare was terrified, and, contracting its limbs, it blinked and blinked its eyes and was looking somewhere. Its fur looked like black silk, and it was very beautiful to see. After a short while, the wild buffalo, which had kept on staring vacantly, as if it suddenly remembered something it had forgotten, charged toward the hare. The hare leaped down and began to run. The buffalo trampled and crashed through the bushes, and pursued the hare with fury. The hare kept on running, but it accidentally fell into a huge, shallow pit. Then, it hid right there. The buffalo greedily opened its mouth and sank its head into the pit. While sinking its teeth right into the hare's scruff, it brought its head out again, and, as it lifted up the hare, the guts and stomach spilled out separately. Then, the buffalo very slowly ate the hare. After it had finished eating, while it was licking its chops, circling and circling its long tongue around its mouth, the forest suddenly started to congeal. Very quickly, all of the plants in that forest shed their leaves. Then, their colors, dark green and pale, mixed as one. And, while gathering together as a vast green cloud, that cloud began to rise upward. In a cranny somewhere in the forest, a fire began to burn. The leafless creepers, the trees, the stones, and the soil began to burn in that fire. They became thin smoke, tan and blackish, and rising into the sky, they began to drift alongside the green cloud. Suddenly, the cloud settled somewhere, and only the smoke rose up, spreading out. Having gone over the sky, it gathered and thickened, and, after swallowing up all the directions, it became a black clot.

He took a final drag from the cigarette in his hand and tossed it away. As the coconut trees alongside the inner walls of the houses swayed in the wind, a light rain began to fall. He walked slowly; getting wet in that light drizzle was very soothing. He walked on, savoring the fall of the raindrops in the light of the streetlamp. One or two yards in front of him, something was lying in the middle of the street. He could instantly guess what it was. Without the least bit of haste, he approached it and had a look. A bandicoot was lying there dead, having been struck by a speeding lorry. Calmly, and without disgust, he began to examine its corpse. He was unable to get a good look at it in the dim light of the streetlamp, which was burning in the distance. Bending down, he squatted and looked at it. It had been split open from its guts to its tail, and it was smashed and scattered on the street. From the remaining tip of its tail, which had rotted halfway up, tiny little hairs were waving in the light breeze. Feeling sorry for it, he stood up and looked at the street. What must this mute creature have felt before it died? Yes, it must have been terrified, certainly. In that grain of time between the moment its head and neck had escaped the lorry's wheel and then before its body and tail were crushed and spoiled, what intense fear it must have felt! That powerful instant, the most important moment of its mean little life! At the moment of death, animals are no different from humans. But in life, compared to that creature, man was more the fool. All throughout his life, he didn't feel anything other than tiny little fears. The very nature of the fear that beset him—one fear swallowing another, one fear catching another and changing it into something else—was ridiculous. A bigger one swallowing a smaller fear . . . he kept on talking within himself, got up, and walked on.

When it saw him going past, a sleeping dog woke up, and abruptly stood up and barked. He didn't expect it at all, and as that sound neatly rubbed out the thoughts that were squirming inside his head, fear paralyzed him. The dog followed him, keeping close to his right leg. It kept up its long and rapid yapping. He became fully self-aware, and went on walking. In the brief moment that beat in the interval between the dog's growling and barking— and between one bark and the next bark—he made a quick decision that he shouldn't become the least bit agitated by the dog's next bark or growl. But as it was, he strove hard each time and failed.

After walking for a way, the dog suddenly stopped on the spot, as if it had understood that he still had a long way to go, and let him be. Then, it turned around leisurely, lightly growled, and ran off while continuing to watch him. He slowly turned his head, watched its departure, and made sure that the dog had left. At that very moment, he suddenly realized that he was hungry.

This naturally slowed him down. He thought about how he had been immersed in his thoughts, having forgotten about his hunger all this time. Next, he swore at himself. Those thoughts, meaningless thoughts, thoughts that ate away at his perception, stumbling thoughts that hardened: they were like shapeless corpses that sucked time dry. He cursed all of his thoughts. The rain that had been falling began to grow heavy with a clattering sound. He began to walk fast. As he came closer and closer to home, dejection and fatigue quickly spread in his mind.

He slipped inside a long alley leading to his house. Alongside the wall, there were pots, tins, a deal box, and next to it, a little stone for washing clothes, all in a row. On the right side, rusty old metal signboards and wooden planks had been patched together to form the wall. Ragged bits of cleaning cloth and clothing were draped over the top of it. The lane was pitted and dug up everywhere.

He reached the door of the house and knocked urgently. The filthy condition of that lane, the discomforting thought of his little house, and his hunger assaulted him in that moment. Again, he banged angrily on the door. It took time for the door to open. Those few moments felt as heavy as boulders. He felt as if all of the nerves inside his head were convulsing. Again he banged on the door furiously, and kept on banging.

After a little while, his mother came without turning on the inside light. She opened the door and stood there in silence. Her hair, which was beginning to gray, shone in the light of the chimney lamp hanging at the top of the inner wall. He went inside, switched on the light, and looked at the stove. Irritated, he switched the light off again, and, in that dimness, he started to change his clothes. The stove had been whitewashed yesterday at noon, and it hadn't been touched. Nothing had been cooked on it today. Then, after changing his clothes, he lay down on the mat that had been spread out for him. After one or two moments, he relaxed his body and began to stare blankly at the ceiling. His mother had lain down next to him, and was looking only at him through the darkness.

She suddenly broke the silence: "What, don't you want to eat, son?"

He lay there without speaking. She spoke again. "You have to eat what's here. Look, Rajika, the poor thing—she sent along some food this evening. Take it if you want it; eat."

"Why should I take food that has been begged for? Go and throw it in a ditch." He spoke in a voice that was mixed with shame and bitterness.

As he waited uneasily for her to give some sort of answer, he guessed that it would take her some time to speak. He could hear the rhythmic sound of raindrops falling on top of the tin sheet that had been used to patch up one corner of the roof. While he was listening to it, he searched for the reasons for his anger, and tried hard to keep them in his memory. Just as he expected, she began to talk again.

"Did your boss give you anything?"

"Mmm."

"How much?"

"Ten . . . out of that, I need 2 rupees for a haircut, I'm telling you right now." He spoke imperiously, like a little child.

She laughed lightly, and fondly caressed his head and chest. In that caress, the sultriness of his mind began to subside. He felt like an innocent, naked child, safely asleep atop her ample chest. He thought that some secret thing, either from her gentle, caressing fingers or from the depths of her heart, had drenched him and cooled him off. Then he continued to talk.

"Take the remaining 8 rupees and cook something in the morning."

"That's all right, but did you eat something in the shop?"

"No, one tea in the morning, one in the evening, and that was it."

"What did you do for lunch . . . you should have said something to your boss!"

"I was embarrassed. I only started today. Besides, there was quite a crowd in the shop."

"Will he make you permanent?"

"Why, of course he will! Where will he find someone who knows the job like I do?"

"Salary?"

"He'll give, what, around 150? We'll see. That's okay, have you eaten?" He asked this hesitantly, with a feeling of guilt.

"No."

"You've been starving since morning?"

"Mmm."

He thought about getting up to switch on the light. Outside, the rain began to fall even harder.

The Mirror

A City Corporation tree stood on that corner, giving off lots of shade.

Palaniyammal had finished bathing Jagadishwari with a sliver of laundry soap and dragged her into the shade of the tree. Jagadishwari's entire head had been shaved clean. Picking out a bundle of clothes from a nearby box, Palaniyammal took a torn frock from it and put it on the child. The child laughed, happy in the soothing morning sun.

Mariyappan, who had been sleeping curled in a half circle around the tree, awakened just then. Palaniyammal watched him as she knotted up the bundle of clothes. He rose silently and sat down. Palaniyammal was very hungry. She had not eaten a morsel since yesterday morning. Shoving aside his ripped bedsheet, Mariyappan leisurely groped for a beedi in his shirt pocket, and, taking it out, he lit up.

He drew in the smoke, but as he exhaled, the thought suddenly occurred to him that he had no change on him for his next packet of beedis. Now, there was only one beedi left, but there was a dim hope lingering in his mind. He remembered that 25-paisa coin that Palaniyammal had so carefully knotted up in the end of her sari the night before.

The child was enthusiastically watching the street that was all hustle and bustle. The thought that the child would soon become hungry and cry for food made Palaniyammal anxious.

Taking a final fervent drag, Mariyappan flicked away his beedi and coughed, then, gathering up a lot of spit and phlegm in his mouth, he spat it out at a distance and stood up.

Palaniyammal was staring blankly somewhere deep within herself.

Mariyappan gave his face a good scrub, and, as he wiped it with the end of his filthy veshti, he came to the foot of the tree. Palaniyammal had finished her sweeping, and was sitting there calmly with her legs stretched out. The area that surrounded the tree now looked clean. Along the wall were two big deal boxes. On top of the first box, three clay pots were kept in a stack, piled one atop the other. The second box, into which several cloth bundles of different sizes were stuffed, didn't have a lid. At a little distance was a black pot with a broken neck. Next to it was a big tin barrel, standing by itself. The barrel was just over three-quarters full of still water. On top of the water, a little leaf that had fallen from the tree was floating, perfectly still.

Mariyappan was very hungry, too. Coming close to his wife, he sat down next to her. Then he began to speak in an amiable tone.

"Can you somehow manage to get some tea?"

"What can I do? Manage for yourself!"

After a few moments had passed in silence, Mariyappan spoke again.

"Okay, let it be, give me some change, at least."

"Where is any change?"

"Who are you trying to trick? Have you forgotten about the 4 annas that you knotted up in your sari last night?"

"Oh, that! That's all gone now! I bought tea for the child this morning. There were 5 paise left. With that, I bought a plug of tobacco."

"Re-e-e-ally?"

"Re-e-e-ally."

Mariyappan didn't believe her, and, grinning sheepishly, he said, "No, you're ly-y-y-ing . . . ly-y-y-ing . . ." The middle tooth in Mariyappan's upper jaw had fallen out. When she looked at her husband, Palaniyammal felt both pity and irritation. The next moment, her hunger and irritation angrily erupted from her.

"Yes, so I'm ly-y-y-ing . . . ly-y-y-ing . . . ! All you do is grin like this all the time, like a monkey that has lost its teeth! You don't do anything worthwhile! A man. Look, what kind of a man is this?"

Mariyappan wasn't expecting this at all, and he switched off his smile at once. The next moment, like a man possessed, he leaped up, and, as he barked obscenities at her in a furious voice, he kicked Palaniyammal in the chest. Clutching at her chest, Palaniyammal slumped down between her outstretched legs and wailed. He stomped on her back. This time, Palaniyammal's cries were even louder than before. He had to shut her up somehow. Like a man driven to the edge, he squatted next to her, and gave her a punch on her back. Palaniyammal screamed again. She abused him with filthy words and screamed some more. He punched her again. He continued to thrash her relentlessly.

Terrified, the child began to cry loudly.

Mariyappan was finally exhausted. He wiped his face that was bathed in sweat and lit up his last beedi. Glowering, he took a deep drag of smoke and slowly walked away.

The crowd that had mutely witnessed them slowly began to disperse.

It was past two o'clock. The street was deserted and calm. In her exhaustion from having been battered, Palaniyammal had fallen asleep.

Mariyappan, too, had dozed off at a slight distance. The child had become disoriented with hunger and fear.

After a short while, the child shook Palaniyammal's shoulder to wake her up. Opening her eyes, Palaniyammal was confused for a moment. But when she saw a woman standing in front of her, she understood. Palaniyammal slowly undid her bun and shook it out. Palaniyammal's hair was very long. Raising her hands, she smoothed her hair down well, and gathered it up tightly. Then, she reknotted her bun. That fair-skinned Brahmin woman waited patiently until Palaniyammal had knotted up her hair, then asked, "Hey, Amma, we have some vessels to be relined with lead. Can you do it?" The woman was wearing sunglasses. She gazed at Palaniyammal's long hair with longing.

"Sure, I can reline them for you! How many vessels do you have?"

"There are, what, twenty or twenty-five."

"Okay, please bring them."

"No, no, they can't be brought. You'll have to come and get them yourself—there's no one in the house to bring them here."

"Okay, where is your house?"

"It's close by! In the next street."

"Okay, just wait. I'll come along with you."

Palaniyammal walked with that woman to the next street. The street itself was exhausted and had begun to doze. They didn't speak at all on the way. The woman walked in front of Palaniyammal at a yard's distance. The woman's house was a simple one, but it was huge, and inhabited by a large family. Palaniyammal was asked to come through the house's alleyway, and the woman went inside through the front door. Palaniyammal began to walk along that long alleyway.

From the interior reaches of the house, one room looked out onto the alleyway. It was open, and the only thing in it was an almirah, infixed with a large full-length mirror. When Palaniyammal walked past, her image flashed from the mirror. She immediately stopped to look at her own form, which was fully reflected in the mirror. She had never had a full look at herself until this moment.

Palaniyammal was shocked to the core. That form that she saw was emaciated and exhausted. The mole that was beneath its left eye made it even more ghastly. The eyes looked as if they were constantly searching for something. Pitiless time had not only gnawed away her body, it had also stolen and run off with her heart's youth. At that single moment, she saw her entire life spooling and unspooling before her, and she understood fully. The blank silence of that minute tormented her. But even so, Palaniyammal became lost in it. A couple of seconds later, she moved slowly and walked across the alleyway. The woman was waiting for her. She was not wearing her sunglasses now.

In a short time, Palaniyammal reached the foot of the tree, carrying the vessels. Settling on her charges with the woman, she even managed to get a 2-rupee advance.

First, from the tea shop in the opposite row, she bought two buns and a tea for the child. She bought a tea for herself and drank it. She made herself a paan with betel nut and tobacco. She didn't forget to buy a packet of beedis for Mariyappan. After she sent the child to buy rice from the Nadar grocers, she eagerly set about her work.

She dug a pit in the usual place. Stacking lots of charcoal in it, she kindled a fire. Then, from a box, she took out a blowpipe, lead, ammonium chloride, tongs, and other such items and set them all out. She told the child, who had returned, to blow on the fire. Then, she began to wash the pots leisurely, one after the other. Mariyappan kept on sleeping like a baby. She was staring at him blankly. Her anger was subsiding.

When it turned four, Mariyappan woke up. The fire had become red-hot, and it was bursting into red sparks and scattering them. Palaniyammal was wiping the pots. Mariyappan squinted his eyes and watched all of this for a minute. He then got up, finished washing his face, and came and sat down next to the fire. From among the pots that had been cleaned and put aside, he grabbed a large vessel with the tongs and put it in the fire. He rotated the pot, and, after it had become fully heated, he dipped a little rag in the ammonium chloride and wiped down the entire inner surface of the vessel. Along with the heat of the fire, that whole place was infused with steam and with an acrid chemical stench.

Palaniyammal pushed the beedi packet toward him. He felt ashamed to look at her. Turning his face, he pulled out a beedi and lit up. She said, "Hey, Jagadishu! Go buy your father a tea and give it to him." The child jumped up cheerfully and ran off. Until they had finished up the work by around seven o'clock, they hadn't spoken to each other at all. After cleaning the place up, Palaniyammal put a rice pot on the fire, still burning away. Then, coiling up the end of her sari and fixing it on her head, she got ready to carry the vessels. Mariyappan stood up quickly, arranged the vessels, and hoisted them up on top of her head. Palaniyammal noisily spat out the betel she had been chewing and began to walk.

When Palaniyammal returned, Mariyappan was playing with Jagadishvari.

When the water had come, which usually came only at that time through the corporation pipes, Mariyappan went off to bathe. Palaniyammal went to scrub his back for him. A lot of dirt had accumulated along his spine. He had no flesh, and, as she scrubbed his back, his rib bones jabbed at her hands. She felt sorry for him. After she had come from her own bath, Palaniyammal indirectly invited him to eat, telling Jagadishvari, "Come and sit with your father to eat." When the three of them settled down to eat, only the child ate with any cheer. They finished their meal in silence.

It was past ten o'clock by the time she had cleaned the dirty vessels and come back. The child had fallen asleep right where she was. Palaniyammal cleaned around the base of the tree to ready it for sleeping. She then sprinkled water all over the ground. The burning heat that was buried secretly inside the soil sucked up the water greedily. Suddenly, the heat dissipated on the breeze, and then the coolness spread out slowly. As usual, Palaniyammal took out a sari that was not too torn and made a screen by wrapping it around the tree. Laying the child down on a frayed mat, she then spread out another sari for herself. Then, choosing one from among the cloth bundles, she stuck it under her head, and, lying down on her side, she began to sleep.

Mariyappan was leaning against the wall. He flicked aside his beedi, and slowly sidled up to Palaniyammal. She lay still with her back to him. After a few moments, Mariyappan began:

"Are you still angry with me, girl?"

"Uh-uh."

"Then-n-n-n?"

" . . . "

"Are you sleepy?"

"Uh-uh."

"Then-n-n-n?"

" . . . "

Palaniyammal refused to talk to him. Mariyappan gently caressed her arms. Then, embracing her tenderly, he turned her over to face him and kissed her on the lips. Palaniyammal lay there without stirring. She was thinking about her own image, which she had seen fully in that mirror. She suddenly remembered that, when she had gone the second time to return the vessels, the room was shut, the room where the mirror had been.

She moved away from him.

The Crowd

Oosa had collapsed and lay there, curled up.

There was no glow in the western sky. The light had withered out and was dying away.

At that hour, in the agrahāram inhabited by North Indians, people were scaling back their activities for the day. Elderly Gujarati men in Gandhi caps had stepped out earlier, leaving their shops in the care of their sons; trousered middle-aged men had left their offices. Pudgy family women on their way to the temple; little girls, prepubescent girls, big boys, little boys; widows short and tall, their heads covered, clad in white saris, making their way home after finishing their bhajans—all of this hubbub had another hour to go.

Mittu Mama stood on his balcony, surveying the street below. The wind blew in bold gusts. At the temple, the plastic lotuses afloat in the tank had lost their color in the twilight and drifted on the water like black stains. Mittu Mama looked out at the intersection of Thangasalai Street and the agrahāram street. There were rows and rows of people, and rickshaws were trying to cross through them. In the dazzle of the electric light, Thangasalai Street was overflowing with excitement. He could clearly hear the swish of its hustle and bustle.

He was sixty-nine. His eyes were deeply sunken. Because of his sunken eyes, his long, blunt nose stuck out. Thick eyebrows. And hair in his ears. Four weeks ago, his head had been shaved. His cheeks had gone so hollow that when he opened his mouth, his healthy front teeth appeared menacing; if he closed his mouth, his face looked blank and emotionless; if he laughed, he bore the facial expression of a constipated man straining; if he cried, there was worldwide grief. His arms and legs were skinny. He wore a handspun dhoti and a handspun sleeveless vest with a pocket; his frayed sacred thread was hanging out from the edge of his vest. On the thread hung a tiny key that opened his treasury, a tin box where he kept exactly 17 rupees and 36 paise and some tattered, old holy books. This was Mittu Mama.

Ten years had passed since Mittu Mama's wife had died. He was not on regular speaking terms with his son and his daughter-in-law, who lived in the back portion of that big building. They had isolated him in this room, where they grudgingly bore the duty of giving him food twice a day. The grandchildren would come during the daylight hours on Saturdays, Sundays, and holidays to ask for biscuits. The old folks of the agrahāram would come during the sultry afternoons to talk about the elderly, sick people in that area, and about the maladies that came with old age. Except for these people, all of Mittu Mama's bonds were with what he could see from his balcony: the Ekambareshvarar temple, the temple tower, the end of the street, the street beyond, the temple tank, its algae, its plastic lotuses. Above all of these, the school clock tower loomed, and so on and so forth.

Mittu Mama drew his head back inside. A 25-watt bulb was dimly hanging inside, unable to completely light up the interior of his room, which looked bare in its patches of light.

Mittu Mama felt like drinking some water. But the clay pot was in the inside corner of the room. There were random fissures that crazed his feet like a modernist line drawing. A festering sore oozed blood and pus, which seeped through the hospital bandage.

He stood there, and inside his mind, he rehearsed every step of the distance to the clay pot many a time.

For Ranjan Behn, time stood still on that day. It seemed as if it wouldn't budge from here on out. She had finished all her chores for the day. Ranjan Behn's husband, Kanyalal, had finished eating and had left just at that moment, telling her that it would be well past midnight before he could come home because they were taking inventory at his company. There was a little bit of leftover food. She regretted that she couldn't sleep alone on the rooftop terrace tonight without Kanyalal. Ranjan Behn decided that she would give leftover food to Oosa, and then she would get the new "Colonel Ranjit" detective novel that she had borrowed from the lending library, latch the door, and read herself to sleep. On a lonely evening such as this, she usually didn't read detective novels in the nighttime hours. But today, there was nothing worthwhile on TV, so she decided to take the plunge. Straightening up her sari, she put three leftover chappatis and a little rice on a plate, poured out some gravy, and, carrying it, she came to the gate to look for Oosa.

Ten years had passed since Ranjan Behn's marriage. She was quite tall, between 5¼ and 5½ feet. She had the kind of complexion that mixed red with white. Her features were of the chiseled sort. Her arms and legs were fleshy; she had small feet and tiny little palms. There were no children. She had an aggressive bearing, and, much like a well-built cow, she brimmed over with insolence, and her body teased the eyes.

Ranjan Behn stepped into the street and looked around for Oosa. Oosa was nowhere to be seen!

Not only did they not know where Oosa came from, no one could remember exactly when he came to this agrahāram. Oosa suddenly appeared one morning, sitting down to bang on pots and pans along with Nayakkar, who did tinkering work and had put up a gunny-cloth tent right along the outer wall of the temple, just opposite the tank.

Nayakkar was decrepit. He was fifty-five years old. He chain-smoked cheroots. And Nayakkar's lungs, too, had gone up in cheroot smoke. He hailed from Erode, and had come to the city to make a living, but his wife, Mrs. Mohana, was a Madras woman. Dark! Thirty-six years old and dark! But magnetic! All day, Nayakkar would tap-tap away, repairing a pot or a drum. All night, he would hack-hack away, coughing, and would continuously hawk up wad after wad of phlegm. Whenever the aforesaid tapping and hacking was not heard, which was rare, he would pick a fight with Mohana. Further details about Mohana's affair with Rajakannu the rickshaw man would emerge, and sometimes, many minutely detailed bits of information would flow beyond that burlap tent and reach the street. One day, Mohana left for good. A few days after she left, Oosa came and joined Nayakkar. After that, Oosa was Nayakkar's everything. But Nayakkar had died one night last October, and Oosa had gone to fetch Mohana. She came and completed all the rites, and then, selling off Nayakkar's assets in Moore Market, she pocketed the cash, got into a rickshaw, and left. From that day on, Oosa had hung around in this very agrahāram. He would speak with no one. No one would speak with him. If you told him to do a job, he would do it. If you fed him, he would eat. He was somewhere between twenty and thirty. He had a medium complexion. He did not cut his hair for months at a stretch. His clothes were filthy, and his face was permanently etched with expectation and disappointment.

Ranjan Behn's eyes searched the street once, and they finally fell upon Oosa, who was lying down. Here he was! She blushed at her own stupidity, having looked for him everywhere but here, right in front of her. She went to his side, satisfied.

Agrahāram boys clad in pajamas and shirts were standing on the right-hand corner. Little schoolkids, college kids, everyone had eaten, and they were listening to Hindi songs on a transistor radio. On the front tinnai of a large building, fifteen or twenty young girls were sitting in their half saris, talking among themselves as they listened to the songs played by the boys. A little way off, a few little girls, aged ten to twelve, were playing hopscotch.

Ranjan Behn knelt down, and twice called out, "Oosa, Oosa."

Oosa lay there, just as he was.

It seemed to Ranjan Behn that the poor boy had wilted from hunger. Coyly, she called out, "Oosa, Oosa," in low tones. Then, she tried calling him four or five times in her normal voice.

When she called out to Oosa for the third time, it was as if Ranjan Behn were speaking to herself. Until this day, she had never talked to herself in solitude, but now, she paid attention to her own voice, and listened to it with care. Then, an unbidden doubt came to her: This voice . . . was this her real voice? Again, she tried to rouse Oosa. It was surprising to her: Did her voice always sound like this? On the pretext of calling out to Oosa, she tried to make a study of her own voice. Ten or twelve times, she tried to call out "Oosa, Oosa." But it was of no use. Her doubt about her own voice was not completely cleared. When she had tired of being immersed in this useless game, she recovered her wits, and really tried to wake Oosa up. This time, Ranjan Behn raised her voice.

Oosa lay there motionless.

A Gujarati family was walking along the street. They saw Ranjan Behn standing there with the plate in her hand, and they passed by her. She wondered if she should just give up and go back inside. But she didn't. She pretended to be looking all around, in other directions, while she waited for one or two moments for their footsteps to fade. Then, once more, she knelt next to Oosa's face and tried to call him: "Oosa . . . hey . . . Oosa."

Oosa was motionless.

It was very embarrassing for Ranjan Behn to stand there like that, holding a plate. She walked past Oosa, came down into the street, and stood there, looking right and left. If any of those boys whom she spotted would come, she could enlist them, and maybe they could wake Oosa up. The street at that moment was without movement and wore a look of desolation.

She spotted Bakula in the circle of children who had been playing hopscotch. Ranjan Behn called out to Bakula. The twelve-year-old girl came running. She was the daughter of Bhaishankar Master, who lived in the building next door.

Ranjan Behn told Bakula to wake Oosa up.

Bakula began to shout enthusiastically, "Oosa, Oosa." After calling him seven or eight times, and perhaps because she was fed up with it, she loudly shouted, "Oosavoosa, Oosavoosa," without any pause between the first Oosa and the second Oosa, as if she were shooing off a bug or a mosquito. Hearing her shout, the other children turned and looked, distracted. Seeing Ranjan Behn and Bakula as they were standing next to the prostrate Oosa, all of them came over. Now there was a little crowd surrounding Oosa.

One or two other children joined Bakula in calling out to Oosa. But deciding that their shouting wasn't good enough, a little girl said in Gujarati, "Just wait a minute: *I'll* wake him up!" and, clearing her throat, she let out a murderous scream: "Oosa!"

Oosa didn't move.

There were one or two moments of quiet. Then, as if the children had decided that Oosa wasn't going to wake up, they began to chat among themselves.

Once more, Ranjan Behn spoke to Bakula: "Touch him once and wake him up." Hesitating for a moment, Bakula recoiled and said, "*Chi*, I won't touch him." She stood there shrugging her shoulders. The other children had heard Bakula and laughed noisily.

From among the youth standing around on the corner, one skinny guy who wore his hair in a step cut walked toward them to go into Thangasalai Street. As he saw the crowd, he slackened his pace, paused in the middle of the street for a moment, and took note of everything. Within that moment, a child ran toward him, calling out his name, "Pratap Bhai!" and told him what the matter was. Turning to his right, he gave his Calcutta paan one last chew, mixed it up with saliva, and spat it out. He strutted toward the crowd.

He came, had a look at Oosa, and then looked at Ranjan Behn. He then spoke to her softly, as if engaged in casual talk. Before this, he had never spoken to Ranjan Behn, nor had he ever seen her at such close quarters. Now, a light happiness came over him at this chance opportunity. Ranjan Behn elaborated on what the kids had told him. He continued to listen as he looked at her intently. Meanwhile, the youngsters who were chattering away came and joined them. It took a few moments for the murmuring of the girls to settle into silence.

It suddenly occurred to Pratap that he was the only man in that crowd. And right then, he realized that everyone was looking at him. So now, it seemed to him that he had to do something clever and manly. He raised his head and looked all around. When he saw that his friends, who were standing on the corner, were now coming, satisfaction and dissatisfaction mixed together and ran as one in his mind.

The young people came over enthusiastically. As they asked him in Gujarati, "What's happened, Da, what's happened?" every little girl tried, one by one, to explain the situation to two or three people at a time.

A few people said, "Bring him around, revive him," and, pushing past the girls as they talked casually among themselves, they looked at Oosa. A few other guys took one perfunctory look at Oosa, then ogled the girls. A few more people who had accompanied them stood about in the street, unable to decide whether to be a part of this.

Now a huge crowd surrounded Oosa.

One particular youth declared, "*I'll* wake him up!" and came up to the front, pushing past the others. He was famous in the street for his really high voice. He knelt down, cupped both palms around his mouth, and roared "Oosa!" as if he wanted to scare everyone. When they heard his roar, all of the girls, the children, and the youths laughed with a "Ho!" The guy who yelled looked like a fool.

Among the young men who were quietly listening to everyone was one Avinash, who calmed everyone down. Now, he spoke up, and in a firm voice told Ranjan Behn to bring a pitcher of water. Avinash had said something that had not occurred to anyone until then! The young girls looked at him in awe, all together in a herd. In his mind, Avinash liked the attention that he had drawn to himself, but he set that thought aside, and stood there majestically.

Ranjan Behn shook the shoulder of a young girl, and politely told her, "Come, Rekha, go and get a pitcher of water from inside." Rekha went inside reluctantly. The girl went and got the water in great haste and ran back with excitement, not wanting Oosa to wake up until she came back there.

And thank goodness! Oosa lay there just as he was.

Avinash took the water from Rekha and began to sprinkle it on Oosa's face. After four or five times, everyone waited for Oosa to move. Oosa didn't move. Again, Avinash tried to splash a lot of water on Oosa's face. Oosa didn't move. Then, something came to Avinash, and he suddenly upended the whole pitcher on Oosa's face. The water drenched Oosa's face and head, and ran trickling down to the ground.

Everyone stood there, with helplessness and fatigue on their faces.

Avinash bent down again, and tried to lay his fingers crosswise just under Oosa's nose without touching it. After one or two moments, it seemed to him that Oosa wasn't breathing. Right afterward, he began to look very carefully at Oosa's chest and stomach. Oosa's body was not moving! For a few moments, Avinash didn't know what to do. But within himself, he felt the tumult and excitement. It suddenly came to him that he might try to take Oosa's pulse. He looked at Oosa. He was so filthy! His whole body was dirty! Avinash thought that it had been many days since Oosa had bathed. Oosa's left hand trailed in the gutter that ran to the outside from the building.

Everyone stood there and stared blankly at Avinash.

When he gingerly grabbed Oosa's right wrist, he did so with distaste. He bent down just enough to perceive the throb of his pulse.

In just this way, one minute passed.

Two girls who had lost their patience were about to open their mouths to say something. At once, Avinash just raised his hand in the direction of the voices without even turning his head, and gestured to them to be quiet. Again, there were one or two moments of silence.

A few middle-aged people, who were standing in the entrances of other buildings, looked at the crowd in panic, and they asked, "What's happened?

What's happened?" They came and stood there thronging, as if they might fall right onto the crowd. Avinash turned his head, and looked in the direction of their voices. The middle-aged people went silent at once. In that same moment, as Avinash's grip loosened, Oosa's hand slipped down and fell with a thud. Everyone stood there in surprise and kept on looking only at Oosa.

Avinash stood up suddenly. Everyone looked at him. Looking at all of them as they waited calmly for his verdict, he said in Gujarati, "He's dead."

Right away, the crowd moved back a little with a murmur and bore silent witness to Oosa. Many of them dispersed, and left to relay the news to other people.

In a short while, people began to arrive from all of the houses. The people who came had a look at Oosa, and then, standing aside, they bunched together and talked. Many of them felt pity. A few did not believe that Oosa was dead, but they, too, moved away and stood there.

The sky had gone completely dark.

Standing next to the door fixed with an iron grate, Mittu Mama's grandson gave it an excited rattle, yelling, "Grandpa! Grandpa!" Mittu Mama had finished drinking his water and had gone to bed.

Mittu Mama turned his head toward the door and looked, without even rising from his bed. Gazing wearily at his grandson, he asked, "What do you want?"

"Oosa is dead."

Mittu Mama got up in alarm. He moved slowly, but as sharp pains shot through his feet, he wilted.

"When?"

"Seven o'clock."

"Where?"

"Right here, at the entrance to our house."

Mittu Mama said nothing in return. He could hear the sound of running as the boy clambered down the stairs from the upper floor.

So Oosa was dead.

Mittu Mama couldn't believe it. He was among the one or two people to whom Oosa had spoken in this agrahāram, even if very rarely. Just at noon today, as they saw a cartful of watermelons go by, he had been talking with him right then about how cheap watermelons used to be.

In the morning, he was fine; how could he just die like this in the evening? The more he mulled it over, the more shocking and sad it was to him.

He got up, deciding that he would go and have one last look at Oosa's face, at the very least. He slipped his feet into his Hawaii chappals and went down the stairs from the upper story. It took him several minutes to descend.

Pushing past those people who were surrounding Oosa, Mittu Mama had a look. The glow from the fluorescent streetlight had been obscured by the crowd, but still, a little light fell on Oosa's face. When he saw Oosa, it felt as if someone were whispering to Mittu Mama within his mind, "Oosa isn't dead. Oosa isn't dead."

Mittu Mama slowly made his way to Oosa, and, bending down, he leaned his body against the building wall with a lot of difficulty and sat there. The crowd just stood there, surprised at how Mittu Mama could sit so close to Oosa.

Mittu Mama hesitated for a moment. Then, undoing the top buttons of Oosa's filthy shirt, he pushed it out of the way. Oosa's shirt was soaked through with the water that had flowed from the pitcher. He pressed his thin fingers and palm down firmly on the left side of Oosa's chest. In one or two moments, Mittu Mama could feel the beating of Oosa's heart. The next moment, he held Oosa's head with enthusiasm and excitement, and lifted it up. He was not able to lift him up completely.

Now, a murmur rose up suddenly in the crowd, which had been watching all of this. Pratap moved forward a little and came to his side. Mittu Mama raised his head, looked at him, and, in anguish, ordered him, as if making an appeal: "This man is alive. Grab his hands, grab his hands!"

Pratap immediately caught hold of both of Oosa's hands and pulled him forward. Mittu Mama placed his hands on Oosa's sides to steady him. Oosa's body, still motionless, was raised up. Pratap shouted, "Water, water!" Water came at once. Someone sprinkled it on Oosa's face. Pratap smacked Oosa's cheeks gently, alternating left and right.

Oosa moved slightly. He began to slump back down again. Pratap stopped smacking him, grabbed both of Oosa's hands, and shook them. Oosa opened his eyes. Looking at the crowd once, he shut his eyes again. Oosa then opened his eyes once more, turned his head tiredly from side to side, and looked at the crowd. Then, he just stared vacantly for a while. People were standing in a throng, watching him. After a few moments had passed, Oosa opened his mouth, brought his thumb up next to it, and made a gesture. Pratap gave him some water. Taking noisy breaths between gulps, Oosa thirstily drank the water.

Mittu Mama said, "Give this man something to eat!" At once, everyone looked for Ranjan Behn. She was standing inside with the other women, talking. A youth quickly took the plate from her, and dashed to the entryway. Someone took a chappati and held it out next to Oosa's mouth. Oosa bit it and began to eat. As if it had grown tired, the crowd lost its enthusiasm and began to disperse.

Mittu Mama waited until Oosa had finished eating and slowly stood up.

His feet began to hurt.

Bamboo Shoots

Since time immemorial, long before Columbus discovered America, the weekly wage system had been in place in tailor shops. And so it was in the shop of Mr. Krishnaji Rao.

Thanks to the mercy of complimentary passes, there were many shop boys who had gone bad by watching week after week on Thursdays the second shows of peerless screen epics such as *Gul-e-Bakavali* and *Kulamakal Radhai*. They mentally embraced the succulent bodies of dream girls and stained their lungis. I was one of them. My older brother had run off to Chennai and vanished. My sister was married off to an estate manager in the Nilgiri Hills. Her beauty had fetched her a bit of good luck. My younger brother worked in a ready-made clothing factory for 50 rupees a month. As for me, I worked in Mr. Krishnaji Rao's shop.

We lived on Thyagaraja New Street, which was crowded with Thevanga Chettiyar weavers, in a house that was owned by a Chettiyar widow who sold idlis. It was a strange, dark hole, an insult to the science of architecture. If you went inside, in the dark you could see Mother's silhouette, a still life clad in white, who had lost her husband at the age of twenty-four. My father was a tall and hefty man. His hemorrhoids had reached an advanced state, and that last scream, wailing as he oozed and leaked blood from his anus, left a scar on my four-year-old mind. In those days, Mother's voice was like the muffled caw of a battered crow as it slid down each row of tiles on a roof. Even now, on quiet nights when I am filled with inner calm, that voice sometimes comes back to haunt me.

Mr. Krishnaji Rao was a Marathi. Stunted. Fat. He was very foul-mouthed. Though he drank a lot, he was utterly brilliant in his profession. Because of this, he had at one time become very close to colonial officials and collectors. These were the unforgettable events in his lifelong career: Once, the wrestling hero called King Kong was so happy with the perfect fit of the suit that Mr. Rao had made for him that he lifted Mr. Rao in his arms and over his head as if he were a child. And then, there was the time when Mr. Rao stitched a khadi shirt for the great leader Kamraj.

In those days, he had money to burn! He lost a lot of it making movies, and squandered the rest on the Anglo-Indian whores of Podanur. Now, his life ran on at the mercy of college contracts and his young customers who had by then become old.

Mr. Rao's house and tailor shop, which had slid from prosperity into destitution, was at the end of Nawab Hakeem Road, facing a movie theater. Everything in the shop—the table, chairs, counters, sewing machines—was battered and could be said to be antiques. It was always a bit dim inside the shop. Mr. Rao used the rectangular back portion of the shop as his house. Mrs. Lakshmibai, who had borne one son and three daughters for Mr. Rao, may not have been a great beauty, but she had a strong, taut, fair body. She had the dazzling attraction of a thirty-year-old, having hidden her own forty-three years well. She had gone deaf in her left ear from Mr. Rao's drunken years of beating and punching her. The oldest girl, Sumitra, was studying for her preuniversity course, and with an expressionless face that seemed cast in cement, she would lie around with her legs showing in the noon hours, her half sari rucked up. (I caught a glimpse of this once when I went to answer the ringing telephone inside the house in Mr. Rao's absence.) The second girl, Gauri, was thirteen years old. She had big, long eyes. And a tongue that wagged a lot. And next was the boy. At the age of eight, he was a rotten-toothed monkey who showered abuse on everyone. And last, there was Sulocana, known as Laddoo. She was three years old. She shat about thirty times a day.

Mr. Rao had hired an army of destitute Marathis to work for him: Gopinath Rao, Padmanath Rao, Govinda Rao, Deshpande, Raghunath Rao, Panduranga Rao, and Mallikarjuna Rao. The ten-year-old Sukumaran, who ran errands and did buttonholes, was a Malayali. And I, a Gujarati, looked after the accounts. When you say "accounts," it doesn't mean shuffling through pages in enormous ledgers. All I needed to do was to keep the money collected when Mr. Rao wasn't in the shop and give it to him after he returned and was in a good mood, bare-chested and sucking noisily on a Scissors Mark. I had to make a note of the paltry sums that my fellow Raos would obtain one or two days before payday. I also had to note the measurements as Mr. Rao took them, write them down on a little slip of paper, and pass them along to Gopinath Rao, the cutting master, along with the cloth. (With eyes that glittered and with those pockmarks on his withered face, Gopinath Rao—like the villains of 1950s Hindi movies—was a man who struck terror in the hearts of those who beheld him. When little squabbles broke out between him and Mr. Rao, he would cut 32 inches to 22, change the numbers on the slips I had given him, and get me into trouble. Afterward, my chastity and that of my mother would be outraged by Mr. Rao's tongue.)

I had to wipe up the eternal dust in the shop, write leave letters for Gauri, and a composition for her about an excursion. I had to keep Laddoo entertained and relish the filthy jokes that Padmanath Rao told. In the time that remained, keeping an account book open and pretending to work, I could stare blankly at my own face in the tarnished mirror that hung above my table.

It was a Saturday.

Mr. Rao had gone out early in the morning. In the cinema hall opposite was a new film, starring one of the tilakams. The people who couldn't get tickets for the 2:30 show had already begun to queue up for the evening show. The hero was starring in a double-action role. On the huge poster, as Hero One, he was shown staring, with a beard and raggedy clothes, and as Hero Two, he was fighting with a ferocious lion. The heroine was standing in profile, sheepishly laughing and brandishing one of her big boobs, as if she had no connection whatsoever with the plot. The famous heroine's nose looked slightly more blunted than her real nose. The poster artist was an intelligent man who knew that, for Tamil heroines, nothing should be more prominent than their boobs and thighs. What he missed on the nose he compensated for on the breast.

Gopinath Rao stood at the entrance, aimlessly looking on. It was quiet inside the shop.

Normally, at this time, all of the Raos would be talking away enthusiastically. About tailoring, about sewing machines, about a machine that they didn't have there that could make a buttonhole . . . but no matter where these conversations began, they would always end in sex, like all Indian discussions. On that day, as if there was nothing to talk about—not even *that*—all of them were silent.

Not much money had come in on that day. It was past three o'clock in the afternoon, and not even 15 rupees had come in. Up until then, everyone had asked me separately one or two times about how much money had come in. We needed at least 200 rupees to give out as wages by evening. Only then could wages be given to everyone. No one had any hope that this would happen.

These sorts of crises were not new to Mr. Rao's employees. In the last week of the month, almost every month, things would go this way. Last month, when Mr. Rao had gone to Bangalore and on a Saturday much like this one, Mrs. Lakshmibai gave everyone 2 liters of rice. But Mr. Rao would not stoop to such extreme displays of compassion. Today, if no money came in, it was a certainty that everyone would have to go home empty-handed, without even rice.

In a panic about their wages, everyone was working half-heartedly.

Padmanath Rao was a newly married man. In order to fetch back his wife from her mother's house, he was expecting a 20-rupee advance on top of his wages. He got up and went outside frequently, with diminishing enthusiasm, to go smoke beedis.

My mother came to mind. She, too, would be expecting my wages. She had declared that afternoon that we were out of rice. And besides, the next day was Father's death ceremony. What we fed the Brahmin priest on that day might or might not reach my dead father, but I still thought that it was inconsiderate of Father to have died as he did at the end of the month. Then I felt sorry for thinking that. I immodestly vowed that the moment I became a big man, I would throw a feast for our entire hometown for my father's death ceremony.

It was that enthralling time when Anna and Karunanidhi were ruling the roost. People thronged like dogs from one place to another to buy Tamil Nadu state lottery tickets. Only rice was cheap. It was smelly, brown in color, and two measures for 1 rupee! Mother had even christened it with a pet name, "rubber paddy." Including an imaginary housemaid on our ration card, we got 12 kilos for four people. Plus 4 kilos of wheat. Added all together, a little more than 13 rupees. My younger brother's boss was a demon who wouldn't give advances. The usual plan was that I had to buy our rations from my weekly wages. I sat there staring at the entrance, hoping that the plan would succeed.

I could see that Mr. Rao was coming—he had just crossed the street from the opposite direction. Because he'd been out and about in the strong sun, his face had gone as red as an old, bruised apple. With each of his steps, his paunch danced and shook. When compared with all other paunches, Mr. Rao's was one of a kind. It had its mysterious beginnings just beneath his hairless chest: rising up tranquilly, it then formed a lazy half circle before angling down sharply and disappearing.

Many of us had heard those stories from the West, about how the beautiful breasts of royal maidens were used as models for mead cups. But it is not fair to expect people who don't care about elegance in form—such as Indian potters or football manufacturers, for that matter—to have heard about such things. Unfortunately, as a result of this, Mr. Rao's paunch kept on jiggling away with no one paying any heed.

Before the other Raos could notice, Mr. Rao came inside, putting the bundle of cloth in his arms on top of the table. I was already on my feet. Panduranga Rao, who didn't realize that Mr. Rao had come back, was teasing Sukumaran, asking him the meaning of a dirty Malayali word that he had come across. Like a stealthy spy, Mr. Rao stood there, listening to their every word.

All of the other Raos were waiting, looking on sideways. The little boy, making a bashful face and raising his head in laughter, then saw Mr. Rao and, taken aback, grew frightened. Anger gushed out of Mr. Rao. Flinging the bundle of cloth that he had put on top of the table at the boy's face, he went after him, shouting, "What, Da? What are you laughing at, you whore's pubes?" The bundle of cloth fell on the little boy's nape and broke open. In addition, when he crouched down shaking with fear, a slap fell, half on his ear and half on his cheek. "Motherfucker! He laughs instead of doing his job . . . what do you say to that?" Right after Mr. Rao abused him, he then turned toward Panduranga Rao. As if he had been waiting for Mr. Rao to turn on him, Panduranga Rao suddenly lowered his head and pretended to be engrossed in his work. When he did this, Mr. Rao's fury increased even more.

Mr. Rao shouted, "Hey, what kind of talk is this? Don't you have any sense, sisterfucker?" Panduranga Rao tried to make some excuse. Mr. Rao interrupted him at once, screaming at him even more vehemently than before: "I'm asking you why, motherfucker? Why, motherfucker?" Then, growling out one or two words in a low voice, he once again raised it, and stated in a resolute tone, "Wretched old motherfucker! Broken-down old motherfucker!" He then angrily made his way to his chair and sat down.

Belittled, Panduranga Rao began to attach a button to the sleeve of a blazer spread out in his lap. Panduranga Rao was in his sixties and bald. His adolescent granddaughter had died just last month.

Mr. Rao's anger would not subside, and he kept heaving out huge breaths.

Right then, Gauri came in, having just borrowed that week's *Rāṇi* from Subbi, the guy who ran the petty shop next door. When he saw his daughter, Mr. Rao suddenly turned his anger toward her. He summoned her in his harsh Marathi. Gauri, who had realized just then that Mr. Rao had returned, stood hesitating for a moment. Then, slowly, she walked to his side, terrified. In answer to five sharp Marathi questions, only four fear-filled answers were returned. Then suddenly, as an answer to the fifth question, a slap fell on Gauri's cheek. She recoiled, crying. Mr. Rao tried to grab her. Gauri's braid got caught in Mr. Rao's fist, but slipped out again. Gauri ran inside. Mr. Rao chased after her, following her in. And right after that, we could hear the sound of four or five blows raining down on Gauri's nape and back, along with her screams.

Gopinath Rao came inside, as if nothing were happening. He noisily moved his scissors from the center of his table and spread out the next piece of cloth that had to be cut.

After a short time passed, the phone rang. Once he had finished talking and laughing along with the caller for a long time and came back out again, Mr. Rao's anger had died down considerably.

Save for the sewing machines that went on running, a silence hung in the air.

It had turned seven, and I very hesitantly asked Mr. Rao for permission to go out to have some tea. Pushing past the crowd that stood waiting for the night show, I felt suddenly liberated as I came down into the street.

When I had gone a short distance, I ran into Natarajan the ironing man, who was wearing a cloth turban. Natarajan was an utter lazybones. His wife washed clothes all day long until her shoulders ached, and in the evening, he would drink up the money she had earned. He was Mr. Rao's drinking buddy. When he saw me, he sidled up next to me, laughing, and asked, "Is that Rao fellow there?" It was customary to address him like this behind his back. When I nodded my head in reply, he enthusiastically said, "Okay, then," and gathering up speed, he walked off.

The Nambiyar Shop radio was broadcasting the farm report. When that flavorless but hot tea trickled down my throat, it perked me up a little. There were lots of people inside the shop: shop boys under eighteen who were trying to be thrifty, and miserly cloth-shop clerks who were well past their fifties. The reason being, while the tea was 15 paise in other shops, at the Nambiyar Shop, you could get it for 12!

I left the tea shop, and began to walk toward Town Hall. I could see that a huge crowd had gathered right next to it. Thick, black smoke was rising up from the midst of the crowd. I began to walk quickly. As I drew closer and closer to the crowd, I was hit with the pungent stench of burning rubber. As usual, gypsies were burning some pieces of tire, and were cooking rice.

In the middle of the crowd standing around in a half circle, two policemen were abusing the gypsies with filthy words and were beating them with their canes. Afraid of the blows, the gypsies were running here and there, quaking in fear.

At a small distance from the edge of the gutter, rice was boiling away in little pots atop stoves, which consisted of three rocks and some dried dung. They had escaped the notice of the policemen until then, but one of them now noticed the pots. The next moment, he kicked over the pots, and he did it with a cruel zeal. The pots rolled away and tumbled into the gutter. Only a shard of one of the broken pots, trickling rice, teetered on the very edge of the gutter. The other man saw it, gave it a kick, too, and pushed it into the gutter. The crowd watched on calmly.

A few of the blows that were aimed at the gypsies missed them and fell on their little kids. Along with the screaming children, a few of the gypsy women were wailing, as well.

After one or two minutes, the policeman who had broken the pots turned around in exhaustion, as if he had achieved something. When he saw the crowd, he got angry again. Before he could begin to curse, I moved aside and walked away.

When I returned to the shop, Mr. Rao was laughing and talking enthusiastically to a customer. There was also evidence that many other customers had come and gone. Padmanath Rao had finished with the inside stitching on a shirt collar, and turning it right side out with a shake, he looked up. When he saw me, he showed his teeth and grinned. The wage money must have been collected.

And I, too, was a little relieved.

It was 9:30.

Panduranga Rao picked up the coarse sheet that had been spread out in the morning in order to work while seated on the floor and vigorously shook it out. I settled down at my table and was ready with each man's weekly account. I then began to provide the details for each one to Mr. Rao. And as usual, he would carry on with the doling out of wages.

Mr. Rao took out the money from his pocket little by little, each and every time, and began to hand it out. He was very keen that no one should know how much money was in his pocket. Needlessly showing off all that money in his pocket in front of these wage slaves might inspire them to ask for advances, and being disappointed when refused, then cursing him at the end. Mr. Rao just wanted to avoid all that torment.

In a few minutes, everyone obtained their wages and left. By sheer luck, Padmanath Rao somehow got his 20-rupee advance, too.

Mr. Rao and I were left alone.

After thinking for a few moments, he looked at me and asked in Hindi, "Can you wait until Monday to get paid?" As my mother's tearful face came to mind, my stomach lurched. In a low voice, I said, "I have to buy rations tomorrow." Mr. Rao was again immersed in thought. After a short while, as he took out all of the money from his pocket, he said, in a voice mixed with strictness and indifference, "I'll ask if any money is needed in the house. If there is no need, I'll give it to you. Otherwise, you can get your pay only on Monday." He then called Lakshmibai.

Lakshmibai needed 100 rupees. When Mr. Rao counted to see how much money he had, there were only 75 rupees left. After he gave 60 rupees to Lakshmibai, he said something to her in Marathi. "There are only 15 rupees left. I need it for tomorrow's expenses. There is no other way for you than to receive your pay on Monday." Saying this, he then went to his chair and sat down. My hopes dashed, I started to close the one last door that remained open.

Suddenly, a thought occurred to Mr. Rao, who had kept on staring right at me. "Why don't you deliver some blazers to the college in the morning?

If that money comes in, you can get your wages. It will be useful to me, too." As he said this, the confidence inside my mind began to spark, and then spread like fire. With enthusiasm, I nodded my head firmly, and took it on. As Mr. Rao was telling me, "It's late now. You can come tomorrow morning to pack up the blazers," Ramanathan, the manager of the theater opposite, came inside, enthusiastically crowing, "Hey . . . Rao!" When Ramanathan came, his arrival always signaled something special!

Ramanathan, the theater manager, was wearing a white veshti and shirt, and his fingers were flashing with rings: the pampered son-in-law! He looked after the theater, which was owned by his father-in-law, a jeweler. Squandering all of his money betting on the snails that "ran" on the race-track at Guindy, Ramanathan had firmly latched on to this sturdy tamarind branch of a father-in-law for the past twenty years. Ramanathan's wife's entire body was covered with leucoderma.

Mr. Rao and Ramanathan had been friends for a long time. They slammed down arrack from the same tumbler. They even slept with the same woman. When new films were released in the theater, if business was sluggish in Mr. Rao's shop, Ramanathan would give him twenty-five tickets per show for the entire first week. Natarajan and I would mingle with the crowd, and we would sell a 1-rupee, 90-paisa ticket for 9 rupees. Natarajan was an Emden! Aside from the cut, he would squeeze another 8 annas per ticket from Mr. Rao.

When I went and stood before Mr. Rao to take my leave, Ramanathan looked at me and smiled slightly. Mr. Rao told me, "On your way, go and tell Natarajan to come over here." He warned, "The students will go here and there to watch films. Only if you set out at 6 A.M. will you be able to catch them." I nodded my head and left.

Natarajan's house was in the washermen's colony. When I entered the little house, I saw him lying there in the light of the lantern, casting a huge shadow. When he saw me, he got up and greeted me. And thank goodness that he wasn't already drunk! I gave him the message and left.

When I reached Thyagaraja New Street, a Telugu voice greeted me. Just some woman, waiting in the street, asking someone for the time. It had now turned 10:30.

The door was ajar. Mother had fallen asleep reading *Akand Anand*—a Gujarati religious magazine—with her spectacles on. I bent down, removed her spectacles, and put them aside. Mother lay there, sleeping like a baby. Her eyes were sunken, her cheeks had gone hollow, her flesh had slackened, and her face was in ruins. Wrinkles were drawing faint lines on her forehead. When she was young, her hair was springing with thick curls, but now, it was lackluster and flat. You could see gray at her temples. She had grown old. Yes. Mother had grown old. How many days . . . how many years . . . she had eaten up years. And the years had eaten her up.

By the time I was done washing my face, Mother had awakened and was sitting up.

When she learned that I hadn't received my weekly wages, she was enraged, and Mother cursed Mr. Rao's family. Then, she withdrew into a confused silence.

For me, it was a relief that Mother's fury had erupted and subsided with a single sentence. One or two moments passed in silence. But just as I was thinking that the problem had not yet struck her fully, she cried, "Rascal, we have your father's death anniversary tomorrow, and you come home with empty hands! Have you no shame, you dog?" She rose, with grow-ing agitation, reluctant to accept the news I had relayed. Raising her hand, Mother suddenly came lunging toward me. Then, forgetting to lower her raised hand, she began to scold me in a mixture of Tamil and Gujarati. She paused for one or two moments between sentences as she scolded me, rais-ing her voice higher and higher.

Struggling to finish most of the sentences that she had started in rage, she ended them by cursing me. I could only listen patiently.

If Mr. Rao was the content of Mother's song of abuse, the Brahmin priest who was to come tomorrow shone forth as its form. The Brahmin was a Tamil. To invite Gujarati Brahmins was beyond our reach. In addition to feeding him rice and offering him a 5-rupee, 25-paisa gift, you had to give at least something like an upper cloth. It had been years since we decided to make do with a dark and sweaty Tamil Brahmin from Sullivan Street, who sat bare-chested on his tinnai, making cheap jokes. When I imagined just how that Brahmin, who had been given a promise, would come tomorrow and face this situation, it was both funny and tragic.

After a few minutes, my younger brother suddenly came in, having noise-lessly leaned the shop bicycle against the side wall. Mother kept silent for a moment, then informing him of the matter, she angrily said, "Tomorrow you will eat dirt! Put out some dirt for that Brahmin, too, who is com-ing!" But the astonishment and frustration that had spread on my younger brother's face diminished her anguish, and she started breathing normally, maintaining a meaningful silence.

My younger brother, who understood the matter to a certain extent, looked at me to confirm it, disturbed. Then, hesitating, he asked, "Didn't your boss give you any money?" When I gave him the answer with a shake of my head, his face began to wilt. Mother, who realized that there was a person now to share and justify her anger, once again erupted with the malice that she had been saving up for those few moments. "How can he get anything!

Only after the funeral bier is built for that good-for-nothing Rao will he get anything. Gambling dog! That drunkard dog!" Mother just went on talking.

My younger brother, who had been keenly observing her, suddenly shouted, "Enough of your lecture. Stop it right now!" He tried to restrain her. Mother would just not stop. Contrarily, she said, "So you're calling this a 'lecture,' you dog," and she turned on him, but he had learned not to react.

Somehow, Mother's ranting stopped, and just after she had begun to fret in a lower tone of voice, I realized that I had been rooted to a single spot for quite a while.

My younger brother tied on a lungi and switched on the kitchen light.

Then Mother, who kept on talking more or less only to herself, raised her voice, and in a matter-of-fact tone, gave us the news: "In this wonderful state of affairs, your sister has already brought us some bamboo shoots to make tomorrow's gravy."

Suddenly, both of our glances fell on the bamboo shoots, which were gleaming inside a bag that was hanging on the wall. I went over at once, took it down, and looked inside. And sure enough, there they were, fresh and green!

Bamboo shoots grew abundantly on the estate of Nayakam, my father's friend. With the smooth texture of eggplant, with the sheen of plantain, these bamboo shoots are a unique pleasure to eat, as their raw smell permeates and gushes forth in the gravy they are soaked in. They slide down your throat smoothly. Besides the fact that you can cook them without dal, which saves some money, it gives you an exotic feeling when you eat them. Bamboo-shoot gravy was a favorite dish for everyone in our family, but my father and mother particularly liked it. Just by chance, on the very day of Father's death, Mother had prepared bamboo shoots. On days other than Father's death anniversary, Mother would not eat them.

Mother was staring vacantly at the wall. A slight redness had spread over her nose and ears, and she was breathing heavily. She might start crying any minute now. Clearing her throat, Mother wept with soft, noiseless, torturous sobs.

When I thought that this year, too, Mother wouldn't eat bamboo shoots, I found it quite absurd.

After she wept for a little while, she wiped her face off with her sari and got up resolutely. Once she had gulped down the anguish from her face, her eyes reflected a silent grief.

Hanging up the bag, I entered the kitchen. Mother served the last meal of the week.

Later that night, from a spot in the dark, my younger brother said something. In a voice that was thick with sleep and exhaustion, Mother told him, "I'll borrow 2 rupees from the landlady and give it to you. In the morning, when the Brahmin comes, buy him a limited meal and a sweet at Krishna Mandir. Next year, we can feed him here at the house." She then went back to sleep.

Giving his whistle a long blow, as if slicing straight through the darkness and the quiet in the street, the watchman made his rounds.

The next morning, it was turning 6:15 when I set out from the house. Our Chettiyar landlady was very strict! Mother decreed that we would have to return the borrowed 2 rupees by noon.

Nawab Hakeem Road was much quieter than usual. There were bearded saaybus, sitting on the bench in front of Mubarak Tea Stall, slurping away noisily at their tea; the faint groan of a nadaswaram on the tea-shop radio, and beyond it, the long road narrowing. Closed shops. Beyond, the sky had begun to glow blue in the light of the sun that had risen in the east. White clouds. Unseen crows and sparrows making a racket. Everything was just pleasant. Today was a holiday for the entire street: from the bustle; from its very bitter, harsh realities.

When I spotted the tea shop, I wanted to have some tea. While formulating a plan that was in harmony with the 15 paise in my pocket, I engaged in a little mental struggle between two cigarettes or a single tea. At the end, I lit up one of the victorious cigarettes and slowly made my way.

When I reached Five-Corner Junction, several butcher shops were opening. Gobs of meat from goats that had been stripped of their lives and hides were hanging outside by their legs. Inside the shops, sticks of incense had been lit, and were smoldering beneath the framed pictures of gods. The raw stench of blood had spread all over that spot.

At the entrance to the theater, people were thronging even now for ground and bench tickets. Nearly everyone was half-asleep, having stayed awake to the point of exhaustion. They squatted there like two rows of frogs, huddled up close.

When I looked from the street, I could see that one door of the shop was open. Lakshmibai had to be awake. I quickly climbed up the steps. When I put my right foot down on the second step, it seemed that there was something pulpy and awful on my foot. Shit! I realized before I bent down that my foot was covered with filth bulging from the gaps between my toes. Hesitating a moment, I then climbed on up. To avoid dirtying all of the other steps, lifting up the front part of my foot so it wouldn't touch the ground, I walked on my heels and reached the front door. Inside, Laddoo was roaming around naked. I had a look at her bottom, and there was evidence there that she had just shat. A lot of evidence.

Lakshmibai was sitting inside, blowing on the stove. With my eye on my shit-smeared foot, I called out to her. She didn't hear me. I called out again. She didn't hear me that time, either. Only when I shouted at her for the fourth time did she become aware of me, because of her deafness on one side. Right then, I wanted to strangle Mr. Rao.

Lakshmibai turned toward the door to see what the matter was, and when she saw me, she nodded her head and smiled, showing her teeth. Then she turned back around again to blow on the stove. Wonderstruck, Laddoo looked alternately at me and at her mother, and stood there laughing. I just stood there as well, looking at my feet.

After one or two minutes had passed, when Lakshmibai came outside to get some firewood, she gave me some water to wash my foot. She angrily gave Laddoo a hard pinch.

Mr. Rao had passed out on top of the cutting table. There were soda bottles next to him, proof that he had been slamming down the arrack.

I quickly folded up the blazers and put them in paper sleeves. There were nine or so in all. Pure woolen blazers. They were nice and thick, but not too heavy. I got a rupee for the bus from Lakshmibai and set out. As I went down the steps of the entryway, she started washing them.

Usually, the college administration would collect all of the money for these blazers. But you get what you pay for: bad stitching quality. The lining that was put inside the blazers would be cheap. But students who didn't want this could give an extra 10 rupees and get a better class of lining. These blazers completely lined with satin. I would collect a total of 90 rupees. I walked along, ruminating over my 15 rupees.

The college was 4 miles from the city. Once you go past the center of the city, you would begin to see green along the sides of the road. The milkmen were walking bare-chested with their cows in tow, little kids, women working in the fields . . . everything seemed to have a natural rhythm. On the bus, the driver, and the conductor, too, seemed calm and not in any hurry. But as soon as dawn broke, everything changed!

The student hostel of that engineering college was at the rear of the campus. The long path that led to the building at the front part of the college was nearly 500 yards from the street. When I got off the bus, I groped in my pocket for the other cigarette, and I began to walk. The campus was quiet and peaceful.

After I had walked half the distance, a gardener clad in a khaki shirt, flustered, came running and angrily shouted, "Put out that cigarette!" Startled, I threw down the cigarette and stamped it out. He put his hands on his hips and stood there without moving, glaring at me until I had gone past. Having gone a short distance, when I turned around to look, he had crouched down again and was getting on with his work.

The hostel stood as four gigantic buildings surrounding a large maidan. In each building, there were 180 spacious rooms. In the middle of the maidan, four or five students were practicing cricket. Because it was so quiet, I could even hear their conversation in low tones. A few other students were running around the maidan. Everyone was running quite slowly. Only one student, with deep self-consciousness, was running and shaking his legs around like the hero of a Tamil movie chasing a heroine who had run off in anger.

Sitaraman and Harihara Krishnan were in A block. Sitaraman's room was locked. A bespectacled student dressed in a banian and veshti answered for Harihara Krishnan, who was in number 132 on the second floor. He was hard at his studies. Harihara Krishnan had gone home.

There was no one in C. There were three people in D. A guy named Krishnagiri was in B. The others were in the "Old Hostel" behind this building. There was nothing stirring in D block. Having climbed up two flights, there was nothing to do but climb back down again. Everyone had gone to town. When I was coming down the stairs, two students were waiting there together, with a copy of *Kumudam* in their hands. Seeing the parcels in my arms, one of them passively asked, "Hey, Pa, are you from the drycleaners'?" When I answered, the other one whistled for no reason, and both of them passed me and went out.

In Krishnagiri's room, four or five lungi-clad students were sitting on a cot, talking. When I knocked on the door twice and came in, they stopped talking. I chose a student who seemed well mannered and told him what the matter was. When I had finished telling him, he thought for a moment. Then he hesitated, saying, "He's sleeping, Pa." Right then, I noticed. On the part of the cot that ran along the wall, Krishnagiri was curled up asleep, looking like a long sack. One student suggested that Krishnagiri be awakened. Another one opposed the idea. I stood there, calmly considering it all. Then one guy smacked Krishnagiri on the side of his hip and woke him up. Two others joined in, and attempted to disrupt Krishnagiri's sleep.

As they yanked on his bedsheet, Krishnagiri awoke with a start. While tying up his lungi that had slipped, he was on the verge of scolding the others, but then he looked at me and was taken aback, and grew silent. He looked like a kid who hadn't even started shaving yet. He had bright and friendly eyes. I began my speech with a "Good morning, Sir." He listened to it all calmly, and then said that since he had no money on him, he would come to the shop to pick it up himself on Wednesday.

In the courtyard of the old hostel, Gurumoorthy and Karunakaran were brushing their teeth. I approached them individually, and when I made my inquiries, they, too, gave the same answer as Krishnagiri's, as the smells of two different brands of toothpaste permeated the air. And finally, I went to Ramesh Babu's room.

It occurred to me that with a name like "Ramesh Babu," he might be a North Indian. If that were so, I decided that I'd speak to him in Hindi. I went, fixing in my mind my words and sentences so that I might somehow speak properly, avoiding my rough Hindi. The door to his room was half-shut. I knocked and opened it.

Ramesh Babu looked like he was expecting someone. Sporting a beard and spectacles, he was taller and broader than I had ever imagined anyone could be. When I saw him, I was terrified for a moment. When he saw me, he got up abruptly. Then he came toward me in a rush. For one moment, he just stood there and indifferently interrogated me with his eyes, as the veins on his forehead bulged. Faltering, I finished telling him about the matter in broken English. The next moment, he was seized with fury. "Did I ask you to bring this?" he abruptly asked with anger. Hesitating again, I said no. "Then get out of here! I know when to pick it up," he said, slamming the door shut.

Feeling stupid, I gathered up the blazers and came outside.

As I passed through the hostel's main gate, about twenty or twenty-five kid goats were being herded inside as the meat for that day's noon meal. Several of the little kids were running around, bleating and gamboling enthusiastically.

I knew that Mr. Rao was not in the shop. After hanging up the blazers again, I shouted out to Lakshmibai and then set off for home.

As usual, there was a crowd at the theater entrance. The gypsies had again spread themselves out at the side of the path. A gypsy woman was nursing her baby, and had put out for sale an odd assortment of garlic and safety pins. Bowing his head, a gypsy man was engrossed in boring his ear. Next to them, scattered grains of rice from yesterday lay there soaking in the mud. The sun was blazing. I was really hungry. I began to walk, slackening my pace.

Inside the house, my younger brother was reading the question-and-answer section from an old issue of *Mother India*. Mother was lying down, curled up in a corner. I changed my clothes, and I, too, spread out a mat. No one said a word.

The next day, when I was getting ready to go to the shop, Mother stared blankly right at me. Even though she had bathed and looked refreshed, her face was shriveled with hunger. I was combing my hair. It took time to do it. Maybe because Mother was scrutinizing me, I felt that I was deliberately taking a long time!

When I got to the front door, Mother took the bag that had been kept right next to it, and maliciously flung it at me hard, shouting, "Go put this in the trash!" The bag glanced off my leg. The bamboo shoots that were in it scattered all over the floor. They had withered. I turned my back on Mother and stood there for a moment. I didn't have what it took to turn and face her. My mind was confused, and a lot of anger came surging up out of nowhere. Telling her to throw it out herself, I walked out. Everything was meaningless.

As I came down into the street, suddenly, from the alleyway of the opposite house, an eight-year-old boy came running, his genitals jiggling, and squatted at the side of the path.

The sun beat down with a smack.

Five Rupees and the
Man in the Dirty Shirt

As on any other day, I had a lot of work to do at the office. I had been out all day running errands, and was really tired when I came back. It was 6:30. I had thought that I might finish everything up early and leave, but when I looked over that day's accounts of income and expenses, we were short by 5 rupees. I couldn't remember what I had spent it on. I thought about it for a while, as I looked at the sky through the window. It was September. Dark clouds were gathering in the sky. It could rain any minute now. I lit up a cigarette. Letters and bills lay scattered on top of my table. I began to straighten them up.

After a bit, when I heard someone coming up the stairs, I turned my head and looked toward the door. I could tell by the muffled sound of the footsteps that the person who was coming up was barefoot. In a moment, a man came in, wearing a white jibba and veshti, and coughing noisily. He glanced around the room searchingly, and then noticed me sitting in the back room. I gestured to him to come inside with a nod of my head. As if he had just come to his senses, he hastily lowered his tucked-up veshti. As he approached me, an acrid stench emanated from him. When he came and stood next to my table, I noticed that he was quite tall. I looked up at him. His face looked blank. His long, gray hair was disheveled.

Creases had appeared on his broad brow. His eyes were deeply sunken in their cavernous sockets. The whites of his small eyes were slightly blood-shot. To me, he looked as if he were consumed by an enormous grief. I thought that his little, bloodshot eyes gave his face its expression. His clothes were crusted over with dirt.

I greeted him in English, telling him to please have a seat. Clearing his throat, he settled into the chair opposite me. Then, in a hoarse and commanding voice, he mentioned my boss's name, saying, "Where is he? I need to see him." I informed him that my boss had gone out of town. Raising his head, he thought for a few moments while gazing at the ceiling. I told him that if he could tell me what the matter was, I could then relay it to my boss. Answering that it wasn't anything important, he asked, "When will your boss come back?" I answered, "My boss will not return to Chennai until tomorrow evening, and because the day after is a holiday for us, you could only see him after that." He looked at me while running both hands through his hair. After some time, I asked him if I might know who he was. And at last, clearing his throat between long bouts of coughing, he lowered his head and briefly answered, "I am Karunakaran from Madurai." Guessing, I asked, "Are you *the* Comrade K.?" "Yes, I am Comrade K." Mustering a bit of elegance in his voice, he verified what I had asked, and saying it again, he told me that, even though many years had passed since he had left the Communist Party, everyone still called him that. Saying this, he laughed loudly. Amused by his laughter, I told him that I was so glad to meet him, and that prior to this, I had wanted to meet him on several occasions. He looked at me plainly and smiled at me. He then asked me my name. I told him my name, and then asked him to sit for a while in the front room. He got up, and, moving slowly to the front room, he took a seat. I hastily put the letters and bills in order. I still could not recall where that 5 rupees went.

Even though I had not met Comrade K. until then, I had come to hear about him from time to time. Since my childhood friend was his wife's brother, I knew of him without the "Comrade" prefix. Many years ago, his marriage had taken place in Coimbatore. I still remember taking part in it. And ten years later, Comrade K. was a member of the editorial board of a little magazine that had published my first story. In fact, I had been in touch with him until around four or five years ago.

In the 1950s, Comrade K. was very active on the Tamil literary scene. I had heard my friends tell me many times that it was he who gave the Tamil short story its definitive modern traits. I had read one of his novels and several of his short stories. A Delhi-based critic had pointed out in an English essay: "The bitter world that Comrade K.'s writings unfold, the spontaneity of the people without class consciousness who inhabit that world, and their coarse logics deeply impressed me. Moreover, the simplicity and maturity of his language have the power to effect a wondrous calm in a reader's mind. With a persistent undercurrent of violence and sexuality, his works constantly unsettle society's basic values, and keep pushing us toward life's enduring questions. His characters trample established social mores and understanding. Comrade K. gently teases life's abstractions through the realities of human physicality. He is, in fact, very successful in that." In the past few months, I had had the opportunity to become acquainted with the writers of Comrade K.'s generation. Through them, I had heard that lately, Comrade K. had begun to destroy himself in the grip of destructive drinking and drugs. More specifically, they spoke with concern and in detail about the decline in Comrade K.'s health.

When I closed up the back room, and when I returned to the front, bringing cigarettes, matches, and an ashtray, Comrade K. was scrutinizing a modern painting that was hanging on the wall. As I drew close, he turned and looked at me for a moment, and then looked at the painting again. After a few moments, he smiled and said with fatigue, "What is this artist trying to convey . . . ? I don't understand it at all." I sat down in front of him mutely. He spoke again. "I am not as familiar with this as I am with literature. Modern art always goes right over my head." As I kept looking at his dull face, my curiosity about him grew even more. I told him to have a seat. He sat down, looked at me, and smiled as he relaxed his arms and legs. I addressed him as Comrade K., and I began to talk to him.

"I have known your brother-in-law Raghavan since I was small, and your wife, as well. I was even among the guests at your wedding. But I don't have a good memory of your face," I told him. As his face brightened, Comrade K. asked, "Is that so?" A few long strands of hair from his head had fallen down over his forehead and over his left eye. Pushing them aside with his right hand, Comrade K. asked me how I knew his brother-in-law. I told him that since Coimbatore was my hometown, too, both of us had studied at the same school and in the same standard. I informed him that his wife had been studying in college at that time, and that I had spoken with her whenever I visited their house. I also told him that, because of my friendship with his brother-in-law, I had come to know about his education, the state of his health, his work, and his marriage. Comrade K. listened to what I was saying, and uttered short phrases of agreement. When I offered him my condolences on the death of his wife, Comrade K. sighed gently and averted his face. After that, a silence hung between us for a little while. Then I started to speak again. I asked him if he knew about the recent death of his father-in-law in Sri Lanka, where he had gone on business. "Is that true?" Comrade K. asked at once, appearing a little upset. He told me that this was news to him; that he did not know. He then immediately added that he had not had much contact with him after his wife's death. After a while, he lifted his head as if he had remembered something, mentioning that his father-in-law was a very good man. I told him that, unfortunately, I had not had the opportunity to become close to his father-in-law. Comrade K. nodded his head slowly, as if in agreement.

We then talked about his wife's family for a little while. After a short time, I opened the pack of cigarettes and took one out. I extended the opened pack to Comrade K. He took one and thanked me. He lit his cigarette first, then, cupping the flame of the match with his hands, he offered me a light. As he was lighting my cigarette, I took notice of his hands. They were somewhat square. The fingers were crooked, the knuckles thick. The skin of the palms had hardened and turned black. I thought that the veins of his hands had slackened, his fingers no longer nimble.

After that, I tried to talk to him about the letters I had written to him. Comrade K. immediately said that he had no memory of any contact with me via letters, and he asked my forgiveness for that. He also told me that he had no good memory of any correspondence with anyone. He added that, in recent days, he had bounced from town to town and had met all of his friends in person, so they didn't correspond with him. I told him that in one letter I had written to him, I had asked him at what age one should write a novel, and I reminded him of his reply. Comrade K. looked at me with surprise, and said, "Oh! Is that so?" I also told him that, in that letter, I had begged him to stop drinking. In reply, Comrade K. told me that many friends, who had love and affection for him, had been exhorting him to quit drinking, but after this much time had passed, there wasn't a thing to be done about it. After several moments, he lowered his voice, as if he were speaking to himself, and said, "I have not been able to stop somehow." Then I asked him when he had come from Madurai. He told me that he had come just that morning. When he arrived in Chennai, he had gone to meet his friend, a famous advocate. He mentioned the advocate's name, and asked me if I knew him.

I did not know him personally, but I had heard of him. Comrade K. stuck the cigarette that was in his hand into his mouth and looked at me, taking a deep drag. He had gone straight to the court, looking for the advocate's chambers. His clients and many other people were crowded there. Seeing Comrade K.'s filthy clothing and undignified appearance, the advocate grew angry. Short of hitting him, he had scolded Comrade K. harshly and chucked him out of his office. Comrade K. said these things in a mild-mannered voice, without getting worked up even a little. Pondering a bit, he told me about that advocate, "No matter what, he is a very good friend." He recollected in detail about his time in the Party with him many years ago. He told me that his friend was a skilled advocate, and that he wanted to come out on top of every circumstance. Comrade K. laughed loudly, saying, "How could he relinquish his pride on my behalf?" He set his face as if he was thinking about something, and said again, "Even so, he is a very good man, indeed." Then he asked, "Can I have a little water?" I brought him some water in a tumbler. He drank it slowly. A little bit of water trickled from his mouth and wet the front part of his shirt. After he had drunk four or five sips, he set the tumbler down. Opening his mouth, he noisily drew in a breath. He averted his face and wiped off his lips and jaw. He shook his head lightly and cleared his throat. With my consent, he took another cigarette and began to smoke it vehemently. I looked at his hands again. A lot of dirt had collected under Comrade K.'s fingernails. I realized that the fact that I couldn't remember what that 5-rupee expense was for was still irritating me.

After a short time had passed, I asked Comrade K., "A few days ago, I reread your first collection of short stories. When you wrote those, you were seriously involved with the Communist Party, but I didn't see any ideological leanings explicit in these stories. Under those circumstances, how did the Communists accept you?" Stubbing out the cigarette he had just finished in the ashtray, he sat up straight. He looked keenly at me for a moment. Then, turning his head, he thought as he looked outside. A few moments went by, and slowly turning toward me, he spoke with a tired expression on his face. He said that in those days, many comrades who had played important roles in the Communist Party were also well read, and because of their wide literary knowledge, they harbored no doubts about his writings. He told me that because the important people of the Party didn't say anything about his writings, none of the other writers criticized him. But when he left the Party, those same writers attacked him severely. "And I even doubt that they did this on their own," he said, and, looking at me, he smiled. Comrade K. said that many writers who were in the Party at that time were influenced by the humanitarian elements of Marxism, and he now wondered if that hadn't been the case with him. He told me that what he found the most fascinating about Marxism were its logical subtleties and broad approach. He also explained that it was specifically Marxism's dialectical principle that engaged him the most. He said, "Somehow it is really strange that I never became interested in Marxist aesthetic theory." And, as before, he laughed loudly. I recalled what Comrade K. had written in a critical essay fifteen years ago: "Philosophy that stems from experience is richer than experience approached through the lens of philosophy. Though such a philosophy might appear diluted in its essence, its greatness lies in its originality." I told him that notion was very agreeable to me, and that the entire essay had influenced me a great deal. He replied he had written that essay many years ago, and that it was unlikely that the thoughts and opinions expressed in it were clear and patiently thought through. I immediately asked him if it meant that he had changed his opinion. Stroking his nose with his right index finger and his thumb, Comrade K. said that he was incapable of absolute certainty anymore, and that the simplicity of the questions really terrified him. Afterward, he slowly raised his head and said, "These two things—ideology and literature—are two different abstract forces that examine life in their own separate domains. These have neither concrete existence, nor concrete consequences. There are myriad possibilities that can meet one another somehow on some level, but the possibilities of complementing each other are rare." I continued to watch his face, and asked him, if that were so, then what was his literary doctrine? Comrade K. turned toward me and abruptly asked, "Do you think that I have a doctrine?" I looked at him silently. Comrade K. smiled as mischief glittered in his eyes.

After a few minutes, Comrade K. asked me what I was writing. I answered, "I write stories when I can." At once, as if he had the desire to read my stories, he asked if there was some collection of my short stories available. I told him that I didn't have copies of the stories that had been published so far, and that only after these had been compiled could a collection be published. Comrade K. told me that he, too, hadn't carefully preserved copies of his stories. Then, he said that it seemed to him that many capable writers in Tamil were getting established, but that he wasn't able to read anything now. After that, he talked for a little while about his favorite Tamil, Russian, French, and American authors. Comrade K. recommended some of the novels that he had enjoyed. I made a mental note of the titles of the several novels that he had mentioned, as well as the names of their authors.

A little later, Comrade K. asked me where my house was, and what my father did for a living. I informed him that I had lost my father at the age of four, that all of my family members lived in Coimbatore, and that I was living on my own here in Triplicane. Next, he asked me if I was a married man. I told him that I wasn't. Comrade K. looked at me and said, "Isn't it difficult to eat in restaurants?" I agreed with what he said. Comrade K. then looked at me intently for a short while, and asked what I did about my sexual urges. I couldn't answer that question. He asked again: "Isn't sex an issue for you?" I curtly answered, "Yes." Even though I understood that there was a real concern at the heart of these questions, their unusual and direct nature caught me off guard. Comrade K. asked me once more if I didn't go out in search of prostitutes. I answered no. Laughing loudly, he said, "If that's the case, do you just masturbate, then?" I looked at him in silence for a moment or two, then informed him that I was to be married next year. Comrade K. slowly nodded his head up and down several times.

Comrade K. suddenly asked, "So you're a Coimbatore man, right?" He asked this not as a question, but as if he was thinking out loud. I looked at him without giving an answer. He laughed, saying, "Coimbatore is a very good town." Right after that, he reminisced about his experiences of many years ago. Comrade K. said that in his experience, only in Coimbatore were there several varieties of very tasty food and some very beautiful women. Mentioning a caste that belonged to Coimbatore, he told me that he liked the women of that community a lot, and that having sex with them was one thing that really made him happy. Comrade K. continued on, describing those women with enthusiasm. He told me that on many occasions, he had savored the special fragrance that would spread from those women lying naked next to him when he would start awake at dawn after a night of sex. As he told me these things, there was a faint glow on Comrade K.'s face. He smiled.

I looked outside through the window. The sky had gone dark, and night had fallen. A light rain was falling, and the drizzle could be seen in the fluorescent glow of the streetlight.

Comrade K. helped himself to another cigarette. I noticed that this time, he didn't bother to ask my permission. Comrade K. put the cigarette between his palms and rolled it four or five times. He then held the cigarette in his left hand. Bringing his right index finger and thumb together, he pinched some tobacco from the tip of the cigarette and removed it. Doing this four or five times, he took the tobacco out, and the cigarette began to loosen. After the tobacco had been completely removed from one end, he then turned the cigarette around and began to remove the tobacco from the other end. In a few moments, when the cigarette was fully emptied of its tobacco and became a curl of empty paper, he unhurriedly stuck it beneath the ashtray. Then, he opened a packet that he had taken from his shirt pocket. In it was a bit of hashish, yellowish tan in color. Putting it in his palm, and crumpling the paper into a little ball, he put it in the ashtray. Holding it down with his right thumb, he rubbed the hashish into a powder. Pressing it down, he did this swiftly and forcefully. Then, picking up the curl of cigarette paper, he filled it with hashish little by little. He seemed to perform this ritual with profound care. After he had filled the cigarette with all of the hashish, he stuck it in his mouth and lit it. With its harsh stench, the smoke of the burning hashish stung my eyes. While I was rubbing my eyes, Comrade K. asked me if I had ever used hashish. I answered no. Again, he took a deep drag on the cigarette. As I watched him, I suddenly thought about his health. His broad shoulders and wide chest that now lacked muscle tone gave me pause—he must have been robustly healthy at some point in the past.

Comrade K. silently finished smoking his cigarette. After a little while, I asked him, "Why are you making such a mess of your life?" The gravity that was carried in my voice surprised me a little. Comrade K. straightened and looked at me. "Yes, that's the truth. I have made a total mess of my life," he said, nodding his head slightly. Leaning back, he sank inside the chair. He stayed like that for a few moments, knitting his brow and shutting his eyes tightly. Then, opening his eyes wide, he looked at me and began to speak.

"The mind always longs for the benefits of hard work, but the body is totally opposed to it. Values, beliefs, action, conviction—I have given up on all of those things. Now, in the eyes of the world, I am a broken man. In reality, everyone is just as broken as I am, deep down inside. But they're clever. They conceal their brokenness. They laugh artificially. They cry artificially. But I am honest and dumb, so everyone hates me. My wife hated me. My daughter hates me. My son hates me. My brothers, my relatives, my friends—all of them hate me. Even my elderly mother hates me. Now, suddenly—very suddenly—I've been made to realize that I am not worthy of anyone's love. This is cruel. Even more cruel than being hated.

"We are human beings. We are guileless by nature. Words such as *work*, *action, ideals, goals* captivate us. We need this captivation, this seduction, this illusion. We are always anxious to give a totally new order to this life. To achieve this, we get angry, we fight, we kill, and we also die. For us, the goal is always more important than the path. We can never know that path's terrifying length. The fools among us die on the path and meet with their own destruction for a nonexistent goal. Standing along a filthy edge of the path, the smart ones shout, "This is the goal," and try to cheat the ones on the path. Again, new rages, new struggles, new murders, new deaths. Disappointments never disappoint us. They just keep on coming. Each and every disappointment comes bearing in its lap a fresh hope. And just like that, hope, too, comes bearing a fresh disappointment.

"Nothing surprises me. I drink, I go to prostitutes. Why? Even my friends say that I committed a murder, as well. They think that I'm a cruel man. And that may very well be true. I don't know. Man always stands stunned between cruelty and love. Murder, suicide, death, woman, her nakedness, a child, a flower—granted, he can accept and savor all of these things. A man must be made of fire and ice. The intellect shrieks, crushed and trampled between this fire and ice. It wants to blend one into the other. But it does not work like that. This brokering of the intellect is absurd. Even though it attempts to oppose, at first, the two usual states of good and bad, in the end, the intellect shrivels and surrenders to these two. What is more, except for the bringing about of a morass of sorrows, it can achieve nothing else. Now, my genius friends are satisfied, they have smeared my hands with blood. It is not my wish to disagree with them. I have become very jaded. I have grown tired, even without accomplishing anything. Now, everything is finished. Even before I can begin to act on my own intentions, it's all completely finished. From now on, all that remain are the sheets of paper that I have smudged with my stories." As Comrade K. was saying this, he was gripped by emotion, and his voice started to falter. He continued, "Now, death alone waits for me. For man, death is the only thing that is certain." As he said this, he suddenly slid from his chair and dropped to the floor. I got up and came close to him. He raised his head and looked at me. With fury, he banged and banged on the floor with both fists, and he wept as he kept on hitting the floor. I took hold of his shoulders. His sobbing echoed everywhere in that room where quiet usually prevailed.

After five minutes, Comrade K. stood up, wiping his eyes. I settled him back in his chair. I then said, "You were overcome by your emotions." He did not reply to that. I got up, went to the inner room, and brought back soap and a thick towel. Giving those to him, I told him to go wash his face. He got up, asked me where the bathroom was, and, finding out, he went. When he came back after washing his face, he looked a little brighter. I gave him some water in a tumbler. He took it from me silently and drank. I then offered him a cigarette. He gratefully took it from me, and began to smoke.

I tried to calm Comrade K.'s mind by directing his attention to other matters. I took in hand three new books that I had recently acquired and sat down next to him. Comrade K. was looking at me as a child would. As I said, "This book is a scholarly work," I handed it to him. Comrade K. took it from me with interest. He then began to thumb through the first few pages. I told him a bit more about the book: "This is a sociological study on how the popular entertainment industry helped the Indian independence movement. This excellent study is the first of its kind to take on this subject." Comrade K. flipped through the pages hastily. He lingered over the pages that had photographs. Then, he said, "This is fascinating," as he closed the book. Further, he said that he didn't have the patience to read sociological studies, and that he wasn't able to read on, holding all of that data in his mind. Next, I handed him a collection of poems. As he read out loud the title of the book and the author's name, he laughed lightly. He informed me that the poet was his very close friend, and that he had a lot of affection and respect for him. Thumbing through the book, he read a few poems aloud, and told me that he was with that poet when he wrote them, and he then described the circumstances in which those poems were written. Saying that the influence of Na. Piccamurtti on that poet could be seen clearly, he laughed, telling me that it was customary that the poet praised his stories, and that he praised the poet's poems.

Finally, I showed him a Tamil translation of a French novel that had won the Nobel Prize. I told him the title of the English translation. Comrade K. enthusiastically took the novel, put it on his lap, and said, "This is the novel that has really captivated me—I have read it thirty or forty times. Wait, wait, I'll tell you how it begins." In a suitable tone and in a well-modulated voice, he recited from memory the first two pages of that novel without leaving out a sentence. I looked at him, amazed. Then, Comrade K. opened the novel, had a look, and said that the typesetting was good. Reading the first page, he said that the translation was excellent, too. Afterward, he talked about the genius of the author of that novel. He pointed out that he was among the outstanding writers of this century, and that his literary prowess was most clearly evident in this novel. Comrade K. had become immersed for a little while in the enthusiasm that was caused by this exchange.

After a short time, I stood up, asking, "Okay, shall we leave?" I went to the back room and shut the open windows; when I returned, Comrade K. was standing next to the door. As I looked at him, he uttered my name and said that he needed help. When I said, "Tell me," he told me that he had become very hungry and thirsty. I was quiet. He told me that he had no money at all on him, and that he needed 25 rupees immediately. I thought for a few moments. Then, I replied that, because it was the end of the month, I didn't have any money on me, and that I was really sorry that I couldn't help him. Comrade K. invoked my boss's name, and told me to give him that amount out of the till. I told him that I couldn't do that without my boss's permission. Comrade K. said that my boss was a good friend of his, and he would inform him himself. I explained to him that it wouldn't be the right thing to do, and that if I did, the relationship between my boss and me would become very strained. At once, Comrade K. told me that I needn't worry about a thing, and that he would do the explaining to my boss and uncomplicate matters. I hesitantly drew near him and asked, if he were in my position, would he be able to make a decision like this? Comrade K. looked at me calmly. He then bowed his head in thought.

After a minute or two, Comrade K. said in a voice filled with an edgy weariness, "How can you say that? Where will I go? At this time, I can't even contact other friends who could help me. It's become dark outside. It's raining, too. You will have to somehow find a way to give me money." Without looking at his face, I said, while looking at the floor, "Tonight, you can eat with me. I have an account at a mess, and even tomorrow you could eat there three times."

"Besides, the mess is very close by. Come on, I'll introduce you to them," I said. Comrade K. told me that he couldn't eat anything spicy and that, for several years, he hadn't eaten anything other than tea and buns. I suggested to him that, in that case, he could just eat some curd rice. Comrade K. told me that he couldn't digest even that. In addition, he told me that he needed a drink right away, and that if he didn't drink, he couldn't do anything. He said that that was what he needed the money for, and that it was essential that he have a drink. Repeatedly, I told him that I couldn't help him. He refused to listen. Finally, I grew weary, walked to the front room, and said, "It's up to you now. I've explained my position." Comrade K. followed me and settled himself down in a chair.

As I was shutting the front-room windows, I looked at him. Comrade K. loudly said, as if he were making an announcement, that if there was no money for him, then he wouldn't leave. I said that this was amusing, that having refused any help that I could offer, now he was being as demanding as a child. He maintained a stubborn silence. I switched off all of the electric fans and all of the electric lights except for one. I went to the front door, and I called to him: "Okay, come on, let's go." He resolutely got to his feet. Turning around, he looked toward me. A strange vehemence could be seen on his face. Then suddenly, in a loud voice, he raised a ruckus: "Motherfucker, are you going to give me money or not?" I hadn't expected anything like this, and approaching him, I asked, "What's happened to you? Why are you talking such nonsense?" As if he had ignored me and what I had just asked, he used the same expletive on me again, shouting even louder than before. I warned him: "You are behaving very indecently. If you speak to me in this way again, I'll chuck you out." As if Comrade K. hadn't heard what I had just said, he stared blankly at the wall. When I had finished talking, he cursed at me again in that very same fashion. At once, I grabbed his right hand and pulled. As Comrade K. abused me again, he slapped my cheek with force. When his hand landed on me, I lost control of myself, and angrily punched him in the chest. Comrade K. folded his arms across his chest and bent over. In that condition, he again cursed me obscenely. I grabbed him by his collar and chucked him out. As I angrily dragged him, his shirt ripped. His body was weightless. After I had thrown him out, I switched off the last burning light and locked the front door. I turned around and saw Comrade K. sitting down, all curled up and cradling his chest. Coming down the stairs, I passed him, and I called out to the watchman of the building. When he came, I asked him to remove Comrade K. from the premises. He approached Comrade K. a little nervously. By then, Comrade K. had stood up and followed me down the stairs. I descended quickly and made it to the street. I walked a few yards, turned around, and Comrade K. was sitting at the entrance to the building. Confused feelings welled up within me, a deep dislike mixed with a sort of fondness for him. He seemed to me like a helpless little child, like a stupid pet animal.

In the street, there was heavy drizzle. I walked off briskly, my mind unceasingly agitated. I suddenly became very hungry. I slipped inside the mess where I customarily ate. I didn't notice the taste of the food. When I quickly finished eating, my mind seemed soothed a little. When I came out of the mess, Comrade K. was standing there. Avoiding him, I passed him by. He immediately called my name. I turned around and looked at him. He came close to me. Then, he said, "I beg your forgiveness for the way I spoke to you." And I answered at once: "There's no need for it." After he looked intently at me for a moment, he asked me, "When are you going to publish your collection of short stories?" I wondered if he was making fun of me. But the tone of his voice was natural, and it reassured me that that was not the case. I answered him, "I'll think about that later." He stood there silently. I said to him, "Okay, I have to go," and I started to walk off slowly. Immediately, Comrade K. grabbed my arm with both his hands, and asked, "Can you give me 2 rupees?" Without saying anything, I reached inside my shirt pocket, took out 2 rupees, and gave them to him. Comrade K. accepted it, and saying, "Thank you very much," he turned and walked away.

I stood and watched him for a little while as he walked away. The damp street was silent and desolate in the drizzling rain. Hugging himself tightly, Comrade K. had lowered his head, and was walking quickly under the fluorescent streetlamp. As he crossed through the circle of light cast by the lamp, he suddenly vanished into the darkness.

When I arrived at my hostel, the whole building was immersed in darkness due to a power cut. My roommate was writing a letter to someone by candlelight. Changing my clothes, I lay down on the bed. Outside, it was raining heavily. That night, I lay awake for a long time before falling asleep.

One day, after two months had passed, I heard the news that Comrade K. had died. Comrade K.'s face and stories appeared in my mind. I particularly remembered Comrade K.'s sobbing, his angry attack on me, and that day's 5-rupee deficit in the accounts. I thought once more of that day, the stench that he gave off, and his smile.

The Solution

In order to tell you this story, I must drag all of you out with me as I walk into the scorching sun on this April morning, as I arrive on this wretch of a train, the delayed Nilgiri Express from Coimbatore to Chennai, irritating the porters with my single suitcase, and disappointing all of the rickshaw men who are fervently jostling up next to me as I hastily cross Wall Tax Road and slip inside a little lane that leads to Thangasalai Street. So please bear with me.

Among the seven or eight lanes that are helplessly strangled between Wall Tax Road and Rattan Bazaar, only Thangasalai Street is just broad enough to walk down with any ease. This is the neighborhood that is overrun with North Indians, mainly with Gujaratis. Therefore, it has more than its share of ostentation and filth. By "ostentation," I mean the clothes these people adorn themselves with, and by "filth," the garbage that they transfer from their houses out into the street. These Gujaratis take a lot of care to keep their homes clean and their thresholds dirty. Furthermore, they are without equal in acclimating their hearts and noses to their own filthy surroundings.

It was 8:45 A.M. Shops and offices were opening. Kids were dashing off to school. Everyone looked sparkling clean. Gandhi-capped merchants and their fashionably dressed, dim-witted sons were beginning to throng. Foreign cars, scooters, and motorcycles stood in wide rows.

These Gujaratis certainly knew how to turn a buck!

The famous Ekambareshvarar temple is in this very Thangasalai Street. It is a large temple with a tank. The main walkway of this temple is very grand. It is majestic in appearance, with its beautiful sculptural craftsmanship, in addition to its deities and enormous pillars. Like all of the other famous temples in the city, it is unexciting to the people who visit it regularly, but to those who don't, it looks immensely beautiful. Lord Ekambareshvarar sits peacefully inside, granting asylum to a Seth-ji selling snacks to the left of the temple's entrance, and on the right, to a Chettiyar selling coconuts, to a Gounder woman selling flowers, to a Marwari merchant selling bangles, and to a few beggars who are unendingly putting their diseases on

121

prominent display. The collective name of the three little lanes that curve around the temple in the shape of the Tamil letter *pa* is Ekambareshvarar Agrahāram. In addition to my uncle's house, it forms the setting of the story that I am about to tell.

I turned to the left, and entered the "pa." The temple wall was on one side, and there were houses on the other. Here, there are a high school and a primary school. So, right now, lots of little kids were flooding the street along with the indispensable ice-cream man. Smothered by two large buildings, my uncle's house was hidden away at the corner of this little lane.

I walked on quickly without taking any of this in. The entrance to my uncle's house came into sight. After that, the faces of all of his family members appeared in my mind and vanished. At the entrance, a few young Gujarati women who were struggling with the water pump observed my arrival in stony silence. I looked at all of them. All of those faces were average. Mind you, there were thirty families in that building alone. Nevertheless, there was not a single beauty. There's Urmila, who lives on an upper floor . . . but never mind. And first, you need to understand the basic layout of this building.

At the building's center is a large, 18-by-18-foot courtyard. It reveals a square patch of sky above the second story of the building. It was built for the people on the upper floors who chew up and spit out their Calcutta paans, but also for the gods of rain and sun! Surrounding this courtyard are six flats that face each other. If you traverse the center of the courtyard, there are two flats on each side. Next, on each side are two smaller courtyards. At the end of the small courtyard on the left are two toilets, and there is a well at the center of the small courtyard to the right. Next to that, there are two more flats. If you wander a little farther, there are grubby steps that lead upstairs. All of the floors above are arranged in this same fashion. This is the dirty building inhabited by a total of thirty Gujarati families.

A corridor 2 ½ feet wide divides the six flats from the courtyard. For the most part, at this time of day, women would be sitting next to the doors of all six flats, intently working away at one task or another. One woman would be scrubbing dirty pots. Another would be washing clothes. Others might be cleaning rice or wheat flour. Even though their bodies have gone bloated after marriage, these women are very hard workers. Their world is limited to vulgar Hindi films, cloying Hindi songs, foods of all varieties, and fine clothing. Apart from this, it is their custom to reproduce the species without any thought. For every female head of household of the thirty families in this building, there has to be a minimum of five heirs. (Even my uncle has his five.) Here, in this place inhabited entirely by middle-class families, this population explosion is natural. In fact, it is inevitable.

The men who live here are docile sorts. They are under the control of their wives. Every day they curse their lot in their banal lives, which grind them down. Imagining that they have enacted some huge betrayal on their wives, they skulk around with guilty consciences. They spend twenty-nine days in a month waiting for their salaries. Every Saturday, they go to warble bhajans, only because they can't go to the movies. Every now and then, they borrow a newspaper and read it. Otherwise, they just endure their lives. Except for the children begotten by them, it is unlikely that we would ever find other evidence to support the fact that they are indeed men.

Mostly, these Gujaratis hold very low opinions about Tamils.

When I stepped inside, what a surprise! The courtyard was its usual dirty self, but vacant. Even the corridors were vacant; the clothes, which were put out to dry yesterday, were still hanging on their plastic clotheslines along the sides. The place was utterly quiet. I crossed the courtyard and looked toward the stairs. There was quite a crowd around the well. Men, women, and kids were standing around. My uncle stood in the midst of that crowd, looking at something inside the well with rapt attention. As I approached them, they all looked at me for a moment. And Uncle saw me, too: at first, he was surprised for a moment, but then he smiled at me wanly.

"Go on upstairs—I'll come right up," he said in Gujarati.

Subduing my curiosity, I reached the stairs to go on up. Gopal Bhai was clambering down in the opposite direction, and I asked him what the matter was.

"What to say, Dilip Bhai! The water saga here has grown to epic proportions. In the house, there's not one drop of potable water. And it is just our luck that a rat has fallen into the well and died. Poor Babu Bhai! From 8 A.M. on, he's been trying to fish it out, but he can't," he lamented in Gujarati. After the usual courtesies, he drifted away slowly, and merged back into the crowd.

I made it to the upper story, and when I entered the flat, my uncle's eldest daughter, Chandra, finished her sweeping and stood up to greet me. She smiled cheerfully, and tended to me. My aunt came from the kitchen and welcomed me: "Come in, when did you arrive?" She then asked after the health of my family members. I replied, and also added a general complaint about train delays. She then went inside to put on some tea for me. My uncle's flat was very tidy, but small. A large hall. On the left, there was one room, and another room on the right. The room on the left was the kitchen. The room on the right was a bathroom, bedroom, and storeroom, all in one. The little boys must have gone out to play. My uncle had two daughters. (Poorna was in the kitchen.) He had three sons. Kanu, Vrajesh, Deepak.

Patti had gone to the temple. She left at 5 A.M., and she would return only by 10:30 or 11:00. Patti was orthodox to the core, and was observant of all of the rites and rules. Every time I visited, because of my height, her first task was to shove her clothes, which were drying on an overhead line, to either side with her bamboo purity stick. In spite of this, if I brushed against her garments accidentally, she would go off to wash them again. She was the eldest, older than anyone else in this building. She had come to be respected as one who was brimming over with wisdom in worldly affairs, and as a very clear and thorough thinker in spiritual concerns.

I looked in the direction of the toilets, and what a miracle. They waited there empty. These were the only two toilets for the general use of all sixty people who lived on this upper floor, and it was unusual that at the peak hour of 9:15, the toilets would be empty like this.

In accordance with the laws of my uncle's extremely orthodox house, in order to avail oneself of these toilets, one had to adhere to a few stringent prescribed rules. A journey to these toilets was truly an elegant experience. First, one had to draw water with the little plastic mug from the crumbling cement cistern, and then one had to put the mug atop the short wall that enclosed a dry tap. In the corner of this floor's low wall stood an overturned 4-kilo Dalda tin. Bringing it with the left hand, putting it at the entrance of the narrow passageway that led to the toilet, picking up the plastic bucket with the right hand, and again scooping up water from the crumbling cistern, one then had to fill the tin. Then, carrying that tin with the left hand, daintily stepping over the estuaries of piss that were produced by the upper-floor children when they relieved themselves, avoiding the first toilet which was overflowing with shit and would leave you without an appetite for one full month, and without slipping in the second, one could then squat there and contemplate, as I did, J. Krishnamurthy or T. S. Eliot. That is, until the girl from the next flat would plead in Gujarati in tones of agony and distress, imploring you to get up: "Who's in there? Get out quickly!"

After that, one had to bow one's head and exit; cross the passageway; avoid the waiting girl and walk straight ahead; put the Dalda tin back in its customary spot; take up a used-up scrap of 501, Rexona, or Lifebuoy next to it; secure with both wrists the full plastic mug that had been positioned on the lip of cement that enclosed the base of the pump; tip it slightly, wet the hands, and rub with soap; and then, by assuming the gesture of a kummi dancer, one could wash one's hands by totally upending the mug. You were now allowed to pick up the mug in the usual way, and wash your feet. Having thus effortlessly completed these rituals, I returned. My aunt had prepared some tea for me. She was wearing a faded blue sari. Bright colors would suit my aunt's fair complexion. But whenever I saw her, she was always dressed in this way, in a bleached-out color. I mentally cursed my uncle's taste in saris.

By now, the crowd around the base of the well had thinned out. The women had left. A few men, two or three teens, and a couple of children remained. All of the men were in their white pajamas and short-sleeved banians with pockets. Only my uncle wore a fraying sleeveless sweater, a veshti, and a cheap leather belt to hold it in place.

My uncle had worked for the Life Insurance Corporation for around twenty years. In this building, he stood in the front ranks of the more educated people. It was the residual fascination with his old-fashioned S.S.L.C. that helped him to lord it over everyone. Here especially, his pretense was accepted, 100 percent.

Right now, he was engrossed in the well. Because of the tin roof fixed above it, there was no light coming into it, and it was very dark. A youth was shining a flashlight inside the well. A black something was floating in it. They had arrived at the conclusion that it was a rat.

No one would consent to lend their bucket to remove the dead rat. My uncle especially wouldn't consent to lend a bucket from his house. So, tying a fruit basket onto a rope, they lowered it down. Since the basket was tied on just one side, it was hanging at a slant. They explained that even though the basket had already become sodden by soaking up water, when they lifted it, the water would drain out, and only the rat would stay in. There was clearly much cleverness behind all of this efficiency. This definitely had to be at the suggestion of my uncle. In instances such as this, man's enterprising nature is very interesting to witness, even though it is all only in aid of his selfishness.

The rat had drifted to the side of the well. They said that it had been in that spot for nearly half an hour. When the others told me of this development, my uncle became very angry, imagining that these others were doubting his skills. But even so, he very patiently labored away. He took it upon himself as a challenge to get that rat out.

Kantilal and Chandrakant were men from a neighboring house. The two of them kept on asking from time to time, "What's happened, Babu Bhai? What's happened?" in Gujarati. Every time they asked that, my uncle squinted and knit his brow, and mentally savoring the fact that he had everyone's attention and taking more foolish pleasure in his task than before, he involved himself in his hunt with a bit more care.

And the battle went on.

At last, his patience ran out, and he performed a series of feats, which variously looked like he was pounding rice with a pestle, or grinding flour, or flying a kite, or, finally, like a sailor steering his ship.

And finally, all of this paid off.

The rat had drifted to the center of the well. Everyone felt that it would be easy to fish it out from this position. Everyone's minds overflowed with enthusiasm.

Like a naval officer, Uncle issued commands to the boy who was holding the flashlight. He rudely told the bystanders to step aside. Then, he lowered the rope. Very slowly, then gently and with great subtlety, he brought the rope right up next to the rat. At once, he yanked on the rope with incredible speed. Everyone peered enthusiastically inside the well, but were disappointed. The basket had come up empty. The rat drifted once more to the side of the well, and stayed there in a sodden lump. Uncle looked sheepish. He grew more and more angry at the rat.

My uncle was repeatedly humiliated by the rat.

The rat put him off the scent for another forty-five minutes. Finally, at 10:15, it was fished out. Shrinking at the sight of the rat's corpse, children and grown-ups alike began to move away. Some young man, who regarded this as a great chance to show off his virility and courage, took the rat outside in the basket.

Uncle emerged victorious, and felt like Muhammad of Ghazni, Caesar, and Napoleon. Then, for a full fifteen minutes, with the eloquence of a politician and with the flourishes of an expert on strategy, he regaled the seven or eight Gujarati lads who surrounded him about the way in which he had fished out the rat.

After Uncle's exegesis had ended, Kantilal, Jeyantilal, and several others anxiously asked a fair question: "Is the well water safe to drink now?" Up until this moment, Uncle himself hadn't thought about it, and was taken aback a little. But now, fears, which were hastily gathering up in the back of his mind, were seen clearly on his face. Even so, he immediately regained his composure. As he considered the fact that any hesitation on his part would damage his position as guru among these disciples, he immediately declared, "No, no, you shouldn't use it in this condition. If we go to the Health Office and inform them, they will treat the well with some chemical or other. Or we can sprinkle in some chlorine by ourselves." He then began to walk away. Even though everyone waggled their heads in assent, upset and panic could be seen on their faces.

"Will you go to the Health Office? We don't understand one thing about this, Babu Bhai," the Tanjore Gujarati Chrandrakant asked Uncle pleadingly. Uncle managed to slip away, replying that, although it was not a difficult task for him, he did not know where the District Health Office was, and besides, he was already late for work. Even though he realized that in his flat, too, there was only half a pot of potable water left, he had tricked himself into thinking that he didn't have the time to take care of this. And Uncle wasn't the only one. Like him, everyone there mumbled some excuse or other, and avoided going to the Health Office and encountering the official who would be there. They all wanted someone other than themselves to go.

In the midst of all this, Govindji Seth, a rich old man who owned a TV, came down from upstairs to offer some valuable advice: "If you skim some fifteen or twenty pots from the surface of the well and dump it out, then we could use it." Enlisting the others, he saw it to completion. After completing the task, everyone stood gasping for breath, staring vacantly into the well.

Supporting her large, weathered body with a cane, Patti entered through the doorway. She was wearing a sari closely printed over with tiny black flowers on a white background. She had a chain of tulsi around her neck and clarity on her face. No one noticed Patti in this hubbub. After drawing close, she herself asked what the matter was, since no one bothered to explain. The issue and the problem to be solved were put before her. Patti thought about it a little. Then, she pronounced, "Come, I'll show you a way out." Everyone trailed up the stairs after her.

In the hall, Kanu and Vrajesh were wrestling. Patti entered and struck Kanu, whose bottom was conveniently within reach of her cane, lightly but forcefully enough that it would sting, scolded him, and took a seat before a teak cupboard next to the kitchen door. Then, she began to open it slowly. In the cupboard were miniature deities dressed up in shimmering clothes, seated atop their tiny cushions. In a corner, something had been kept all wrapped up in a saffron cloth. Patti took it out slowly and unwrapped it. Inside it was a miniature clay pot. It was tied up in a white cotton cloth. Patti called out to Poorna, sending for a cup. Then, undoing the cloth that covered the mouth of the pot, she poured a little water from it into the cup. A hush prevailed there. Everyone was watching her impatiently, but without hurrying even a little, Patti closed the cupboard door and turned around.

Among those who were thronging outside of and right next to the door was Pranjivanlal, and Patti gestured him inside. Because she had had her head bowed for a little while, Patti's spectacles had slid to the center of her nose. Pushing the cup forward a little, and slightly raising her head, she raised her eyes a bit, focused her gaze through her spectacles, and spoke: "Here you are. This is Ganges water—it's holy. Pour it into the well in the name of god, and use the water." Pranjivanlal humbly nodded his head, accepted the cup, and left. Everyone trailed after him to the base of the well.

In a short while, pots in every household overflowed with water from the well. The abnormal silence of the building had ended, and the buzz of normal function was restored.

Patti began to immerse herself calmly in *Jan Kalyan*.

The Path

I regained consciousness with a severe headache. The pain must have begun a bit before my consciousness returned. I slowly realized that I was lying in that narrow cell, in the dense dark. My eyelids would not move. Trying again, I squeezed my eyelids tight, and when I opened them, the nerves convulsed, and a sharp pain shot through my temples. A nauseating stench, like garlic and urine mixed, permeated the cell. The floor was completely damp, cold, and sticky. An icy breeze assaulted my naked body.

I slowly extended my folded legs and straightened them out. I let my body go a little slack. Instantly, a sudden, severe pain shot through my feet and my knees. It felt as if the quickening flow of blood through my veins increased the pain. It seemed that my muscles had lost their coordination and had gone haywire. Lying there in that condition brought agony to my entire body. The distress from the pain had surpassed what I could bear, and I screamed. The enveloping dark, the stench, and my headache were suffocating. It seemed that I was about to lose consciousness again. With a lot of struggle, I rolled over again and folded up my legs as before. I groaned softly to lessen the pain. With that slight movement of my lips, I could feel that they had gone swollen and stiff. My lower lip was drooping like an overly salted slab of meat.

In that room shrouded in darkness, I could hear aloud that soft thud of anxiety in my heart. Slowly, slowly, every part of me made its presence known. Fingertips, anus, the backs of my thighs, shoulders, throat . . . every part was pulsing with pain. I contracted my body and tried to bury myself in the floor. The stickiness of the damp floor covered my body everywhere and made me suffer.

Clasping my hands together, I buried them between my thighs. The little bit of heat that spread from my palms was soothing. As I made little purposeless movements with my hands, I felt something sticky and stiffening on the backs of my thighs. When I tried to touch them again, I began to figure it out. That had to be blood oozing from my anus. Even though this realization gave me a shock at first, I slowly recovered from it.

My throat and tongue had gone dry. I was thirsty. I looked outside. A small lamp was dimly burning out in the courtyard. The guards must have been somewhere in the corner. I lay there just as I was, without moving a muscle.

The day before yesterday, when they came to look for me, a crow in the neighborhood had died. Standing on the balcony, I was looking out. Many crows had settled in rows on the TV antennas of the opposite buildings, and were cawing loudly. From every direction, singly or in pairs, other crows came flying in. They uttered sharp caws as they glided in without fluttering their wings. I could not tell whether these crows had come to pay their respects to the dead crow. Countless crows joined in, and were cawing.

Only when they opened the iron front gate with a clang did I notice them. A jeep was waiting outside. They entered quickly. In moments, I heard them pounding up the stairs in their boots. Before they could knock, I opened the door to the front room myself. One of them who looked like an officer informed me that they had come to take me in for questioning. I regarded him calmly. Then, I went inside to change my clothes.

They took me with them. But I knew with certainty that this time, there would be no interrogation. They had interrogated people like me several times. But now, there wasn't a thing left for them to ask me about. Three months ago, in this very same way, they had taken Nayakam in for questioning, too. Nayakam never returned.

As I sat in the jeep, which had started off slowly, I keenly listened for the crows. Their caws slowly faded and were growing inaudible.

Once it crossed our street and turned back into the main road, the jeep gathered speed. Crossing big roads and small lanes, the jeep finally stopped at the police station, which was at a big, busy intersection. Two men who had been in the back jumped down. They then made me climb down. As we entered the police station, one among them suddenly laid his hand on my nape and shoved me with malice. In the main front room of the police station, an elderly, bespectacled policeman sat at a table, writing something or other. A few chairs and benches were arranged before him, set to the left and right. There was a lockup in the right-hand corner. In the left-hand corner was a small office for the station superintendent, marked off by a wooden partition. They made me stand inside the main room, and the officer who had brought me in entered his superior's office. Inside the lockup, a young man sat, grasping the iron bars and staring blankly. His hair was uncut, and it seemed that his eyes were sunken. His bones were protruding from his shirtless upper body. Outside the lockup, right next to the iron bars, was a dirty plastic bucket with a bit of water and a tumbler in it.

After a while, I was dragged into that small room made of wooden partitions and a swinging half door. Inside the room, an officer was sitting behind a large table, smoking a cigarette. He looked up at me. And I looked at him. He had a broad face and a receding hairline. He had thick eyebrows and a moustache. His eyes were bloodshot. To look at his huge, fleshy nose was revolting to me. The size of it gave him a cruel, despicable air. After eyeing me for a few moments, he signaled to the officer who had brought me in. The policemen dragged me out at once. Then, crossing a big courtyard, they dragged me to the back portion of the police station. In that courtyard, ten or twelve policemen, clad in short-sleeved banians and trousers, were sitting around talking about something. I was then confined inside this dark and narrow room. Inside the room, one single bulb burned, giving off a dim glow.

Fifteen or twenty minutes later, the door opened. That officer with the fleshy nose and three policemen came inside with lathis in their hands.

They began to beat me.

First, that officer with the fleshy nose struck my left knee hard with his lathi. As soon as I bent that leg in unbearable pain and gripped it with my hands to rub it, a blow fell on the other kneecap. I slid down. My head was bent toward the floor. Suddenly, everything went silent. I had been expecting many more blows, and I raised my head and looked, wondering why it had stopped. That officer looked at me, pausing with his lathi high. I could not see his face well in the dimly lit room. At the right moment, when I wasn't expecting it at all, he brandished his lathi again. This time, a blow fell on my jaw. Screaming, I covered my face with my hands. Next, blows rained down on my back, nape, and shoulders. Wailing, I kept moving about, but when a blow fell on my foot, I collapsed to the floor.

Somehow, even in that state, I knew that he was the only officer who was beating me until then. He beat me silently, without any frenzied blabber. I had been beaten many times by policemen and their superiors. Usually, they did it while constantly blabbering something. It served to justify their cruel fury, or to dispel the extreme fear caused by their own malice. But this man was not like those others. Like an animal, he was assaulting me without any feelings of uneasiness at all. I realized that this man was dangerous.

At one point, that officer stopped beating me and stood there in silence. I lay writhing in pain. One among the policemen stripped me roughly and flung my clothes aside. As soon as this man had stripped me bare, the other two began to beat me. They beat me brutally with their lathis on my thighs, buttocks, calves, and hands. Groaning, I began to scream again.

Suddenly, one man planted his foot on my chest, grabbed both my legs, and lifted them high. The other two men beat the soles of my feet with their lathis. They kept on with their beating, targeting the center portion of my soles. I screamed continuously, and more than ever before. The sound of my screaming must have been heard outside, over the din of traffic on the road.

After they grew tired of beating me on my soles, the man who was holding my legs grabbed them even tighter, and turned me over on my belly. Then, as the other two men spread my legs and held them, he shoved his lathi into my anus. The next moment, my throat slammed shut. It occurred to me that I might die within seconds. My vision began to go dark. This man thrust his lathi inside me even farther. He then suddenly drew it out. After all of this, I screamed horribly in pain. One man held my legs, brought them together, and roughly slammed them down on the floor.

They then kicked me. Two of the three men were barefoot. They took turns kicking me on my chest and back. Even more kicks fell on my face and neck. Pain was smashing me to pieces.

When they were finally done with me, I lay there like a rag. My body felt pulpy: it seemed to be welling over, becoming a disgusting liquid. They began to leave. They smoothed out their clothes and talked among themselves. They abused me with disgraceful curses. The man who was wearing boots came back close to me suddenly, and lashed out and kicked me in the genitals while shouting a filthy curse. I slumped over onto my side, screaming. I then lost consciousness.

It was silent everywhere. Like this, I had previously spent silent nights in lots of jails. The silence of prison always contains great horrors within it. It is like a spy who, unsheathing his dagger and stealing off into the dark, waits to make his move.

Surely it was on a silent, moonless night like this one when they must have killed Nayakam, too. Somewhere, in a distant forest, he must have died like a wounded bird, parched and uncared for. His corpse was found after many days—he, too, had been brought in for "questioning." A bullet had pierced his temple. His well-built young body was riddled with wounds. The face on that lifeless corpse was strangely contorted, registering the agony of that final moment. On that night, Nayakam's wife, with face lowered, cheeks buried in her hands, wept silently for a long time.

The next day, the newspapers carried the official account: Nayakam was shot to death in an armed encounter with the police.

It was painful to keep on thinking about Nayakam. He was a splendid man. I was with him when he went underground into the dense forests. He had curly hair, a broad forehead, and smiling eyes. It was marvelous to see his well-built, young body. He was like a gorgeous, powerful animal with his well-muscled upper arms and the sheen of his skin. It seemed that death could never come for him. But, in the end, he, too, died. He would talk at length, laughing, with the locks of his hair bunching at his brow. During debates, he would suddenly say things that would shock the others. I can see him right before my eyes, perched atop that small rise on which he customarily sat, leaning his body forward, his head raised toward the sky in sorrowful laughter. And here is what he would say: "Protect yourselves from two things: loneliness and nature. These are the two that can cause the most misery and pain to man. You can never conquer those two things by any means, neither through armed struggle nor through a sense of rebellion. Why? You can never even hate them completely. They surround you, like a pervasive toxic gas, invisible to the eyes."

Nayakam's death was a huge loss to the movement. Recently, the movement was losing many young men. Those who could have become upstanding citizens were getting dragged off to the forest interiors without anyone's knowledge and were getting murdered. Each and every time, we regarded the one who was dragged off as a Jesus, and the one who would escape as a Barabbas.

I realized that just like Nayakam, I, too, had arrived at death's door. It occurred to me that all of us are constantly right next to death. The reason for the panic and the curiosity that death creates in us is its extreme unpredictability. The nature of death's unpredictability is a cut above that of life. In truth, we can never know what death has in store for us. Death is just the final move of a strange game in which the player—and the game itself—just vanish. The stark nature of death transcends our imagination. If we disagree and insist that death is indeed imaginable, we are still not going to find a shred of evidence for it.

Life is not just a struggle between death and being alive; between sorrow and joy; between evil and good. Life somehow, in the end, becomes a struggle between the fulfillment of actions and the futility of the consequences. Perhaps, when my veins wither and my hands go slack, death's interruption might even offer great peace.

But right now . . . the thought of death only created a feeling of profound bitterness. For people who are without commitment, life and death are one and the same. But for men like me? Right now, death would only make me more disappointed than sad. If I were to die now, it would be considered a hero's death. But this much I knew: that when the moment comes, there is no such thing as a "hero's death." Death is nothing but death. In death's presence, I am certain to lose.

Outside, it started raining again. The raindrops fell with a patter on the prison roof.

The sound of the raindrops was like the throb of a single, huge heart. The lure of that rhythm cultivated a profound sorrow within me. The sound of these little drops of rain restored to my memory, in quite an unexpected way today, the phases that I had passed through in life. I was amazed that such a little sound could infiltrate the compact coils of a human brain. In thinking about it all, my solitude seemed monstrous. These drops of rain, which just rained on without my being able to see them, were pitilessly producing before my eyes the many men from throughout my life, and the many moments. Relationships and experiences were losing their substance. An abstract world, which man has created to differentiate him from beast, is without end and without sense. For a man who is very close to death, it becomes suddenly clear that his abstract world is not at all what it seems. It is a void! And the face of that void would lie shattered, imprisoned in fragments of memory. It would be cruel to be unable to verify if its beauty and its wonders were mere illusions. At the end, man is left abandoned in that great void and becomes a squirming infant, senselessly wailing in a broad, vast wasteland.

I was shivering in the cold. They would come for me before dawn. And dragging me to a forest interior, they would shove a country rifle without bullets into my arms, set me at a run, and they would mow me down, shooting me like a wretched animal. Then all would be finished. I, too, would be completely absolved of the abjection of self-pity.

Enveloped in darkness within that reeking cell, I lay still, waiting for the thud of their boots.

TRANSLATOR'S ACKNOWLEDGMENTS

My thanks go first of all to the United States–India Educational Foundation, which awarded me a Fulbright-Nehru Senior Scholar Fellowship. USIEF's generosity allowed me to spend an eight-month stretch of time in Chennai in 2013 and 2014, where I had the great freedom to concentrate on "one thing," so rare and precious in our world as it now is. Special thanks are due to Dr. V. Kamesvari, director of the Kuppuswami Sastri Research Institute in Mylapore, for welcoming me back as a research affiliate. I thank Cherie Mahadevan and her family for giving me a splendid roof over my head in C.I.T. Colony, and L. Vijayalakshmy and V. Rangaraj and their families for all of their efficient help and hospitality. I am also most grateful to my small, supportive network of friends and colleagues in the world of Tamil studies, who through the years and through many conversations have made my work better and who have also made me a better person. Chief among these friends is Diane Mines, whose constant, steadying friendship for the past thirty-five years, and whose integrity and inspiring research, continue to make me who I am, through thick and thin. In Chennai, my thanks go to fellow Fulbrighters Shirley Huston-Findley and Stephanie Shapiro, and to Michael Collins, Mathangi Krishnamurthy, Mini Krishnan, Kamini Mahadevan, Shanti Pillai, S. Ramakrishnan, Perundevi Srinivasan, and Rupa Viswanath. I thank Sascha Ebeling for inviting me to speak at the Franke Institute at the University of Chicago, where I received valuable comments and suggestions from E. Annamalai, Yigal Bronner, the late Lakshmi Holmstrom, and Jim Lindholm. Thanks are also due to Christoph Emmerich, Sarah Lamb, Srilata Raman, David Shulman, and Archana Venkatesan for their incredible support; to my family in Iowa for putting up with my long absences and for always welcoming me back; and to all my wonderful students, past and present. Special thanks go to Emilia Bachrach (for all things Puṣṭimārg), daniel dillon, Andrea Gutiérrez, Gardner Harris, Kathleen Longwaters, and Nikola Rajić. I owe a huge debt to Dr. Subasri Raman of Stella Maris College, Chennai, for reading through many of the stories with me, and to my deeply talented, versatile student and fellow translator Aniruddhan Vasudevan for helping me make those final, crucial adjustments to tone and register. But my biggest thanks go to Dilip Kumar himself, for writing these marvelous stories in the first place and for suffering my endless lists of questions and my moments of pure and utter cluelessness, and for giving a classicist the terrifying, enthralling opportunity to work with a living, breathing author writing in a living language.

Dilip Kumar and I are grateful to our editors at Northwestern University Press, Jill Lisette Perry and Gianna Francesca Mosser, for supporting this project from the very beginning, and to the marvelous Laura Brueck, associate professor and chair of the Department of Asian Languages and Cultures at Northwestern, for facilitating our contact with the Press.

Finally, Dilip Kumar and I dedicate this book to the memory of John Bernard "Barney" Bate. His ideas about Tamil rhetoric and movement through the textures of Tamil spaces remain vibrant in our minds, in the ways in which we think about things. Barney, you left us far too soon, and we miss your brilliance and contagious energy.

Note: terms in the glossary are Tamil unless otherwise noted. In the stories, a simplified transliteration has been used that avoids diacritics; here, some terms are supplemented by more precise transliterations.

Adey (*aṭē* or *aṭēy*) A context-sensitive article used to express surprise, or to address a man or a boy either informally or with disrespect.

Adiye (*aṭiyē*) A context-sensitive article used to address a woman or a girl either informally or with disrespect.

agrahāram (Sanskrit *agrahāra*) A street or streets occupied by orthodox Hindus.

Aiyo (*aiyō*) An exclamatory particle used to express pain, sorrow, or pity.

Aiyye (*aiyyē*) An exclamatory particle used to express surprise or disapproval.

almirah (Hindi *ālmari*; Portuguese *almario*) A tall wardrobe, usually made out of wood or steel, where clothing and family valuables are kept.

Andhra Andhra Pradesh, a Telugu-speaking state just to the north of Tamil Nadu. Andhra Pradesh was divided into the states of Andhra Pradesh and Telangana in 2014.

Anna The popular name of C. N. Annadurai (1909–69), who served as chief minister of Tamil Nadu from 1967 to 1969.

Are (Hindi/Gujarati *arē*) A context-sensitive exclamatory particle used to express surprise or to draw attention to an occurrence or a thing.

arrack A distilled liquor made from the fermented sap of coconut or sugarcane.

Ashok Leyland Headquartered in Chennai, India's second-largest manufacturer of automobiles, engines, buses, and lorries.

Ayurveda A form of humorally based medicine founded on Sanskrit texts that are nearly two thousand years old. The current forms of Ayurveda are largely based on herbal and dietary remedies, and have become quite popular since Indian independence.

Ba/Bai In Gujarati, Hindi, and other North Indian languages, a respectful term of address for an older woman, and often attached directly to a proper name.

banian   A man's cotton undershirt, usually V-necked, sleeveless or with short sleeves.

Baroda   The former name of the city of Vadodara, the cultural capital of the state of Gujarat and home to many colleges and universities.

beedi   A thin cigar filled with flaked tobacco, wrapped tightly in dried tendu leaf and tied with a string.

Behn   In Hindi, Gujarati, and other North Indian languages, *behn* (or *behan*) means "sister" and is often used as a polite term of address or appended to a given name.

besan   Flour made from chickpeas.

betel   A leaf from a vine (*Piper betle*) that is rolled up and chewed, and sometimes given as an offering in ritual and ceremonial contexts.

Bhāgavatam   See *Bhāgavata-purāṇa*.

Bhagavatar crop   A male hairstyle made popular by film star M. K. Thiagaraja Bhagavatar (1910–59, popularly known as MKT), in which the hair is worn long and swept back from the face in a shoulder-length bob.

Bhāgavata-purāṇa   A Sanskrit text from the tenth century C.E., which details the exploits of the god Krishna in its tenth chapter, and has been translated into many of the modern vernaculars of India.

Bhai   In Hindi, Gujarati, and other North Indian languages, *bhai* means "brother" and is often used as a polite term of address, appended to a given name, or used as an expression of friendship.

bhajan   A devotional song that can be sung individually or in communal worship.

Bhuleshvar   A neighborhood in south Bombay, famous for its markets and temples.

biryani   A fragrant pan–South Asian mixed rice dish made with spices, vegetables, and usually chicken or mutton.

black money   Money earned through illegal activity and paid in cash.

bonda   A savory snack usually made of a spiced mashed potato mixture dipped in besan flour batter and deep-fried.

bulbultara   A musical instrument with two sets of strings, one for drone and one for melody, based on the *taishōgoto*, a Japanese import.

Burma Bazaar   A Chennai market run by Tamil refugees from Burma (now Myanmar). It was established in 1969 with support from the Tamil Nadu state government, and located at Parry's Corner, a popular landmark in the northern part of the city.

Central Station   The main railway terminus in the city of Chennai, and within walking distance of Ekambareshvarar Agrahāram.

Chandrababu   J. P. Chandrababu Rodriguez (1927–74), a Chaplinesque Tamil film comedian. A female character in "Crossing Over" is given this nickname because of her long and expressive face.

chappals/Hawaii chappals   A pan–South Asian word for sandals. "Hawaii chappals" are rubber flip-flops.

chappati   A pan–South Asian unleavened flatbread made from whole wheat flour.

Chengelput   A district in Tamil Nadu southwest of Chennai. Chengelput town is the capital of the district.

Chettiyar   A title used by mercantile, agarian, and land-owning castes in South India.

chi   (*cī*) An expletive used to express disgust or anger.

Chittappa   Uncle; father's younger brother or husband of mother's younger sister.

City Corporation   The civic body that governs Chennai city.

co-brother   (*saṭṭakar*) Wife's sister's husband.

Cochin   An important port city on the Malabar coast of Kerala, the state directly to the west of Tamil Nadu.

Coimbatore   Also called Kovai, Coimbatore is an important textile city, and the second largest city in Tamil Nadu.

"Colonel Ranjit" detective novel   Colonel Ranjit was the pen name of Maqbool Jalandhari, who wrote pulp crime novels in the popular Hindi *jasoos* genre. His chief character was a detective named Major Balwant.

Da   (*ṭā*) A context-sensitive term used to address a man or boy, used to express contempt, familiarity, or affection.

Dalda   A popular South Asian brand of hydrogenated vegetable oil.

Deepavali   (*tīpāvaḷi*) The Hindu "Festival of Lights," also celebrated by Jains, Sikhs, and some Buddhists in the lunar month of Kārttikai, mid-November to mid-December.

Deksa   (*tēksā*) A large pot with a wide mouth and a tapering bottom, here used as a code word for "bottom" or "rump."

Dey   (*ṭēy*) An informal or disrespectful address to a boy or a man.

Dhobi   A pan–South Asian word designating a person who washes clothes for a living.

Di   (*ṭī*) A context-sensitive address to a woman or girl, used to express contempt, familiarity, or affection.

Dongre Maharaj   A revered twentieth-century Puṣṭimārg holy man and teacher who wrote popular commentaries on Hindu epics and religious texts.

drumstick (*muruṅkaikkāy*) The long, edible seed pod of the moringa or drumstick tree, often used in curries and pulse gravies such as sambar.

Ekambareshvarar (Sanskrit Ekāmbareśvara) "The Lord who wears a single garment," a form of Śiva.

Emden The German cruiser SMS *Emden* bombarded Madras Harbor on September 22, 1914, firing at the storage tanks of the British-owned Burmah Oil Company.

ever-silver The local English term for stainless steel, very popular for cooking vessels, utensils, and kitchen storage.

501 A brand of laundry detergent in bar form.

Gandhi cap A cap woven of white handspun cotton, worn by activists during the movement for Indian independence, and now worn by politicians.

Ganges water Water from the Ganges River is considered holy, and is believed to have purifying effects.

Ghatotkaca (Sanskrit Ghaṭotkaca) A hero from the Sanskrit epic *Mahābhārata*, Ghatotkaca was the son of the Pāṇḍava hero Bhīma and the demoness Hiḍimbā. He had magical powers and could change his size at will but is popularly known as a giant with superhuman strength.

Goloka (Sanskrit) Literally "cow world," a name for Krishna's heaven.

gopuram An ornate, monumental tower, marking the entryway into a Hindu temple in the Dravidian style of architecture.

Gounder A title used to refer to various caste groups in Tamil Nadu.

governor In postindependence India, a governor is an appointed constitutional head of state and functional representative of the president of India.

Govinda (Sanskrit) "Cow finder," an epithet of Krishna, referring to the god's youthful activities as a cowherder.

Guindy Guindy Race Course is the oldest horse-racing track in India, and was established in 1777. It is located in the Guindy neighborhood in Chennai, just to the south of the Adyar River.

Gul-e-Bakavali A very popular 1955 Tamil-language adventure film starring M. G. Ramachandran and based on the Arabic *Thousand and One Nights*.

gypsies I have used this problematic term to translate the Tamil caste name *narikuṟavar*, which refers to their old occupation as "jackal catcher." They were criminalized by the British, and even though they were "denotified" in 1952, they are still stigmatized, and wander from place to place selling beads, ornaments, and odds and ends. "Gypsy" is the English term that most Tamil speakers use to refer to them, which is why I have adopted it here.

Hanuman Chālisā   Attributed to the Hindu poet-saint Tulsidas (1511–1623, dates approximate), the *Chālisā* is a forty-verse hymn dedicated to the god Hanuman, the monkey-hero of the Sanskrit and vernacular epic *Rāmāyaṇa*.

haveli   In the North Indian vernaculars, a haveli is a mansion-like home with a central courtyard, but in the Puṣṭimārg faith, the word refers to a home-like temple devoted to Krishna.

idli   (*iṭli*) A steamed disc-shaped cake made of a fermented batter of ground rice and black gram.

jaggery   Unrefined brown cane or palm sugar, purchased in blocks.

Jan Kalyan   A Gujarati monthly magazine devoted to religious matters.

"Jaya Jagadishvara Hare"   (Sanskrit) "Victory to Hari, Lord of the Universe," a popular bhajan refrain. Hari is an epithet of Viṣṇu, of whom Krishna is considered an avatar or incarnation.

jibba   A loose-fitting shirt, pulled on over the head.

"Justice before Caste"   (*Nītikku-p pintān Cāti*) This is a play on the slogan-like film titles of the films of M. G. Ramachandran.

Kamaraj   Kumaraswami Kamaraj (1903–75) was a member of the Indian Congress Party and served as chief minister of Tamil Nadu from 1954 to 1963.

kanji   Gruel, usually a watery, grain-based soup, given to people who are ill or bedridden.

Kannadiga   A native speaker of the Kannada language; a person from the state of Karnataka.

Kapila-vastu   (Sanskrit) The name of the town in which Śākyamuṇi Buddha was born; here used as a code word to refer to the female genitals.

Karunanidhi   Muthuvel Karunanidhi (1924–2018) was head of the DMK (Dravida Munnetra Kazhagam), one of the two main Dravidianist political parties in Tamil Nadu. He served as chief minister of Tamil Nadu on five separate occasions (1969–71, 1971–76, 1989–91, 1996–2001, and 2005–11).

khadi   Handspun, handwoven cloth, usually cotton, and a symbol of the Indian independence movement. Khadi was made popular by Mohandas K. Gandhi while he was leading boycotts of foreign, machine-manufactured cloth.

Khan, Salman   Abdul Rashid Salim Salman Khan (born 1965) is a wildly popular Bollywood actor.

King Kong The professional wrestling name of Emile Czaja (1909–70). Born in Hungary, he wrestled all over India and Pakistan until his death. His chief opponent was Dara Singh, and their bouts would often draw crowds of a hundred thousand and more. He was dubbed "King Kong" after he played that part in a 1962 Indian remake of the famous movie.

kolam (*kōlam*) A decorative design drawn in the morning by women all over South India, on the threshold of or at the entrance to a home. The design is usually made with rice flour sifted through the fingertips.

Kontittopu A neighborhood in Georgetown, Chennai, slightly to the northwest of the location of the agrahāram stories.

Krishna/Balakrishna Krishna is worshipped as the eighth incarnation of the Hindu god Viṣṇu and is recognized as the supreme god in his own right by some sects. He is often depicted as a prankster, lover, and divine hero. In Puṣṭimārg Vaiṣṇavism, Krishna in his infant form of Balakrishna is especially revered, and rouses intense feelings of *bhakti*, or intense emotional devotion.

Krishnamurthy, J. Jiddu Krishnamurthy (1895–1986) was a philosopher, speaker, and writer. In his youth, he was "discovered" by the Theosophists and was groomed to become a "world teacher" by Annie Besant, who became his legal guardian. He broke with the Theosophists in 1929, and traveled the world as a popular speaker, religious figure, and author.

Kulamakal Radhai A 1963 Tamil-language blockbuster film, starring Sivaji Ganesan and B. Sarojadevi.

kumkum A brightly colored red powder, usually made from turmeric treated with slaked lime. It is used in religious contexts, but it is also worn on the forehead by "auspicious" Hindu women (either women who are married or are of marriageable age).

kummi A type of circle dance performed by girls and women, characterized by rhythmic clapping.

Kumudam A very popular Tamil-language weekly magazine in continuous circulation since 1947, featuring cinema gossip, cartoons, and essays on events in the state of Tamil Nadu. It is famous for its glamorous center-page photographs.

lakh A hundred thousand.

Lalitha-ji The famously unsmiling spokeswoman for Surf laundry detergent in Hindustan-Lever's television advertising campaigns of the 1970s.

lassi A pan–South Asian yogurt-based drink. A lassi can be either sweet or savory.

lathi A heavy stick, usually made of bamboo bound with iron, used by police to disperse crowds.

Lifebuoy Although no longer made or marketed in Britain or the United States, Lifebuoy soap is still very popular in South Asia, where it is produced by Unilever.

limited meal A term used on South Indian restaurant menus to indicate a thali-style lunch that is more "limited" and basic in its list of items than a usual or "special" thali.

lungi A kind of veshti or sarong worn by men. The two ends are sewn together to form a tube.

Ma Mother, often used as a term of respectful address for an older woman and sometimes appended to a proper name. It can also be used to indicate affection and familiarity.

maidan (Arabic *maydān*) An open space in or near a town, used for public meetings and events, and as a parade ground.

Mārgaḻi A Tamil month equivalent to mid-December to mid-January in the Gregorian calendar.

Marwari A person from the Marwar region of Rajasthan in northwest India.

maxi A cotton nightdress, usually floor-length, worn by many women in Tamil Nadu as casual wear around the house.

Moore Market A Chennai market established in 1898 by Sir George Moore, president of the Madras Corporation, to accommodate street hawkers. It was famous for antiques, books, and pets, and had the air of a flea market where one could find anything for a bargain. Located in Park Town in north-central Chennai, it burned to the ground in 1985.

Mother India Begun by publisher, writer, and politician Baburao Patel (1904–82), *Mother India* was a national magazine devoted to a blend of film criticism and political commentary, and ran from 1960 to 1985. It had its beginnings as *filmindia* in 1935.

Muhammad of Ghazni Muhammad of Ghazni (971–1030) was the most prominent ruler of the Ghaznavid empire. He conquered eastern Iran, Afghanistan, and northwest India and was the first ruler to hold the title of sultan.

nadaswaram (*nātasvaram* or *nākacuram*) A double-reed instrument, much like an oboe, usually played on auspicious occasions.

namaste (Sanskrit and North Indian vernaculars) A respectful greeting, usually accompanied by a gesture of folded hands held at the level of the chest.

Nargis The stage name of Fatima Rashid (1929–81), considered one of the greatest actresses of Hindi cinema.

Natesan Park A park located in Thyagaraja Nagar in west-central Chennai.

Natti (*nātti*) Short for *nāttanār*, one's husband's sister.

Navaratri   The "nine nights," a festival celebrated in the autumn all over India and for various reasons, but in Tamil Nadu, it is the main festival to celebrate the Hindu goddesses Lakṣmī, Sarasvatī, and Durgā. It is also known in parts of India as a military festival that celebrates the forces of good over evil.

Nilgiri Hills   The "blue hills" that form part of the Western Ghats in Tamil Nadu, Karnataka, and Kerala. The region is a popular vacation spot and is known for its coffee and tea plantations.

number one account/number two account   Phrases common in "black money" accounting practices. The "number one" account is the official account for tax purposes, and the "number two" account is the one used to record business income that the proprietor wishes to keep hidden.

Ooty   (*utakamaṇṭalam*) Also called Ootacamund, Ooty is a popular hill station located in the Nilgiri Hills north of the city of Coimbatore.

Pa   Father, often used as a term of respectful address for an older man, also used to indicate affection and familiarity.

paan   A pan–South Asian preparation made with areca nut (and sometimes tobacco or sweet items, such as rose jelly and flaked coconut), wrapped in a betel leaf and chewed. It is a digestive, a mild stimulant, and when made with the right ingredients for it, a breath freshener.

Parikshit Maharaj   King Parikshit was the grandson of the epic hero Arjuna, one of the five Pāṇḍavas of the *Mahābhārata*. The story is retold in the *Bhāgavatam*. Parikshit was cursed to die by snakebite, and this episode occurs near the beginning of the text, indicating that Gangu Patti, the heroine of "Crossing Over," dropped off to sleep in fairly short order.

patti   (*pāṭṭi*) Grandmother, also used as a term of address for any elderly woman regardless of kin relationship.

Pawar, Lalitha   Lalitha Pawar (1916–98) was a famous character actress who starred in more than seven hundred Hindi, Marathi, and Gujarati films. She was best known for portraying wicked matriarchs and mothers-in-law.

petty shop   A small neighborhood shop that sells necessities, odds and ends, and groceries (items such as toothbrushes, batteries, soap, candies, eggs, and condoms, as well as cigarettes, which many shops used to sell singly).

pinman   A man who sells pins, but in the context of "The Letter," it is used as a local synonym for dhobi, or washerman.

Podanur   A railway town four miles from Coimbatore, Tamil Nadu, the city in which "Bamboo Shoots" is set.

Pondy Bazaar   Named after Justice Party politician Soundarapandian Nadar, Pondy Bazaar is one of the principal shopping districts of Chennai, located in Thyagaraja Nagar in the west-central part of the city.

Prabhudas Patvari   A Gujarati lawyer, freedom fighter, and Gandhian, Prabhudas Patvari (1909–85) served as governor of Tamil Nadu from 1977 to 1980.

puja   (Sanskrit *pūjā*) Worship of deities either in temples or in small home shrines.

puri   A pan–South Asian deep-fried, puffy unleavened bread, often eaten for breakfast with a potato side dish.

purity stick   (*maṭi-k-kōl*) A long bamboo stick used to maintain ritual purity (for example, to prevent direct human bodily contact with clothes that have just been washed and hung to dry).

Rāṇi   A weekly Tamil-language magazine, with features on news, cultural affairs, and cinema gossip.

Renigunta   A small town in Chittoor District, Andhra Pradesh, located just north of the Tamil Nadu border.

Rexona   A popular brand of soap manufactured by Unilever.

saaybu   (*cāyapu*; Urdu *sahib*) A colloquial term used to address and refer to Muslim men.

samosa   A savory snack, usually spiced potatoes or meat wrapped in flour-based pastry, formed into a triangle, and deep-fried.

Saturn   (Sanskrit *śani*) The planet in the form of a deity and considered to be inauspicious and the bearer of bad luck. "Saturn" is a term of abuse in the modern vernacular languages when directed at a person or thing.

Scissors Mark   A popular brand of imported filtered cigarette manufactured by the British firm W. D. & H. O. Wills. The Wills firm is now defunct, but the brand is still marketed in India by the Imperial Tobacco Company.

Seth   "Seth" is a caste name, but it is also used as a title to designate a merchant or a landlord.

shaven-headed widow   Hindu widows are traditionally considered to be inauspicious, and in some conservative communities, they are still required to shave their heads, wear white saris, and go without any kind of adornment.

Shrinath-ji   A form of the god Krishna as a handsome youth, iconographically depicted as lifting up Govardhan Hill to shelter his cows and devotees.

Sivakaci calendar cat   Sivakaci is an industrial town in Virudhunagar District in south-central Tamil Nadu. It is famous for its fireworks, matchbox, and printing industries, and is a large manufacturing center for calendars, including a popular cat series.

Sowcarpet   A large neighborhood in north-central Chennai, home to many North Indian mercantile families from Gujarat and Rajasthan. Ekambareshvarar Agrahāram is located in the Sowcarpet neighborhood.

S. S. L. C.   The Secondary School Leaving Certificate is awarded to students who have successfully passed the grade ten public examination administered by the state of Tamil Nadu, making them eligible for further education.

Suraiya   Suraiya Jamaal Sheikh (1929–74) was a Bollywood actress and playback singer, known as the "Melody Queen" of India and one of the few actresses in the Hindi film world to sing her own songs. The two songs referred to in the story, "Sōchā thā kyā, kyā hō gayā" and "Ō Dūr Jānēvālē . . ." are from the films *Anmo Ghadi* (1946) and *Pyar ki Jeet* (1948), respectively.

Tanjore   (*Tañjavūr*) Located in Thanjavur District to the southwest of Chennai, Tanjore is famous for its temples, art, and architecture. It was the capital of the medieval Cōḷa dynasty (848–1279 C.E.) and was home to many North Indians during the reign of the Maratha mahārājas (1674–1855).

tank of a temple   (*teppa-k-kuḷam*) The tank is an essential feature of Hindu temple architecture. It is a large, rectangular reservoir with steps, and the water is used for ritual cleansing and during rites of consecration.

Tenkalai Vaiṣṇavas   One of the branches of Śrīvaiṣṇavism, which favors *bhakti* practices and Tamil texts. In Tenkalai theology, the devotee's salvation is left in the hands of god, much like a kitten surrenders itself to be carried by the mother cat.

Thakur-ji   (Hindi *ṭhākur-jī*) A term referring to images of Krishna used for worship purposes in temples and in private home shrines in the Puṣṭimārg faith.

tilakam   A term that usually refers to the beauty mark worn on the forehead of married or marriageable women, but that, in this context, is used to refer to the best among a category. The two "tilakams" of Tamil cinema were M. G. Ramachandran (1917–87) and Sivaji Ganesan (1928–2001).

tinnai   (*tiṇṇai*) A raised platform, usually of poured concrete, on which people can sit, sleep, or relax, either under the verandah of an old-fashioned house, where it functions much like a porch, or it can take the form of a rectangular slab on either side of a door.

Tiruvorriyur/Tiruvanmiyur   Tiruvorriyur is a neighborhood in the northern reaches of Chennai, while Tiruvanmiyur is a neighborhood far to the south.

Triplicane   One of the oldest neighborhoods in Chennai, Triplicane is in the heart of the city, just to the north of Mylapore and adjacent to the Bay of Bengal.

tulsi/tulsi beads   Tulsi is the variety of Indian basil sacred to Krishna, and his devotees wear necklaces made of beads carved from the wood of the tulsi plant.

Udamalaipet   A town in Tirupur District, Tamil Nadu, near the Western Ghats and to the southeast of Coimbatore.

Udupi restaurant   A vegetarian restaurant serving Udupi-style cuisine, taking its name from Udupi, a coastal city in the Tulunadu region of Karnataka. Such restaurants serve favorite South Indian snack items, such as idlis and dosas, but they also offer sumptuous full-course meals, which include different flavored rices, vegetable dishes, fried items, and a sweet.

vadai   (*vaṭai*) A savory doughnut-shaped snack made of legume batter and deep-fried.

vastu   (Sanskrit) Any object, substance, or "thing," here used as a code word to refer to the penis.

veshti   (*vēṣṭi* or *vēṭṭi*) An unstitched, sarong-like garment for men that hangs from the waist to the ankle. It is usually woven of white cotton with a colored border.

Yardley   A British brand of soap, talcum powder, and other cosmetics made popular by the model Twiggy in the 1960s. Yardley products are still very popular in India. The character is nicknamed "Yardley" because of her fondness for the scented talcum powder.

BIBLIOGRAPHY

Arnold, David, and Stuart Blackburn. "Introduction: Life Histories in India." In *Telling Lives in India: Biography, Autobiography, and Life History*, edited by David Arnold and Stuart Blackburn, 1–28. Bloomington: Indiana University Press, 2004.

Ashokamittiran (Jagadisa Thyagarajan). "Muṉṉurai." In Dilip Kumar, *Mūṅkil Kuruttu*. Chennai: Cre-A, 1985.

———. "The Pre-Occupations in Tamil Short Story Today." *Indian Literature* 37, no. 3 (1994): 181–83.

Bachrach, Emilia. "In the Seat of Authority: Debating Temple Spaces and Community Identity in a Vaiṣṇava *Sampradāy* of Contemporary Gujarat." *Journal of Hindu Studies* 10, no. 1 (2017): 18–46.

Bate, John Bernard. *Tamil Oratory and the Dravidian Aesthetic: Democratic Practice in South India*. New York: Columbia University Press, 2009.

Blackburn, Stuart. *Print, Folklore, and Nationalism in Colonial South India*. New Delhi: Permanent Black, 2003.

de Certeau, Michel. *The Practice of Everyday Life*. Berkeley: University of California Press, 1984.

Ebeling, Sascha. *Colonizing the Realm of Words: The Transformation of Tamil Literature in Nineteenth-Century South India*. Albany: State University of New York Press, 2010.

Eichinger Ferro-Luzzi, Gabriella. *Cool Fire: Culture-Specific Themes in Tamil Short Stories*. Göttingen: Edition Herodot, 1983.

Freeman, Donald C., ed. *Linguistics and Literary Style*. New York: Holt, Rinehart & Winston, 1970.

Gros, François. "Tamil Short Stories: An Introduction." In *Deep Rivers: Selected Writings on Tamil Literature,* edited by Kannan M. and Jennifer Clare. Translated from the French by M. P. Boseman. Pondicherry: French Institute of Pondicherry and Tamil Chair, Department of South and Southeast Asian Studies, University of California at Berkeley, 2009.

———. "Wandering in the Tamil Archipelago." In *Deep Rivers: Selected Writings on Tamil Literature,* edited by Kannan M. and Jennifer Clare. Translated by M. P. Boseman. Pondicherry: French Institute of

Pondicherry and Tamil Chair, Department of South and Southeast Asian Studies, University of California at Berkeley, 2009.

Grossman, Edith. *Why Translation Matters*. New Haven, Conn.: Yale University Press, 2010.

Jagannathan, N. S. "Smothered Creativity." *Indian Literature* 37, no. 3 (1994): 165–79.

Kothari, Rita. *Translating India: The Cultural Politics of English*. Rev. ed. Delhi: Foundation Books, 2006.

Krishnaswami, P. "Collective Vision in Contemporary Tamil Literature." *Indian Literature* 37, no. 3 (1994): 186–93.

Krishnaswamy, Subashree. "A Note on the Translation." In Dilip Kumar, *The Tamil Story: Through the Times, through the Tides*, xxv–xxxi. Chennai: Tranquebar Press, 2016.

Kriyāvin Taṟkāla-t-Tamiḻ Akarāti. 2nd ed. Chennai: Cre-A, 2013.

Kumar, Dilip, ed. *Contemporary Tamil Short Fiction*. Translated by Vasantha Surya. Chennai: Manas, 1999.

————. *Kaṭavu*. Chennai: Cre-A, 2000, 2010.

————. *Mauniyuṭan Koñca Tūram*. Chennai: Vānati Patippakam, 1992.

————. *Mūṅkil Kuruttu*. Chennai: Cre-A, 1985.

————. *Ramāvum Umāvum*. Chennai: Sandhya, 2011.

————. *The Tamil Story: Through the Times, through the Tides*. Chennai: Tranquebar Press, 2016.

Mufti, Aamir R. *Forget English! Orientalisms and World Literatures*. Cambridge, Mass.: Harvard University Press, 2016.

Mukherjee, Meenakshi. *Realism and Reality: The Novel and Society in India*. Delhi: Oxford University Press, 1985.

Rajam Aiyar, B. R. *The Fatal Rumour: A Nineteenth-Century Indian Novel*. Translated from the Tamil and with afterword by Stuart Blackburn. New Delhi: Oxford University Press, 1998.

Ramanujan, A. K. "Form in Classical Tamil Poetry." In *The Collected Essays of A. K. Ramanujan*, edited by Vinay Dharwadker. Delhi: Oxford University Press, 1999.

————. "On Translating a Tamil Poem." In *The Collected Essays of A. K. Ramanujan*, edited by Vinay Dharwadker. Delhi: Oxford University Press, 1999.

Ramnarayan, Gowri. "Book-bound!" *The Hindu*, November 6, 2000.

Sadana, Rashmi. *English Heart, Hindi Heartland: The Political Life of Literature in India*. Berkeley: University of California Press, 2012.

Saha, Shandip. "A Community of Grace: The Social and Theological World of the *Puṣṭi Mārga Vārtā* Literature." *Bulletin of the School of Oriental and African Studies* 69, no. 2 (2006): 225–42.

————. "The Movement of *Bhakti* along a North-West Axis: Tracing the History of the Puṣṭimārg between the Sixteenth and Nineteenth Centuries." *International Journal of Hindu Studies* 11, no. 3 (2007): 299–318.

Shankar, Subramanian. *Flesh and Fish Blood: Postcolonialism, Translation, and the Vernacular.* Berkeley: University of California Press, 2012.

Shulman, David D. *More Than Real: A History of the Imagination in South India.* Cambridge, Mass.: Harvard University Press, 2012.

————. *Tamil: A Biography.* Cambridge, Mass.: Harvard University Press, 2016.

Spivak, Gayatri Chakravorty. "The Politics of Translation." In *Destabilizing Theory: Contemporary Feminist Debates*, edited by Michèle Barrett and Anne Phillips, 177–200. Palo Alto, Calif.: Stanford University Press, 1992.

Tamil Lexicon. 6 vols. plus appendix. Reprint. Chennai: University of Madras, 1982.

Todorov, Tzvetan. *The Poetics of Prose.* Translated by Richard Howard; new foreword by Jonathan Culler. Ithaca, N.Y.: Cornell University Press, 1977.

Venkatachalapathy, A. R. "In Print, On the Net: Tamil Literary Canon in the Colonial and Post-Colonial Worlds." In *India in the Age of Globalization: Contemporary Discourses and Texts*, edited by Suman Gupta, Tapan Basu, and Subarno Chattarji. New Delhi: Nehru Memorial Museum & Library, 2003.

————. *In Those Days There Was No Coffee: Writings in Cultural History.* Delhi: Yoda Press, 2006.

————. *The Province of the Book: Scholars, Scribes, and Scribblers in Colonial Tamilnadu.* Ranikhet: Permanent Black, 2012.

Zvelebil, Kamil. *The Smile of Murugan on Tamil Literature in South India.* Leiden: E. J. Brill, 1973.